THE HOURS OF UNDER

The Hours of Under

Underoveron Book One

K.E. MacLeod

SgianDubh

SEATTLE

The Hours of Under is a work of fiction. Names, characters, places and incidents are the product of the author's imagination or are used fictitiously.

Book design by Alex MacLeod

Cover design and illustrations by Roslyn McFarland, Far Lands Publishing

Published by Sgian Dubh

Seattle, Washington

Printed in the United States of America

First Printing 2022

ISBN paperback: 978-1-945827-05-1

ISBN e-book: 978-1-945827-07-5

ISBN audiobook: 978-1-945827-08-2

Library of Congress Control Number: 2022940022

www.kemacleod.com

MJD
You know...

BOOKS BY K.E.MACLEOD

THE HOURS OF UNDER

Mid-Dark
Dreaming Hour
Philosopher's Hour
Hour of Despair
Hour of Hope
Mother's Hour
Hour of the First Turning
Hour of Beginnings
Bright Hour
Father's Hour
Hour of Lessons
The Found Hour
Mid-Light
Hour of the Second Turning
Hour of the Second Beginning
The Lost Hour
Hour of Remembering
Children's Hour
Hour of the Last Turning
Hour of Ease
Hour of the Spirit
Hour of the Arts
Lover's Hour
Hour of the Conspirator

PROLOGUE

The rock, the stone slept. Exhausted from fire and quake, it slumbered for a time not measured by nights or counted by days. It took slow breaths and favored rich dreams. When, at last, it awoke, it was not in the way of the brief-lived beings who had, in fearful flight, come to burrow into the rock for safety's sake. Bemusement was the slow, patient first response. Then, with the measured compassion that graced its veins, the stone graciously gave hollowed chambers of peace, filling the spaces with air, light. The tiny folk filled the caves with their rapid scrabbling, wisps of breath and small deaths. Treachery came too swiftly for the deeps of the rock to comprehend at first. It required an adjustment of awareness. It required addressing the unexpected pain. It required a conjuring.

CHAPTER ONE

It took him three hours to leave the ledge. Far from up-inward, cool and quiet as it clung to the rock, the ledge held him as he tried to grapple with the unsettlings that had brought him there. He threw stones into the sea, aimed one or two at water birds, kicked at salt-rimmed puddles without aim. After three hours, the only conclusion Andeved found was that avoidance was impossible.

A last time he scanned the two bluenesses, air and water, stamped his boots on the cold, rough rock beneath and drew what strength could be gotten from the high reaches of stone that loomed above and inward from the narrow opening that looked out into the unknown. When he re-entered the caverns and began, with a determination he tried to fully feel, to climb the first of the chilled, dark passageways that would take him on the return trip, the Fool was waiting. As always. Emerging from the shadows, his unavoidable presence almost entirely blocked the tunnel.

"I am ready, lordling." The Fool's voice rumbled in the echoing tunnel like a rockslide.

"Of course." Andeved sighed, and once again rebuked himself for his tendency of late to show so little courtesy to his inevitable companion. They each were doing what generations of tradition demanded. What could not be changed must be endured. But there was a prickle of irritation across his shoulder blades all the same.

As they started to climb the 378 Steps to the Beginning of Below, the Fool began, "When we return it will be the Hour of the First Turning," and then commenced the litany:

> "In the Hour of the First Turning,
> The Lord of the Under awakes
> And remembers that beneath the above
> And over the below,
> The lives of the people turn
> With the tide and the light.
> Turned, turning.
> Hour of the First Turning."

Not even at the first of the Inferior Hallways and Andeved was already out of breath, so that the ritual reply - "The lives of the people. Turning. Turning." - came out in a half-realized whisper. Hearing himself, he did not need to glance at the Fool to know there was a frown on that too familiar face.

"This is quite a climb, eh, Belwether?"

As usual, his most constant companion said nothing. And said enough. For Belwether was not puffing one bit after the arduous climb, though he was certainly a generous handful of seasons older. So Andeved tried to regulate each breath, to take in more air with less noise, knowing even as he did that this pride of his would make the long trek to the Superior Hallways even longer.

Indeed, the final minutes of the Hour of Beginnings were running their course when the pair made the refectory. Today, of all days, it was inappropriate to be late for breakfast. The leftovers, usually remaindered on the wide serving shelf cut into the wall of the lengthy cavern, had been removed by the cadre of Foodists. Already they had taken off their masks of office and, with circles of sweat blossoming between torso and arm, had begun the scrubbing of the tables. Slap, brush, slap, brush – four to a table, two tens of tables. Slap, brush, move down.

"We'll not get fed here." Belwether's rumble overrode the Foodists' cadences. "And your mother will want to see you. Will you go, then?"

Andeved's stomach protested, a metaphor and a reality.

"I suppose." The young man took one last look at the serving shelf just in case he had missed something. Nothing remained but the now fading smell of yeasty morning bread. He turned back toward the junction of tunnels leading to his home chambers. A hot scolding, a cold bath and a change into a formal tunic that chaffed more than just his neck were only the first of what awaited him. For today his older cousin, Lord Paell of Under, would receive at court his bride-to-be, the Lady Arrant of Over. Ceremony on ceremony, insult on injury.

x • x • x

His mother sighed, her hands moving in aimless worry. "I don't suppose you remember where you put the sash for your dress tunic?"

Andeved pulled the sash out of his clothes chest without a reply. It did no good to defend himself, to tell her he knew very well where it was and had just been in the act of retrieving it. It did no good at all. Though he believed his mother loved him, she had developed notions about him that no amount of time and proof could shake. In more than sixteen seasons of life he felt he had amply demonstrated competence, knowledge of ceremony, a working memory, appropriate behaviors of all sorts that could be deployed when necessary.

"Well, there it is." A small sound, something between the upward tone of surprise and the downward slide of disappointment, escaped from his mother as she examined the item in question and then shrugged. "It will have to do."

His mother was already dressed for the ceremony – had probably been so for several hours. The clothes she had chosen tended toward the gaudy. The tunic that hung over her long skirt was voluminous, a vain attempt to hide her widening girth. Silver threads glinted in the fabric, a familiar irony given his mother's name. Even her ceremonial mask, denoting her family relation to Lord Paell, had sparkles on it – an addition beyond what was actually required by tradition.

Not for the first time, Andeved wondered at the pairing that was his parents. Glitter and Sere. Names too right for humor, too opposite for comfort. The only weight his mother carried was on her skeleton. Ideas pushed against her mind and sprang out again, leaving no dent on that internal softness. The only liveliness his father managed was in the animation he gave his anger.

"I cannot help you any more with your preparations, dear," Glitter announced as she started toward the chamber door. "You made me take too much time already worrying where you were. Your cousin has great responsibilities today. It's naughty of you to take so much of our attention on such an occasion."

That Andeved had not asked for, needed nor wanted that attention never seemed to occur to his mother. As she left, he noticed that a section of her hem had come undone and trailed behind her, collecting ragged bits of thread and dust. He said nothing.

A slight sound made him start. Once again Belwether made his presence known.

"How do you do that?" Andeved growled. "Been my Observer since I was seven and you still manage to startle me at least once a day."

Belwether's expression did not change even slightly. "Yes, you still startle – though most often when you've taken the last sweet cake or broken something."

"Mother left before I could tell her about the hem."

The Fool tilted his head and blinked once, slowly. "Hem?"

Andeved felt the warmth of guilt flush up his neck. "You know very well what I mean. You saw the same thing I did and you didn't say anything either."

"Hmmm." That was the total of the Fool's reply.

Andeved's insides growled, effectively distracting him from his companion's infuriating neutrality. The prospect of a long and difficult ceremony on an empty stomach was not pleasant. If he hurried, he might be able to finagle something edible elsewhere before he was missed. Out he went, half running but hoping not to sweat in his dress clothes, toward the Outer Halls.

Down the passage, turn left, then right, then straight out a wide corridor whose rock turned from the dark gray of interior selphstone to the brown of edgestone. Light grew the farther outward he went until it burst out in fullness as he reached the terrace. The Terraces. They never failed to amaze him. Great waves of stone jutting out beyond the caverns and to each side, crowded with growing things and those who tended them.

But first he turned back to the interior hall where, of course, the Fool stood, not an arm's span away.

"You can guess what I mean to do and you know you cannot stand near me like a beacon." Andeved pointed at a darkness of shadow just inside the cavern entrance. "Stay there until I return and, if you keep hidden, I may bring you something to eat as well."

Without a word, Belwether stepped back into the darkness and Andeved plunged forward and outward toward his prospective breakfast.

"You cannot go outside today, boy." A Terracetender blocked his way. "Too much going on, what with the feast and all. Can't allow anyone out but Foodists and Terracetenders. Sorry."

Andeved wracked his memory for the woman's name.

"But I was sent by Lord Paell, especially for some sweetrounds." He peered up under the huge brim of the inevitable shielding hat and recognized the face beneath. "You know how it is, Fleeney. My cousin's all nerves and jitters. Needs something gentle to settle his stomach. I, myself, would not bother folks just now, but..."

"Nonsense, son. You need to do what you're told." Fleeney stepped aside and motioned him on. "Go on then, but be quick about it and stay out of the way. Lots of busy people - and your father's out there somewhere having an argument about visqhens that won't lay on his schedule."

His father out here? Not good at this precise moment, though usually there was an advantage to having Sere as a father, this access to the terraces whenever he wanted. For the edgeside farms were his father's responsibility. It was Sere who directed the guild that hauled soil recovered from the gesh excavations to the ledges, those who planted and tended, those who harvested. On the ledge farthest down was the ocean garden with its sheltered fish ponds, oyster beds and salt reclamation basins. The terraces up from that held the cool growers: meshroons, berries and the diminutive sheep of Under. Here, on the topmost gardens, were the warm growers: fruits and vegetables of all kinds and the threadworm and small fowl.

But Andeved was quite adept at avoiding those he did not want to meet. So he dove into the bustle of the Foodists rushing here and there, shouting for more of this and another of that. He dodged Terracetenders running up and down the narrow aisles between plants, picking what was ripe and sprinting back to the waiting baskets.

Ah, there. A long, tall row of sweetround plants. The fist-sized melons hung heavily, ripe and warm. Andeved picked four of the most likely looking ones and, stuffing them inside his tunic, turned to go back - back to the city entrance and a chance to eat.

But from the other side of the sweetround row came the sound of anger. Two people were heading down-row, just as Andeved was, hidden by the broad leaves of the trellised vines. And he knew one of the debaters. The horrible flatness of the voice, the words hitting like huge, dull rock hammers. His father. Andeved froze.

"If you have devoted your life 'til now to becoming a moron, Chasen, it is the only success you've had." His father's black temper was legendary throughout Under. "What did you do to those hens? They won't settle, they won't lay. What did you do to them?"

"Nothing, I swear Head 'Tender." Chasen sounded frantic under Sere's verbal attack. "Something's set them off, but no one knows what. They're jumpy and cross and..."

"Nothing, I swear, master." Sere's parody of Chasen's defense was brutal, derisive. "Do you hear yourself? You admit you've done nothing. Get back to the coops, idiot, and soothe the lice-ridden fowl if you have to eat and sleep in the coop for a hundred days. Keep at it until I see eggs or I'll speak to my nephew, the Lord Paell, and he will have you and your brats exiled. You can spend the rest of your miserable life in the wideopen with no surety of stone to keep your lazy brood contained."

"But no...I can --"

"Go. Now." Sere's tone had gotten even harder. The last word could have shattered stone. As it was, it elicited the sound of footsteps hurrying away. Andeved knew the sweat and fear Chasen must be enduring. Knew it well. And because he had grown up too close to this father, a black anger grew in his own heart. His father should not hurt others this way. It was not right.

Andeved picked another melon - this one larger and heavier than the others. He drew back his arm, calculating the force needed to launch the too-ripe missile over the plant row. The sound of dirt grinding into stone meant his father was walking away. If he could just...

A huge hand caught his outstretched arm and held it hard.

"Is this one for my breakfast?" Belwether's voice was low and steady. He pried the sweetround from Andeved's grasp. "I could not see you once you entered the planting rows so I moved closer."

"You came to spy on me." The tang of anger was still bitter in Andeved's mouth.

"No. Attached do not spy. They observe."

"And they are not supposed to interfere. Or do you pick and choose which traditions you will obey?"

To Andeved's astonishment, Belwether appeared to blush, if that was what the darkening of the Fool's cheeks meant.

"An Attached does not interfere. I was only observing my breakfast in your hand. That was all. That you held it in the manner of small boys bent on mischief, that you looked ridiculous, that you could have hurt him...or he, you...observances only."

It was perhaps the longest speech Belwether had ever made and it took Andeved by surprise. He realized his mouth was gaping. He shut it with a snap, turned on his heel and started back to the interior entrance, Belwether trailing silently behind him. There was not time to consider what this departure from his Observer's usual ways meant. But he placed the question in a recess of his mind for later.

x · x · x

It was the Hour of the Second Turning. As the tiny bells hung from the mirror ropes rang the change, the light of the Chamber of Ceremony went from pewter-glinted to burnished copper.

From his place on the first balcony, Andeved watched the skin on the back of his hand go from shadowed to warmly luminescent, transfixed by the play of light on flesh. This chamber, its shape and colors, what was in it and what happened in it was a source of endless fascination. His first memories of it were filled with changing light. Of all the great halls carved out of Under's vast caverns, this one was the greatest. Not one but three levels had been carved, each of them with its own tunnel of light mirrors. The sunlight captured by the polished plates was usually diluted the farther back in the city one went. But here, in the Chamber of Ceremony, that never seemed true. Even the loftiest reaches of the vaulted ceiling were not completely enshadowed.

And when the sun shifted in the sky and the hours for turning the outer disks toward the light came, the jangling of the tiny rope bells chimed so loudly that for long moments the sound continued to careen from wall to wall.

Even now, before his eyes and ears had drunk their fill of the place, the tunnel bells died away and there was a silence made - created, he knew - for the speaking of the hour's ritual. From her position beside the Water Clock, this season's Ceremonialist, dressed in robes of deep red and decked with the black and white full-face mask of that office, spoke into the void:

"Turning and turned again.

The second solar revelation

Piercing, as a miner's candle might,

Morning's chill reflection.

Heat and light, sustenance, sight,

Turned again and turning."

The sound of the proscribed phrases sank into the ears, clothes, skin and bones of the hundreds of Underions in the great cavern. Those bones and flesh knew exactly when the echo of the ritual would die. Knew exactly when to reply, "The lives of the people. Turning. Turning." And though each time Andeved swore he would be the rebel by leaving the response unsaid, he had not yet mastered the doing of that irreverence.

Then, before the reverberations of the reply had ceased, there was noise from the outer hall. All heads turned toward the cavern-high doors - but Andeved glanced back and saw Lord Paell's hands tighten into fists. How his cousin must dread this moment - to see the stranger who was to be his wife here, in the company of those who desired and those who dreaded his humiliation. And yet, in the band of light that flowed over the wide dais Lord Paell posed as calm, resplendent in a tunic of garnet and a half-mask of green with long visqcock feathers arrayed lavishly on each side. Andeved wondered if anyone else saw that the very tips of those feathers trembled, oh so very slightly.

The doors completed their slow, stately swing open.

"Ahhh." Those who first saw what entered sighed as one. Tall as the looming doorway came branches, leaves, trees. It was as if a forest moved into the chamber, bringing with it the rustle of wind playing in the open.

As the onlooking crowd moved apart to receive the procession, Andeved could see that the moving trees were, in fact, many long branches held by attendants dressed in mottled greens and browns.

"Ahhh," again from the courtiers. This time there was an undertone. Cavern dwellers could never so wantonly waste the tallest of plants. Hard enough to grow foodstuffs in a mostly sun-missed place. But this...

"Ohhh." A swelling of fragrance preceded the next of the procession. From wide baskets youngsters tossed handfuls of petals. Pink and yellow, lavender and ivory. And upon this carpet, laid on the unblemished smoothness of the chamber's stone floor, came the party of the Intended.

First came High Minister Voeller of Over. Attired in a robe the color of storms, sleeves edged with blackest fur, he held in one hand the engagement contract, its seals glinting in the bronze light. The other hand was empty - and so, too, for all purposes his face. This broker of kingdoms had not come masked to honor the customs of Under. Angry mutters stirred as he approached. Wait. Andeved looked harder. Voeller was masked - but it was painted so cunningly that it seemed the Minister's own features. As the crowd discovered the ruse, the mutters died down even as the unease grew.

Next in the procession came a woman who would not have been immediately noticed but for her place in the pageant. There was no glitter about her, no suggestion of the openwide, no haughty manner. She was short, stocky, but steady. Her gown was of deepest burgundy, made deeper as the copper-colored light of the Hour of Turning melted into it. Her mask was the half-mask of a ruling family, colored mid-dark blue-black, traced with the silver stars arranged in the pattern of...Andeved looked harder to see what it might be...ah, yes. The pattern of the Night Lord's Bow. The only star cluster seen so low in the sky that it was an icon of night protection for both demesnes. The young woman carried a small wooden chest, polished to a high sheen, no doubt containing the Overite's guesting gift.

Who was this subtle, unforward herald?

"The Lady Kendle, younger cousin to your cousin's betrothed," came a whisper from behind Andeved where Belwether had anticipated his question. "She comes as companion to the Lady Arrant. Some say there is more of the servant-to-master in this, but I speak as one who seeks to learn what others know." And with this, the Fool managed, somehow, to withdraw without actually moving at all. Andeved sighed to himself.

But his attention was again fully caught with the entrance, finally, of the Lady Arrant, the Intended.

She came, walking stiffly, in a gown of pale pastels that, in the intensity of the hour's light, had turned to muddy golds and russets. Her mask was of white and copper, made in the shape of a sunburst. Was it a dawning or a sunset? Andeved could not tell.

The attendants of the trees made a circle around the lady. And all stopped. In the silence that sprang from perceiving motionlessness when action is expected, awkwardness built. This was not the way the moment had been agreed upon in those long hours of negotiation. Paell was to have met Arrant in the center of the chamber and escorted her to the dais, each in the full focus of both contingents. But the lady was encircled, without an access way to be seen.

It grew quiet and then more quiet, save for the susurrus of the grove whose branches were not shivered by wind but by the beat of blood. Those courtiers who had been murmuring amongst themselves or jostling for a better view fell silent.

Lord Paell stood alone on the dais in a space built of his disbelief and the terrible expectations of the crowd. Like a cautious crow, he tilted his head, listening for more than a dozen heartbeats, as if seeking direction from the empty air.

Andeved's fingers began to twitch. Three times he flinched, needing to step in, to break his cousin's paralysis. But the moment was too witnessed, too intimately observed. So the taut, unseen connection of cousin-friend between large-knuckled Andeved and fine-boned Paell stretched even tighter. To the point of pain.

Then, from beneath and within the stone of the chamber came a low, sweeping sound, a groan that shook the air and built and grew louder until it became a howl of rock. And another rumble of despair came, pushing through the very walls of the chamber. Then another, until the air could hold no more howling.

The crowd, with a single voice, moaned a word that named their fear: Bittercalls.

No sooner had that name been voiced than the rock walls creaked and crackled with bulging and pushing - here an immense forehead, there an unseeing eye as big as a cistern. Stone walls were forced by a power too large to consider into the shapes of three howling faces. The Bittercalls were present - those who existed only to be harbingers of disaster, who ate fear and drank chaos.

Courtiers scrambled into a mass in the center of the room, the pretend grove trampled underfoot. Overites and Underions alike huddled together, as if that would protect them from the doom the Bittercalls inevitably preceded.

Only Paell remained alone, his mask askew but his pose unbroken, a small dark smile on his lips. Until the last howl died he stood unmoved, one leg cocked at the knee and the other locked with the foot turned slightly outward. Then, when only the cries of the frightened broke the silence left when the nightmare visages melted once again into the stone, he raised his hands to straighten his mask. That done, he lifted his hands even higher. Carefully he uncurled his fingers from the fists they had formed, leaving the forefingers on each hand bent at the middle knuckle. In his mind he saw himself, from fingertip to pointed foot, and approved of the picture. It was time to speak. He drew in a clean, deep breath and, tightening the tendons and muscles below his lungs, pushed up the words to be heard.

"Do not fear." The echo of his voice came back to him. He listened and found it strong. "We are well and we will be well. Rise up and do not be afraid."

But immediately he saw there were no people who had fallen down and the mischoice of words irritated him. Still, those who cowered in the center of the great hall began to regroup in more normal ways. Paell scanned the balconies, too, for signs of people in distress. Slowly the crowds that had so eagerly lined the railing were returning to see what was happening on the main floor. He saw Andeved on the first level, moving among the shaken onlookers. That ludicrous boy, all knuckles and knees. No grace, no sense of duty. But loyal.

A strident voice, edged with anger, took Paell's attention from his cousin. There, in the middle of everything, the lady Arrant pointed and gestured and spoke - too loudly. He could hear every syllable much too distinctly.

"No, pick them up. All the branches. They are ruined, take them out. Kendle, come here and bring the casket." Leaving her attendants to gather the now trampled branches that had so recently been her sanctuary, Arrant strode forward. Toward him.

Before he could think to do otherwise, Paell lowered his arms. His Intended had climbed the seven steps to the dais and was almost upon him. His reaction to this unseemly haste and invasion of what was surely his place and public moment was a surprise to himself - he had begun to panic. More so the closer she got.

"The ceremony is ruined." Arrant's tone had an edge to it that suggested movement barely restrained. "We have to do something with the people. How do you want to organize clearing the hall?"

Arrant's eruption into demands and questions with so little ceremony made Paell almost ill. The whole ceremony, for that matter, was a descent into uncivilized chaos - circled tree branches, departure from the planned way, the Bittercalls, the Intended's abruptness. Was he the only one to keep to the right in all of this? With great determination he recalled the words that should have been spoken.

"Lady Arrant, as Lord of Under I welcome you to the heart of our city and to my own heart. You come today as representative of Over and as she who will share--"

Paell stopped. The lady was staring as if she had never seen the likes of him before. At first he could not think why she was so amazed. But he could tell from her expression that something had stunned her into silence. He could only conclude it must be himself.

"Ah, yes, Lady Arrant. You have not truly seen me before this and I do not doubt you are struck by what you see. I have been told I am a handsome man." He said the words gently so as to appear humble, but still the lady's face took on a deep ruddiness. Perhaps she was embarrassed by appearing so crude in his presence. He tried to help her.

"Those who have seen behind your mask tell me you are very beautiful. More so than the drawings sent to us could show." She did not warm to his courtesy. He tried another tack. "Perhaps you feel uncertain of what is required here. Our society is so much more... shall we say...ordered than yours. But rest assured, my people do not hold your lack of ceremony against you, for you are not familiar with our ways as yet."

"Are you mad?" The Intended waved her arm toward the rest of the great room. "Did you hear the Bittercalls? Look at all the frightened people. You must do something."

Paell looked out over the milling crowd and his heart warmed.

"They are mine and I am theirs. We can rest in that."

Arrant stared at him.

At that moment, one of the Overites, a short younger woman - the one who carried the guesting gift casket - appeared at Arrant's side.

"Cousin? Lady? Perhaps we should--"

Paell felt anticipation stir. Since he first set his eyes on that polished, wooden box he had barely been able to restrain his curiosity. What had the Overites brought him? The box alone was worth a great deal. But what was in it?

Paell inclined his head in the gracious way, though he did it a bit too quickly in his eagerness. "Yes, you want to present the guest gift. How splendid." He held out his arms.

"No...I..." The plain young woman pulled back, apparently unable to speak to her betters with any ease at all. While she spluttered awkwardly, others also began to approach the dais - several of Paell's advisors, the Chief Advisor Etcherelle, the Overite High Minister Voeller. Would they not let him be?

They closed around him, a living prison.

From his vantage point at the balcony railing, Andeved watched his cousin. And as he did so, all the fears he had tried so hard to conquer returned. Something was wrong with Paell. Something fundamental. How else to explain the man's calm hard on the heels of the Bittercalls, the strangely skewed comments and priorities of recent days?

At least he was no longer alone in his apprehension. The Chief Advisor's alarm at Paell's non-response and her charge toward the dais made that clear. Andeved's father, a late arrival to the ceremony who had stationed himself on the uppermost balcony, had also registered a reaction. It was not difficult to read the black study on his father's face. Unlike Etcherelle, Sere would not step forward to help, however. As usual, he left the scene, waiting for the object of his sufferance to come to him.

Worst of all, the chamber was filled with desperately worried people who needed reassurance, counsel, someone to tell them they need not fear, to name and then prevent the disaster the Bittercalls had come to predict. Would no one step in and take charge?

Chief Advisor Etcherelle was on the dais now and, for good or ill, she signaled for the attention of the crowd.

"Quiet," she shouted over the tumult. "Quiet and listen."

Beside her the Lady Arrant frowned deeply, clutching at Paell's arm and whispering swiftly and violently into his ear. He seemed not to hear, his gaze never wavering from the shining box.

Slowly the anxious crowd moved toward the dais, though Andeved was hard pressed to know whether it was from the Chief Advisor's shouting or the peculiar tableau arrayed at the top of the seven steps. He shivered under the stress - and heard a similar movement from behind him where Belwether stood. The notion that the Fool was uneasy was unexpected and alarming.

"The Lord Paell wishes you to know that his advisors will be gathering in the next hour." Etcherelle, her sharp eyes glinting from behind her mask, arrowed her glance to one after another of the many near the dais. As if her glance were an accusation, an uneasy quiet formed in the front of the hall, spreading backward and upward.

"At the Hour of the Last Turning we will bring our conclusions and a plan back to this hall. For now, go to your home chambers." For a space no one moved. Etcherelle's native impatience asserted itself. "Go on. Go home. Now."

At last, some turned toward the doorway, worriedly muttering, reluctant to leave the comfort of numbers. The Bittercall's wordless prophecy might mean a single death or many, a small but potent disaster or one to strike down a world. Until they knew what to expect, it felt better to be with others.

And then there was the mesmerizing scene on the dais. Andeved, like many of the folk in the great hall, could not leave because he could not bear to look away from it. So it was he saw that, in her fierce whispering to Paell, Arrant gestured too broadly and jostled Kendle, causing the gift casket to fall from her hands, hit the stone floor with a loud report and fall open. A bright effervescence of light flew up from the broken box, up into the highest spaces of the vaulted dome of the chamber. Back and forth it streaked, leaving a glowing trail in the eyes of the beholders. Then down it came, over the crowd, like tiny ball lightning, zigzagging from person to person. Just over their heads, stopping for the beat of a heart at each one. Then rushing on. Then streaking toward the dais, hovering over Etcherelle, then Arrant, then Paell. And stopping above Paell. Stopping long enough that it could be identified.

Once again the crowd saw and knew and named. Flett. The word breathed up from those watching like the exhalation of a dream. Unmistakable. The sinuous body, no longer than a child's finger, a blunt, eyeless head - like a blind worm powdered with light. And the wings of shifting, oil-on-water colors, fluttering faster than the mind could grasp.

As if one body, the crowd held its breath. Nothing moved except the fey luminescence of the flett as it described an intimate circle around Lord Paell's head, closer with each revolution until, at last, it settled delicately on the top curve of his ear. In a movement peculiar to fletts, it nestled between Paell's ear and head, bringing both wings to one side of its body to lay them over the ear of its now-host like a gossamer coverlet of colors.

Again, as one, the crowd sighed. No matter that disaster was moving toward them all, this was a thing of wonder and awe. Only a very few times in a handful of generations had one of these mysterious beings singled out one of the grossfolk with a bonding. And they had seen it here, and it had been one of their own.

Andeved found it hard to breathe. His hands were clenched so tightly his nails dug into his palms like tiny skinning knives. Too much had happened too quickly and his heart lurched painfully against his ribs. Was this seeming gift of grace what the Bitttercalls had come to decry? How could something so rare and beautiful be the stuff of disaster? Or was it the marriage that was to connect Under and Over that prompted the visitation? Or the off-balancing arrival of Overites to the protected realm of Under? Or his cousin's increasing strangeness?

His cousin. Andeved found that his burgeoning unease did not lessen, but grew, as he looked at Paell, now the pinpoint center of all attention. He could not help but look - and could not help but be frightened. For an expression of ecstasy had come to Paell's face and to it he had utterly surrendered. Eyes closed, mouth open, all eerily lit by the bodyglow of the worm.

Behind Andeved, Belwether was rocking back and forth in manifest distress, repeating and repeating but one phrase: "They knew. They knew, oh save us, they knew."

x·x·x

The urge to find privacy and the lust for display fought a giddy battle within him. He reached up to touch the creature but stopped just short for fear of disturbing, harming or even offending it. Paell frowned in frustration. He knew too little about fletts - though what he did know shivered him with elation. They were rare. Almost unheard of in Under. Surely the mark of a special destiny. A visible sign of what Paell had always believed. The ruin of his well-rehearsed ceremony by the undisciplined Overites and the manifestation of the Bittercalls did not seem so predictive now.

He looked around, needing to search the faces of those near him for their reaction to his wondrous addition - and found that he was almost alone, having somehow walked out of the Chamber of Ceremonies toward his own rooms. Only Etcherelle remained at his side. He was disappointed. His chief advisor never showed emotion. He would get no satisfaction from her face.

Her face. Odd. Her mouth moved, as if in speech, but no sound came forth. Her brows were furrowed and the lines that splayed out from the corners of her eyes were deeper than usual. What was she doing? Did she realize she was soundless? Or was she mocking him for not paying closer attention?

"Etcherelle, I would thank you to stop--" But Paell could speak no more. His words reverberated so strangely in his head he knew immediately it was not his advisor who was voiceless but he who could not hear. Thunder crashed against his chest, hammered in his head. It was the only sound he could hear - the sound of his heart pounding out its fear.

He must regain control. In an attempt to calm, he shut his eyes. But opened them again in panic. The darkness behind his eyes was too silent, too deep without any noise to tether him to the outside. Sweat ran, hot and swift, down his spine. In front of him, Etcherelle stood immobile with astonishment. In some way he must let her know his problem. He reached up and placed his fingers against his throat to at least feel the words he would try to make heard.

"There appears to be a problem, perhaps due to the physical adjustment I must make to my flett. It seems I cannot hear, at least for now." It did not feel like a whisper that went through his throat, but Paell could not tell for sure.

Etcherelle moved her lips again, then caught herself doing so and stopped. Instead she nodded so vigorously that Paell thought surely her head would snap off with the force.

"I can see you well enough. You needn't visually shout." His choice of words pleased him. He began to believe he could bring advantage from this. Then she began to speak again. It irritated him that she would so disregard his state that he settled his fingers against his throat again so he might remonstrate. In so doing he brushed up against the flett as it nestled behind his ear and draped down toward the cords of his neck.

His reply died before it was born, for as his fingers touched the powdery skin of the wormlike creature he began to hear the slightest of noises. Etcherelle's voice came at him as if from a distance - not the voice he knew from his youth, first as severe foster mother and then as relentless advisor. This was gentle, soft, papery.

"...what I say? How will we - I could get pen and--"

Paell could feel the smile drift to his lips as he made to answer her. "Be calm, Chief Advisor. It seems that when I am in contact with the flett, I can hear. It must be part of this new, joined state."

The flood of relief that swept away Etcherelle's distress proved amusing to Paell. He pressed his advantage.

"So do not tarry with me. I shall, as always, be well. Go, call the Council. Bring together the guild leaders. And when all are assembled, I will come and we will calm the fears the Bittercalls created. And as soon as possible, send Andeved to the Archives. Tell him to find everything on fletts and bring it to me."

"I shall. Indeed." Etcherelle stumbled in her reply but it was not unpleasant to hear, filtered through the fey creature's perception. A great welling of benevolence filled him as he watched his second-mother leave at his bidding. All would be well. He knew it.

He brought his fingers away from his neck where they touched the flett. But his hand felt suddenly cool so he looked at it. For the second time in this strange hour, the thundering of his heart bashed against the darkness in his head. His fingers were covered with red - blood - that could only be his.

CHAPTER TWO

She had not imagined a place could be hot and cold in the same instant, but it was all too true. The stone bench on which Kendle sat was clammy and hard, but the tongue-lashing coming her way from Arrant was blistering - all the more so for being undeserved.

"Seasons and seasons of work almost ruined! You stupid, clumsy girl!" Arrant's voice had jumped up several octaves and had a shrillness that was hard on the ears as well as the heart.

Kendle tried to defend herself. "But it was you jostled me--"

"And see," Arrant gestured widely to the others in the antechamber, "she will not even take responsibility for what she's done." Her cousin made that awful tsk-tsk sound she hated so much and then delivered the ultimate wound. "Disappointed, Kendle - I am, the High Minister is, your people are. Don't you realize how important this proposed marriage is, how much of our entire way of life rests on it?"

"No one is more aware of that than I," Kendle began.

"Then why were you not more careful? Why did you drop the box and let the flett escape at the wrong time? Chance - luck - only that saved us. If the flett had been damaged - do you know what disaster that might have been?" Arrant jabbed at her with a finger that seemed more dagger than flesh. Even as the stone bench got colder, Kendle's insides twisted and burned. If only she could escape this humiliation and fix what she was wrongfully accused of doing.

The triple-thick doorway curtains sluggishly parted and High Minister Voeller entered. Below eyes that perpetually squinted, his lips were pursed. He had assumed this expression of disdainful superiority the very hour the party of the Intended had set out from Over and, as far as Kendle could tell, it had not left his face for a moment since.

"Good news, honored lady." His tone was smooth, silvery. "The Underions would like nothing more than to include you in the emergency council meeting."

Voeller made the peculiar half bow he customarily did upon delivering valuable information, though he never broke eye contact during the maneuver.

"Really?" Her cousin's manner moderated. "They changed their minds?"

"It was the delivery of your good reasoning that produced this result, I believe." Voeller pressed his thin lips together harder in what Kendle recognized, after long years of observation, was a smile. "The meeting will not begin until you arrive."

"Yes, yes." A half smile flickered across Arrant's face. "Excellent. What we need now is to regain control of our plan." Voeller and the several clan leaders left their aimless milling about the room and found seats at the long stone table. Kendle did not bother to move. She was never given a seat at these meetings, but neither was she ever excused from her uncomfortable place at the periphery.

"Clan Leader Spentser," Arrant began even as she assumed her seat at the head of the table, "do you have a report yet?"

The dark, burly clansman nodded. His stubby, callused fingers twisted and untwisted like demented slugs.

"Yes, there was a chance to see what needed seeing. We were shown the gesh pens down below. As we...as you suspected, the herds are large in number. The geshherders are almost frantically busy. They would not take us to see the excavations themselves, but surely such activity in the pens can only mean a highly productive operation."

"Good work." Arrant's praise was terse and, as usual, prefatory to a further demand. "I want to know how much is actually being extracted in a moon cycle. When we ask for the bride-gift, we need to be sure of the amounts - too much and they will balk, too little and we will suffer."

"Aye, lady." The clan leader's head bobbed up and down in agreement.

There was a pause. Arrant continued to stare at Spentser. The man began to squirm under the scrutiny, his thick neck reddening.

"Well? Were you going to the excavation sites now? Or perhaps you have something more important..."

"No, lady. I mean, yes, I am going. Now." Spentser awkwardly clambered over the bench and made for the doorway. The moment he had pushed out through the door hangings, several of the clan leaders put their hands in front of their faces, whispering to one another and snickering.

"Spentser brings us very useful information." Arrant frowned at each of the others in turn. "It will not do to make comments about his person."

"Of course, lady." "Naturally." "Just so." Those singled out for reprimand responded in a chorus.

"And next," Arrant was going full bore, "we must address the issue of the botched guest gift and the...shall we say...the unique behavior of Lord Paell."

The remaining clan leaders shook their heads and muttered. Several sneaked glances at Kendle.

"My Intended and I share a common affliction - both of us are shadowed by cousins." Arrant frowned over at Voeller. "What is that boy's name?"

"Andeved, my lady. He is called Andeved." The High Minister spoke the name as if it were an apology.

"Yes, yes. A lanky, raw-boned creature - nothing like our shadow." Arrant sighed. It was a quick, harsh sound. "But the young man is close to Paell and, for that reason alone, knows more than most. We can only hope that setting our cousin upon Paell's will gain us useful information."

Everyone in the room turned to look at Kendle, the stares sticking into her like needles. Her sense of self-preservation rose along with the red that flushed across her cheeks. She stood up and made for the doorway.

"I will go and find out what I can," she heard her voice drop into the room and fall, graceless, into disdainful reception. But Kendle took a deep breath and lifted her eyes to take in all those who made this room the burning, freezing place it was. "I will help. Of course. I always have."

And with that she turned and ducked through the heavy draperies, out of the anteroom and into the hallway.

Walking and swearing under her breath, she turned a corner too sharply and banged her elbow against the hard rock. *Stupid, stupid, stupid.* It was the worst epithet she could think of and it applied to this merciless maze of stone and most of the people who lived here. Or were guesting here, for that matter. She rubbed her bruised elbow and derided herself for doing what she despised most in others: claiming such devotion to the people of Over when she could hardly stand a single one of them.

The corridor turned again and then opened to a nexus of hallways. At one side began a broad, curved stairway leading down. She knew this must be the Grand Stair leading toward the Chamber of Ceremony and, beyond that, the apartments of Lord Paell and his family. If she must find her counterpart cousin, that would surely be the place to start the search.

But the stairway was full of people trudging up and down, intent on errands or looking for someone to gossip with or going from here to there just to be seen. Some wore those masks of office. Some were drably dressed. Others were decked in finery that was trumped by chains and bangles of the precious metals and gems that only Under possessed.

Not for the first time Kendle felt dowdy, an outsider, ill at ease in her own skin. That it happened now, here, was not too odd. But it happened more often at home, in Over. Which wasn't really odd. Sad, probably. Stupid, maybe.

At least she could shine at some things.

Kendle straightened her shoulders and started down the wide, shallow stairs, ignoring the appraising looks she got. She had work to do: Find Andeved. Find out if the guesting gift that had been loosed too soon was still pleasing the chosen host - and whether it pleased Paell enough he would overcome his strange behavior when it was time for Arrant to request the bride-gift. Because it all rested on that. Nothing else mattered. There wasn't much time.

It was a long decline, however, to get to the level that held Paell's living area. Kendle had made a point of learning as much about Under as possible before coming. So she knew that the older sections of Under, in which Paell and his family lived, were lower and more inward in the maze of caverns, nearer to where the Underion ancestors had found the cliffside opening that led them deep into what became their refuge and home. It was said that the higher an Underion lived in the caves, the less prestige they had. But Overites found it hard to see the sense of that because not too far beneath the oldest of the vast, vaulted chambers were the gesh caves.

Kendle shuddered at the thought and almost missed a step on the still-descending grand stairway. She'd never seen one, but she'd heard that these gesh were dark-dwelling monsters, repulsively ugly, bred to be huge with bile sacs the size of a person's head, bile that ate through rock and turned it into soil, enormous bugs that fed on excrement and garbage. It turned her stomach to think of it.

And yet - Kendle shook her head at the contrariness of circumstance - and yet it was these same grotesqueries upon which the welfare of Over now depended. But that thought was interrupted as she stumbled, catching her heel on a stone step worn to a dip with generations of use. She paused to rub her calves. Walking for days on the giving bridgeways was a pleasure compared to this bone-jolting upping and downing.

It suddenly dawned on her that there should be more people on the stairs. But there were only a few going each direction - and they didn't have the look of courtiers or anyone who might frequent the levels on which the governing class was found.

No wonder her legs ached. She'd gone too far down the main stairway. A whiff of something foul tweaked her nose. Much too far.

With an irritation she felt no need to conceal, Kendle turned around to begin the corrective ascent. Only to be passed, with a whoosh of air and a trail of mutterings, by a gangly young man in a vivid mask hurtling headlong downward. Close behind him came a man with a look of determination on his face that appeared to be a permanent resident. It was common knowledge that the only one to whom an Oni had attached was Paell's cousin, Andeved.

"Excuse me. I say..." But the boy and his silent shadow were well past her already. They must be on some important errand. Kendle's curiosity woke up and poked her. She had to talk to him anyway - she'd been directed to find him - well, so be it.

Ignoring the jolts of even more downstepping, Kendle started after Andeved. Quickly. The two ahead of her were nearly flying downward. In a matter of moments she was breathing hard - and sorely regretting the need to do so, for the smell coming upward was increasingly horrible - a cross between a full slop jar and a warm-season funeral held too late. It could only mean their destination was the gesh pens.

The stair curved down, curved again, passed landings and sidehalls, downward until the refraction tunnels no longer sliced into the halls with warm illumination, downward until there was only the sickly green light of jinncar moss to show the way.

Then the stairs broadened and finally opened into an immense cavern – rough-hewn, ancient, so enormous that the farthest reaches were indistinct voids. All around the walls of the massive cavern were thick, twisted, impossibly lush masses of jinncar. The fungus must have much to feed on in this fetid place if the rank air was any indication. Kendle held her tunic sleeve up to her mouth and nose, too staggered by the stench to go forward. Besides, as her eyes became accustomed to the greenish light, she began to see the number of pens spread across the immense floor, a multitude of corrals each holding...holding gesh, hundreds of them, teeming dark and wet.

To make matters worse, along the side walls a steady ooze of brownish, lumpy liquid dripped from huge conduits coming down through the cave's ceiling. Kendle knew by sight, if not by smell alone, that this was where the contents of every slop jar in Under eventually ended up to feed the monster gesh. It was just too much. Kendle made herself look elsewhere before the contents of her stomach joined the general miasma.

She focused on locating Andeved among the teeming pens. Eventually, she saw him standing next to a man who was surrounded by four of the largest of the insects. The man was leaning over to pick up a gesh the size of a clothes chest, lifting it onto what Kendle's research on the subject indicated was a milking bench. Even from where she stood, it was all too obvious that the monster bug was ready to be emptied. Four red, mottled sacs beneath its blue-black flightless wings bulged with the thick, malodorous and precious fluid that allowed Underions to carve space in the unyielding rock. The herder pressed down on one of the fleshy sacs, letting the stinking bile flow out and into a leather-lined catchment pail.

Kendle fought hard to keep from gagging - and to keep her watering eyes on Andeved. The young man was trying to speak to the worker but could not seem to get the man's attention. Finally, the boy began to shout - so loudly that Kendle could hear him above the terrible slithering sound of bugs dragging full bile sacs across hard stone in a cavern that echoed.

"Geshherder Lampey." Andeved tugged on the older man's sleeve, though it had little effect. "Excuse me. Sir. I bring a message from Lord Paell."

The herder continued with the milking, not letting the smallest smear of the viscous bile escape.

"Herder Lampey? A message, sir. SIR!" The man was deliberately ignoring Andeved. Ignoring the official messenger of Lord Paell. Interesting. What was going on here?

Andeved raised his voice even louder. "You cannot refuse to hear a message from---"

Grunting with the effort, the herder lifted the now-emptied gesh from the milking table and set it back on the cavern floor. Setting it very nearly on Andeved's boot.

"I heard you, boy." Old Lampey's voice cut through the clamor of the corrals like gesh bile through stone. "You don't have to shout. Now I'm finished with this one you can talk at me. But make it short - there's more work to be done."

Straightening his mask of duty, Andeved drew in a breath - and started to cough. Kendle felt some sympathy. The geshherder might be used to the smell, but few others were - or wanted to be. Andeved recovered and began again.

"Lord Paell requests the Council of Leads to gather for a meeting at the Hour of the Spirit in the Great Hall. The visitation of the Bittercalls requires discussion."

"Don't need to meet. Need to work." Lampey shook his head and, twisting up his mouth, spat a huge glob of spittle onto the floor. The nearest gesh scuttled to it and had devoured it before Kendle's stomach even had a chance to turn. Paell's cousin did not even seem to see it.

"But that may be part of the problem, the Bittercalls do not come for nothing. There is disaster coming. We must prepare."

"Wrong. And so very wrong." Lampey jabbed a thick, callused finger toward Andeved with every word. "Those rock-faced doomsayers don't predict disaster, they cause fear and fear causes mistakes and mistakes cause disaster. We don't plan to make mistakes. Just work."

"As you say, Lampey. That is your belief. But the meeting remains, all the same. Lord Paell has called it. Your duty is to come."

The lead herder waved him away with a gesture that looked part acceptance and part dismissal and turned back to his odious charges. He made a curious clicking noise and it drew the four crawling beasts after him like sweet music draws lovers.

Andeved was left standing like a fool, his mask of office slightly askew with the effort of shouting and his fists clenched tightly. Shaking his head, he turned back toward the stairs, past the corrals, past the milking benches, past the effluent chutes that brought down the waste the gesh ate like cake. And right toward Kendle - who suddenly wished to be elsewhere. It would not do for the Lord's cousin to think she was spying on him.

But Andeved's long legs brought him too close too fast. Abruptly, he was right in front of her. Her mind flew over possible excuses, anything that might mitigate the embarrassment of being discovered here, following him. And just as abruptly he was past her. Going up the stair, pulling off his mask, leaving a trail of mutterings behind him in the noxious air.

He hadn't recognized her at all. Kendle was instantly relieved and rather insulted. Well, fine. If someone was too involved with himself and didn't notice what was right in front of him, too bad. She would just keep following him. With that kind of attitude, he might never notice her and that would just make her job easier.

"You are Kendle, cousin to the Lady Arrant." The words were spoken not as question but as fact. The Oni had somehow come to be standing on the step just below her, though how he managed it without her seeing him was beyond her.

"Yes. Yes, I am." His sudden words threw her off her conversational balance. "You are from On - attached to Lord Paell's cousin aren't you?" Kendle chided herself for such a blatant statement of the obvious.

"You need to speak to him." The Oni's voice was rumbly, oddly loud and quiet at the same time. "You may follow, if you wish." He glanced at the upward reaching stairway and then back at her. His gaze stopped on her for a moment - one that stretched out longer than normal conversation might allow. For no reason she could name, a flush swept up her neck and left her feeling uncommonly awkward.

"I am Belwether," he said softly. And then turned up and began taking the stairs two at a time, though it appeared not to strain him in the slightest.

Sighing, Kendle made to follow. Too many stairs in this place. Too many by far. Step. Step. Step.

By the time they had all conquered the upward climb, Kendle's legs burned and shook. But Andeved had led them to the Hall of Office - a place she wanted to see, if not be seen in. Her counter-cousin, who had not turned round to see who or what followed him the entire time, made a backward gesture toward Belwether indicating he should remain outside and then the boy disappeared behind heavy, ornate door draperies.

A hand gripped her elbow - it made her start. Gently but firmly, Belwether pulled her into a deep niche in the hallway - one made for decoration but clearly used by the Oni for waiting unobserved while still observing. It was cold and dark in the cramped corner. But then where in this stone fortress wasn't it cold and dark? Best try to turn this momentary misery to an advantage.

"So, you are Belwether? I've never met an Attached Oni before. How long have you been with Lord Paell's cousin?"

"Since he was seven." Belwether's face was hidden from her by shadow and his voice, though deep, was oddly devoid of inflection.

"That's an awfully long time to be away from your own home. I guess you miss it very much."

Nothing came from the darkness. Several clerks, arms full of parchments, padded by out in the corridor, their felt boots making soft soughings as they walked.

The longer the silence, the more distressed Kendle became. Had she offended him with mention of home? Suddenly Belwether gripped her elbow and pushed her out toward the hall.

Through the drapery came Andeved, his messenger's mask in one hand, his head down as if he were searching the floor for meaning.

"Now. Mention food," came a rumble from the nook behind her.

"Excuse me," Kendle began as she stepped forward, "you are Lord Paell's cousin? I am Kendle, Lady Arrant's cousin and--"

Andeved's head swung up and he looked at her in surprise and, she thought, some curiosity.

"You're the one I saw." He smiled just a bit, somewhat shyly. "I didn't think I'd get the chance to meet you. It's been--" he waved vaguely toward the chambers lining the corridor, "--rather busy, and busyness for them usually involves running for me."

Though their acquaintance was only moments old, Kendle felt a surge of compassionate understanding. She knew what it was like to be on the edge of power, at the beck and call of those who were both rulers and family.

"Indeed, sometimes I think..." She stopped as a gaggle of courtiers turned into the far end of the hallway, heading their way. "But perhaps we could talk elsewhere? I'm sure it's mealtime and..."

"Say no more." Andeved straightened his shoulders, his expression brightening. "I know a shortcut to the refectory." He motioned her to follow him and she was happy to do so. This was progress indeed - she should accomplish her mission soon. At no pain to herself.

X • X • X

"We cannot tell precisely why the Bittercalls come." Chief Advisor Etcherelle's caustic voice cut through the weary babble of the council meeting. "Pointless to attempt to name just one cause.

Pointless." Etcherelle pounded the table in her irritation, narrowly missing her discarded mask of office.

Kendle shifted uncomfortably on the stone bench cut into the back wall of the council chamber. Her cousin had been invited to the Underion's meeting - but only after making an issue of it through the irritating intervention of High Minister Voeller. Voeller, as a result, did not get invited.

Arrant sat at the end of the table opposite Lord Paell. She had not spoken much yet, but all the signs were there - an outburst was coming. Paell, on the other hand, had not spoken at all. Every once in a while he touched the flett that now nestled behind his ear. It must be strange to have a creature take up residence on your head. Kendle shivered a bit with the thought. There was no reason to be apprehensive. Fletts were a rare and special honor. But a brief, dark vision of the flat blood-leeches that slithered in the high-country lakes came to her all the same. She quickly turned her attention back to the meeting.

Voices collided across the huge stone table, voices of fear, need, resistance, denial. Kendle sighed. Replace the rigid cavern walls with a slightly rocking tree-hung meeting room and it could have been home.

"But we must at least make a list of what we think brought them if we are to try to prevent the disaster that must inevitably follow. We must." The speaker was a short, red-faced man who Kendle thought had been introduced as Corson, leader of the wallworkers - though what a wallworker was had not been explained. His demand brought mutters of agreement from around the table.

"Really? We *must* make a list?" Etcherelle wielded her sarcasm like a weapon. "So we can be the very first in all of history to avert a Bittercall-heralded event? Why, yes. We must make a list, of course."

Corson flinched under the Chief Advisor's verbal onslaught. Yet Kendle saw the man take a breath and try another approach. He looked to Lord Paell.

"And you - do you agree we must not even try to head off whatever calamity is coming?"

Deep inside himself, far deeper than Paell was wont to venture, trepidation created uncommon heartbeats, breaking the rhythm that could have soothed him. Some of the off-beatings were soft, almost unfelt but for a sense of imbalance. Others were so hard, it made him stagger if he were walking, or stammer if he were speaking.

It concerned him, this intrusion into his carefully cultivated grace. He tried to puzzle out what caused the unwanted syncopation. Blaming the wildly unceremoniously bestowed but glorious addition of the flett was not possible. The very idea of doing that made him flush with an anger so intimate and pure that it might have become savage rage in a lesser man. But he was a man of history, a leader becoming legend. No display of untoward emotion would sully his mythic moment. He owed his people that much; they would expect no less.

Paell reached up and ran his forefinger down the soft valley that lay between the body of his flett and the tender, bare skin behind his ear. Once again, directly touching the creature sent a swift, molten pulse down his arm, into his body, ending in his groin - a small, warm blossoming of pleasure. He parted his lips and sighed very softly, but kept his eyes wide open so that no one looking at him would know of his moment's bliss. He would have the little god, for he knew now that's what it was, always within reach. He would forgive Arrant's lack of love and grace, for she had brought him the flett. He would wed the lady and, in doing so, also join Under and Over, saving them all. He would take his place in destiny's record. Of this he was sure. He reached upward again.

"Lord Paell?" The room was silent but for Arrant's insistent attempt to get Paell's attention. All eyes were on the Underion leader, who did not move but only stroked the creature behind his ear and breathed out softly through lips parted in a small, odd smile.

"Intended One. Tell us what you believe we should do." Though Arrant's words were diplomatic, the tone bespoke a mounting irritation. From long experience, Kendle knew anger was imminent.

With jerky movements Paell rose from his place and started toward the door. "Very well. Then I must go and there...to make sure..." His words trailed behind him, incoherent, unfinished and unsettling.

At first no one could speak into the stunned quiet that followed Paell's departure. But when someone did, it was Arrant.

"I know Lord Paell and I are not yet wed. But we will be, and soon. In his absence, I am willing and fully able to be of help in this time of trouble."

Council members drew back at the force of her declaration. A low murmuring began.

"I propose that we do, indeed, make a list of possible reasons why the Bittercalls might have foretold the coming of a disaster. Once that is completed, then--"

Etcherelle leaned across the table, interrupting without hesitation.

"I wonder, Lady Arrant, that you propose to do so when your coming is most likely the event to top that list?"

Now those around the room caught their breath. Some grabbed the table edge in surprise. While a few lost color in their cheeks, Arrant gained red. When she spoke again, Kendle could tell it was all her cousin could do to keep from sputtering out curses between every other word.

"I, head the list? You are saying that I am the reason the Bittercalls came to howl?"

Etcherelle narrowed her eyes and tilted her head. The Chief Advisor's expression reminded Kendle of one she had seen in the eyes of a six-clawed forest-raptor.

"Yes. Head the list. There was no difference in our routine, no break from the right and just traditions of the hours. Our ceremonies had been set and met. Only your intrusion was different. You and your flouting waste of growing things, your disrespectful minister, your wall of forest excluding our Lord Paell, demanding he demean himself by wrestling a way through to you. Indeed, it must be your arrival that set in motion whatever calamity is coming. No one--"

The world side-slipped, hard. A fist-sized stone fell from the ceiling of the chamber onto the table, gashing the polished surface. Then the bench Kendle was sitting on began to shake. No, the whole room was shaking. Bits and pieces of wall and ceiling fell off.

A deep rumble. Cries from the hallway. A council member called out in panic and scrambled under the heavy, stone table. A jolt - strong enough to topple several of the free-standing chairs and the people in them.

Then a sudden end to the shaking. And the queer moment of quiet and dazed calm that follows an unexpected terror. The council member under the table began to moan.

CHAPTER THREE

The farther back he went, the colder it became until his breath steamed and his fingers curled in for warmth. The light turned from a bright and shifting bronze to the seeping green dimness of the far-inward hallways. Andeved knew these back-reaching corridors better than almost anyone. He appreciated, if others did not, the contrasting nature of his favorite haunts. The openwideness of the outer terraces and the inner recesses given over, since no one else would have them, to the Archives.

A small, fast smile raced across Andeved's face. He was nearly there, one more turn. And there were the doors, tall as the high-ceilinged corridor, each of the pair three armspans wide, metal beaten so thin and worked so well that one person could manage them with ease. He could not help but reach out and touch, with never lessening awe, the wonder that was an Archive door. And in the coldness of the corridor, the doors were warm. Warm enough to please his chilled fingers as he pushed the metal marvels open.

Usually it took a long time to find Bertrynd – for the archivist seemed, like an ancient, cowled fish, to swim silently through the maze of shelves and ledges, crannies and alcoves. Never where you thought he would be, always too absorbed in the book, scroll or tablet of the moment. The faster way was to use the visitor alarm that had been hung in the entry. Andeved grabbed the heavy rod and clanged it against the hollow brass cylinder, beating it until the cavern reverberated with the clamor. And then he stopped and listened for the sweep-swish of the archivist's robes and the inevitable muttered invectives intrusion elicited from Bertrynd.

Beyond the big belly of the furnace that radiated both heat and light into the place came the sound of movement. Soon after came the archivist, squinting and puffing, as was usual. When he saw it was Andeved, his expression changed for the better. Also, as usual.

"It is you, my boy. Come to visit the old man of the archives. Welcome. Welcome." Bertrynd enveloped Andeved in a hug that was hearty for one so bony and cerebral, and then stepped back. "Again you've grown. Since last I saw you maybe three fingers of height added. Has your skull expanded with added wisdom? But, dear me, what is this you have with you?"

At first Andeved thought the old man referred to Belwether and turned to confirm that, indeed, the Fool had silently followed him here.

"No, no – *what* you have, not *who* you have," Bertrynd chuckled as he pointed at the mask of office clutched in Andeved's hand.

"Oh, that. Well, I was actually sent, officially, that is, for some knowledge. Lord Paell—"

"What does that upper-cousin of yours want now?" The archivist began squinting once again.

"Well, perhaps you have not heard the most recent news." Andeved tried to use what diplomacy his few years had brought him, for it was well known that Bertrynd held a profound disinterest in the state of affairs beyond the Archives. "The Lady Arrant of Over arrived and her guesting gift turned out to be a flett. And it attached to Lord Paell."

"You say what? A flett? Paell has it?" Bertrynd's agitation at the honor done to Paell and Under surprised Andeved. But behind him, the Fool murmured an equally agitated assent.

Clutching his mask of office as a way to focus on the duty that had brought him here, Andeved continued. "And so Lord Paell sent me here to get what knowledge there is about fletts and what will happen with it and him and how he should care for it, I suppose, and...."

Bertrynd turned on his heels, the voluminous robes twisting around his spare frame. "Come on then, boy," he shouted over his shoulder as he disappeared down an aisle of stone tablets. "And don't think I didn't notice Paell asked for knowledge with no thought for wisdom. Don't think that..." his voice fading as he faded in the long, darkening passage.

From behind him the Fool nudged Andeved to hurry after the archivist. And so he did, having to almost run to catch up with the surprisingly swift elder. Down the one aisle, then a turn, then another turn and another aisle, faster and faster. High hanging light globes popped on as movement passed under them, spluttering into dim, blueish-white illumination that marked the archivist's hurried, erratic trail. Until Bertrynd's sudden stop at a collection of scrolls nearly caused Andeved to collide with him.

"Here, no there. Not that." The archivist muttered to himself as he sorted through the scrolls in haste, almost careless haste. Not a manner Andeved had ever seen in the usually meticulous scholar.

"This one I think." Bertrynd pulled out a scroll so old that, though it had once been the color of clouds, it was now darkened to nearly the color of dirt. From a deep pocket in his robe, the old man extracted a fist worth of jinncar from a mesh bag. He blew on it, blew on it again and rubbed it between his hands until the moss glowed green and then hung the bag around his neck for a reading light. The scroll shook as he unrolled it, for his fingers trembled violently. Deep unease crept up Andeved's spine.

"See, here." Bertrynd's long fingers ran along the manuscript's surface. "This indicates that no caretaking was ever necessary to maintain a flett. Never did a flett seem to require food or physical protection or…well… anything at all. Yet, living beings require sustenance, rest, shelter. So the question becomes…"

The archivist abruptly rolled up the parchment and jammed it back onto the crowded shelf. Turning on his heel, he headed farther down the aisle, toward a darker recess where oddly shaped artifacts were lined up against sealed containers – large, small, clear or clouded, filled with swirling liquids or dusty with desiccated specimens that Andeved had always avoided examining too closely.

Bertrynd hesitated in front of a shadowed shelf, made as if to move on, then stopped. He turned toward Andeved and Belwether, a look of calculation and despair in disturbing evidence.

"We…we, here in Under, we do not have the records of On. Not the depth or breadth, nor number, most certainly not on the great range of subjects over so many generations." The archivist was not speaking to Andeved, but directly to Belwether. In humility. In apology. Andeved found, to his surprise, that being ignored was, for once, a relief. This conversation seemed to be headed toward something dark and weighty, too heavy for him.

"Yet," the old man continued, "We have sought to preserve what we have found in the form of written records. Or in ways without words." He pointed at three framed squares. In the middle of each square a long-winged creature was pinned. Fixed to the surface, open to the aging of air and examination.

Belwether pushed past Andeved to peer more closely at what was displayed. The boy startled to hear the Fool gasp.

"These are fletts. They have been…cut, splayed open. What does this mean, Archivist? What have you done?"

Bertrynd flinched. "I have done nothing. These creatures died with the death of their…mounts." The last word came spitting out of the old man's mouth. "There are those who learn the hidden ways of living creatures by opening them after death. The three… examples…here took seven generations to obtain and as long to study."

"To learn what?" Belwether could not turn his eyes away from the squares. "What could possibly...."

"That fletts do not appear to be the blessing tradition has them." The archivist pointed at the tail of one of the flayed creatures. "See the hollow bone-like structure at the end of the tail? It is posited that it is through this apparatus a flett gets its sustenance, how it feeds."

Silence. A pause. Then Andeved cried out in his conclusion. "It burrows. Into the head. It feeds on...."

"But they knew!" Belwether whirled on Bertrynd. "How could they know it would pick Paell?"

"They knew? What?" The old man's voice came out breathy and strained. "I do not know how that could be done. Nothing we know shows that a flett's choice can be directed. Are you sure?"

All three squares tumbled over at one time, shattering on the cavern floor. From above and outward somewhere came a crashing rumble, a shaking of rock, a bucking of stone. Andeved threw down his now useless mask and ran. Out. Up. In fear.

Lungs afire, legs pounding in spite of pain. Andeved made the distance from the Archives in a very few fearful moments that seemed to last forever. It was when he arrived up-inward from the main levels, that the dirt swirling downward in filthy drafts began and, in the same sweep, worsened. With the downdrafts of grime also came downrushing people, faces caked with mud and smeared with panic. Stumbling, careening, shoving, they came and then passed him.

"What happened?" Andeved grabbed at one of the downstepping to get an answer, but the woman pulled away from his grasp shouting "Collapse. Run."

And run he did – but toward the dense billows of dust and grit. Once he stumbled as his exhausted legs missed a stair, only to be borne up by hands from behind him. Belwether. Setting him upright. Beside him now going toward the disaster. Each of them covering nose and mouth with shirttails.

Then a corner turned and through the unnatural murk could be seen many moving forms swarming over an enormous pile of fallen stone. At one side of the still creaking and shifting mass a line of workers pulled away stones, some still settling from their fall, passing them back along the line. Hands grasping rock, digging out dirt, the churning despair and relentless hope of a rescue in motion. Inside Andeved something twisted. Rescue. This must mean there were people beyond the fallen rock, perhaps beneath.

Bump. Hands grabbed his arms. A face looked up to his. "Andeved? Is it you?" The mouth moved under a mask of dirt. The voice was familiar.

"Kendle?"

"Yes. Please, can you help?" Her plea was cut off by a wracking cough. Belwether moved in and put an arm around Kendle, steadying her until enough of the coughing died away that she could get more words out. "Outside – we can get to them from the outside. I've tried to get someone to listen but no one…they are…" She waved a hand toward the frantic, roiling efforts in front of them.

"There you are!" The boy, the girl and the Fool turned as one to see Lady Arrant emerging from the haze, striding toward them. The lady's gown was torn and filthy, the grime on her face streaked with sweat. "Come with me. Hurry. We don't have much time." Arrant grabbed Kendle by the arm and pulled her along, away from the rockslide. "You, too. Come."

Andeved could not move for a moment. The disaster, the fear, the need to help, the abruptness of being ordered by a stranger – it was too much. Then Belwether, in a motion that eerily mimicked Arrant's, took his arm and dragged him along as well. Out and down they went, passing would-be rescuers going upward and being passed by survivors going downward. Until they reached a wide alcove that gave some shelter from frantic people and terrible air.

Arrant leaned against the alcove's inner wall, taking quick shallow breaths. She tried to speak but choked and turned away to cough out what stuck in her throat. Kendle moved to help, but

Arrant motioned her back. Motioned with hands smeared with the black of dirt and the red of blood. Even in the dimness of the recess, the meaning of such stains was plain.

The lady turned back to the three and this time managed words. "Here is what we know at this moment," Arrant began, her voice rasping and taut, "A work party had been hollowing out new chambers high up when the ceiling collapsed. Some of the workers are believed trapped behind the rockslide. Not all...no...not all. The first of us to get there...we found..." The words died away.

A terrible roaring filled Andeved's ears, one not made by falling stone. Made by the tearing of his heart, the trembling of his very blood and bones. Dead. There were dead.

Arrant looked up again, first at Kendle and then at Andeved and his Fool. And wiped her grimy sleeve over her eyes, for there were tears tracking through the dust on her cheeks.

"When we were trying to help dig through we saw, also, among the fallen rocks, some great amount of soil and the roots of trees and brush. It could only mean that the collapse has opened to the surface.

"Underion rescue teams are trying to dig through. Burrowing through rubble is something they know to do - and know how to do. I," she glanced at Kendle, "we begged them to send a rescue team with us to the surface. But they said it would weaken their effort – that they saw no evidence that the top of Under was opened."

"Ask us, Lady. How can we aid?" Belwether's voice startled them, but Andeved most of all.

"Under is such a maze to us, stairs and halls and turns and upward and inward..." Arrant clenched her fists in frustration. "We need a guide to get us out to the surface as quickly as possible. There is an encampment not far from the outer doors and –"

"Stop – what encampment? What did you do?" Kendle's question hit Arrant like a blow.

"I had them follow us here. Not many. Just for safety." Arrant met no one's eyes. That evasion announced the secret more clearly than words. She had brought troops. And hidden them.

Kendle sputtered with outrage. "Marchales? What possessed you to conceal marchales here, at the gates of Under? How could you?"

"It was decided. And not just by me." Arrant's fists opened and turned upward in pleading. "But now they can help, do you see? That's all that matters now, the rescue." She turned to Andeved.

"Could you lead us to the outer gates? Your people, soon my people, need this. Your teams are digging out the dead, but we can still find the living. Will you guide us?"

The fury of rescue, the shouts, the running, the hideous dull crack of stones displaced, the slithering rain of soil and debris, Andeved did not want to hear it. Did not want to know what it meant, did not want to be the one to make this decision. Say no - and there might be more death. Say yes – and the whole of Under might be undone by treachery. And yet, before he knew he had made a choice, words and motion came from him.

"This way." He turned to lead, without the slightest doubt that they all would follow. Downward, inward. Against the rushing of others, toward the consequences that would be known all too soon.

X • X • X

In three directions impassibly craggy mountains define a distant, unreachable horizon. The unmountained direction ends in a precipitous drop to the sea. Within the bowl between upward rock and downward rock, trees point skyward, ancient arrows of brown fletched with green and gray. Among the branches small things hurry through brief, eventful lives. Above the scurry of living, wide skies impassively spread, glimpsed only in pieces by eyes beneath. On the floor of the forest the most immense of growing things shows the tiniest part of its vastness. The varied-colored faces of meshroons push through the dirt, minute indications of an immeasurably wider life underground. As the forest branches twine above, so do the hidden, connective nets string together vast webs known only by the briefest of glimpses.

Over the seasons the question inevitably arose, usually over a hot skillet of 'shroons and eggs, of who had dared on a long past day to first eat something that thrived in moldering detritus and shadows. Grannies chuckled at the thought, children found it delightfully disgusting. Most were just grateful there had been such a brave soul, for the realm of Over depended so thoroughly on them. So many kinds, colors, tastes, toxins, textures and uses. Overites understood their need for the ubiquitous fungus on the deepest level. Dwellings were hung from the giant, patient trees. Walkways were strung between homes and along routes from one nexus to another so that the tread of feet almost never reached the ground lest the shallow-buried webs be breached and never more send their meshroons upward.

The practice of swaying through life in suspension was so ingrained that Mote spent every hour of his encampment at the edge of Under's realm uneasy at the rigidity of rock, the absence of height. Not to mention having to haul water by the heavy bucket-load to reconstitute the supply of dried 'shroons for every blasted meal. No one had ever mentioned this hardship when he approached the senior marchale in his village to join up. Come to think of it, old Yester probably had not imagined it could happen. Ever.

Yet, here he was, hidden away behind stone upjuts, on a mission that could not be discussed, by command of an unnamed authority, for an indeterminate period of time. In place of the gentle sway of his bed, hard rock that could not, it seemed, be cleared once and for all of sharp bits. Instead of daytime's dappled shade, unrelieved light. Immense and empty darkness at night. No give to the ground, so his feet were giving out. And worst of all, the waiting – waiting for something that might be nothing, that could be bad but maybe not.

Mote shifted from one bruised buttock to the other, cursing the cold stone on which he sat watch. From where he had stationed himself, the mighty doors of Under that had closed behind the Lady Arrant's party, that were never opened more than the width of a small cart, were far enough away that he could see but not be seen. He repeated the senior marchale's instructions to himself: *If there emerged a person waving a white cloth, then I am to run back to the encampment and alert the company. It will mean all is well and they would not be needed.* Mote dearly wished to see white. *But if there emerged a person waving a torch, that meant the Lady and her attendants were in trouble.* What the company would do at that point had not been explained, but it didn't bode well.

How long had he been out here? Wasn't he due to be relieved soon? By the angle of light it must be near supper time. At least when he was on watch he didn't have to haul water. Rumor had it that there would be mullock stew tonight, warm and rich with meat and roots and 'shroons and....

Blast the thought of food. It was making his stomach rumble - rumble enough that he felt it all the way down to his toes. That it shook the stone on which he sat. No. Wait. The sound, the trembling, was coming from somewhere...he stood and turned this way and that, trying to find where the noise and shaking were coming from. There. Northward. A deep, mad noise. And, against the horizon a low whorl of...what?...throwing a dirty billow against the sky. Birds rose, screaming, wheeling.

Mote was surprised to notice that he had started off in the direction of the rumbling. It took a few more steps before he could convince his legs that they should not be moving. His instructions required him to stay on watch. And if he went to what he heard in the distance, what would he find and, more precisely, what would he have to do? No, it was not his to decide to leave his post. Abandon his duty – that's what the senior marchale would say. Not good.

So back he went to the watcher-hiding rock, congratulating himself on making a good decision. Somewhere deep within, though, he thought he heard an accusation of cowardice. Likely it was the voice of his curiosity for it had gotten him into trouble many times before growing up in Ressa which, as everyone knew but no one said, was the village of those who secretly loved to dirt-walk for their livelihood. Disdained by the deep forest Overites as uncivilized but necessary, Ressans tended fields and herds. Likely it was this shame of place that had pushed him into joining the marchales.

But Mote considered himself an adult now. He would not fall prey to a youngster's yearning for adventure, the desire to discover what was beyond the next tree, the need to dig under the top layer of dirt just to see. Besides, he'd heard about the hideous beetle monsters, the ravenous gesh that ate rock. And who knew what else. No, if stones rumbled somewhere over Under, then likely those beasties caused it and the best choice was to stay on watch. Yes. The wise choice.

The stone seat looked colder and harder than ever but he sat down again nevertheless. And sat. And watched. And sat. And watched. And rued the directives that bound him to sit and watch. Worried about immense bile-drooling monsters. And waited for time to pass. For his relief to come. As the day dimmed slowly and relentlessly.

Eventually, Mote could no longer see the doors he was supposed to be watching. It was clearly apparent that the night relief watchman had not come. There were no instructions for this dilemma. Should he go back to the camp and find out what was wrong? Or should he move down to where the night watcher watched, hidden by darkness more surely than stone?

He turned the matter over and over in his head concluding, with a shiver, that watching was what he was to do until someone told him otherwise. So, gingerly finding his way in the gathering gloom, he went down toward the pathway that led to the closed doors of

Under. Partway down he slid on loose rocks, righting himself with effort and what seemed like deafening noise. Some stealthy watcher he was. He stopped to listen – had his small avalanche given him away?

Boom. Craaack. Groan. The sounds made his heart stop. One of the massive doors was creaking open. And he was just at the bottom of the rocky slope in plain sight even in the murky light. He froze, willing himself invisible, dreading that he was not.

First a lady emerged, then another lady, then a boy and a fourth being, though of what sort was not clear. It walked upright so it could not be a beast. One hoped. But the first of the party, the taller lady, held a torch against the darkness. A torch. Mote's heart sank. The signal that said the Overites were in trouble. Wait, though. He squinted through the gloom and saw for sure what he'd thought he'd seen. The torch bearer was the Lady Arrant. Now what? There were no instructions for this, either.

Just as it seemed his legs might have come up with a plan that his brain could not, the lady called out "halloo" and came straight toward him.

"Halloo." Mote began and then stuttered to a halt. It was no way for a junior marchale to greet the Lady. "Rather, I meant to say, Junior Marchale Mote, my lady. May I serve? You have a torch but you don't seem to be…"

"No time to waste." Arrant cut short the ramble. "Take me to the encampment as quickly as you can. We need all the help we can get."

"Umm…yes…of course…except they," Mote nodded toward the other three, "are…are not…us, actually. Should they know about the…you know…?"

"Know about the camp?" Arrant finished his stammered sentence. "They already know – and we need to get there right now. There has been a cave-in. Lives are in the balance. Move!" The lady thrust the torch toward him.

That instruction was quite clear. Mote took the torch, turned and quickly led off campward. Behind him the small, odd group followed, their way lit by the signal for trouble.

And trouble seemed to have run ahead of them, for when they reached the encampment, it was dark and deserted. No sentry to see their arrival. No senior marchale to explain or direct. Even the cook fires were banked, no soup simmering. A severe disappointment to at least one of the party.

Then, from behind the cook wagon, movement.

"Mote? Is that you?" A familiar voice from behind the wagon.

"Yes, it's me. And the Lady Arrant, too. Come out, Cord. What has happened?"

Tentatively, the hidden one emerged until he reached the outer edge of the torchlight. It was, as Mote had guessed, the company cook, one whose only bravery was evidenced in the brash spicing of his food.

"I had to stay behind – they said I should," Cord began his explanation, voice strained, hands twisting. "After the quaking, which I must say was just horrible – the rootmeal sacks fell and burst open. There was meal dust all over. And those bins of..."

"Enough. Where are all the rest of the guard?" Arrant stepped into the circle of flickering light, startling the already nerve-jangled cook. "Speak up, man. Where are they?"

"Yes, yes, the rest of them. They," Cord nervously took in a gulp of air, "they went to the sinkhole that the scouts went out and found after the noise happened. They said the ground had collapsed and they heard...the scouts said they heard...sounds. Like cries." The cook was trembling with remembering and telling. "So they took all the ropes and nets and..." he made a sweeping gesture at the empty camp behind him, "...and everything. And left. Left me here."

Arrant turned to the three still in shadow.

"This bodes well. Better than I expected. Our people already have gone in aid. We need to hurry to join them – the more hands the better. You," she turned again toward Mote and the shaking cook, "you stay here. Stand the camp and direct any who might come from Under to the rescue site. Understood?"

Mote nodded so hard it hurt his neck, then realized a verbal reply was required.

"Yes, Lady. Stand the camp. Direct others. Understood." The comfort of useable instructions helped a great deal. Almost enough to make the vasty darkness bearable. Until the Lady took the torch and led her party away onto the frail path that twisted between cold stones.

X · X · X

It was hard enough to see anything in the flickering torchlight when she was right behind Arrant. How Andeved and the Oni, following behind them, could pick their way through the darkness Kendle could not imagine. Her feet hurt with the wrenching against pathway stones hidden in the darkness, her hands hurt from hitting the large rocks to keep from falling. And yet she felt ashamed for even thinking of a complaint. Where they were heading, much worse was waiting.

Then, ahead of them, yellow points of flame, some moving and others steady against the night. Beneath, it had been a gruesome intrusion. Above, it would surely take the form of a horrific sinkhole. For all the urgency to get here, Kendle felt a sudden hesitancy to arrive. *Please let the marchales find those who were trapped, please let them be alive.* But what if they weren't? Behind her, Andeved took in a deep breath, an outward evidence of what she knew was his own fear.

Down the trail and too soon, with hope it would be soon enough, they reached the illuminated rescue site. Multiple torches, stuck in dirt or wedged between rocks, seemed to strain toward the shouting marchales, the staked out ropes leading into a monstrous hole, a few still and shadowed forms laid at some remove from the crumbling, uneasy edge.

Andeved pushed past her, past Arrant, past purposeful marchales, to the row of those who had been pulled out and laid down. At the first of the five forms he stopped, leaned down to see who it might be, how they might be. Kendle caught her breath as Andeved had to reach down and lift the corner of a blanket to see who he had come upon. He let the cover down again, slowly. Seeming to draw himself upright again by will alone, he moved to the next. The next one, the same. But the third in the line, this form reached a shaking hand up to clutch Andeved's arm as he came near. Kendle let out her breath. There were those who lived.

She turned to tell her cousin that she would try to help the injured, but Arrant was already shouting and directing, joining others hauling on ropes that were taut with the heavy pull of rescue. So she hurried to where Andeved leaned over the injured one. The young man seemed caught by what he was seeing, or perhaps what the man was saying. No, it was what he saw, for when Kendle was close enough she, too, could not look away. The man's face was... dented...on one side, the deep red-brown of blood meeting air contrasted with the white, white of jaw bone gleaming through the gray dust. No words, terrible liquid sounds.

"You can do this." Belwether's voice should have startled her, but Kendle could not be astonished by any other thing in this moment. "You know what to do." His rumbling voice shook the air even as her body trembled with it.

"Do?" Her lips were too dry to produce more words. Without the possibility of resistance, Kendle felt herself firmly but carefully steered toward a large bundle near the line of litters. The bag had no doubt been brought from the encampment for just this sort of thing. Filled with bandages, jars of ointments, dried meshroon powders of various sorts and uses, needles and thread. Kendle shivered.

Hands reached down and took hold of the bag. Belwether's hands. His face came into her view.

"Now."

The single word broke through. Kendle grabbed the bag and nearly ran the few steps back to the man with half a face. Kneeling down, she first reached over and turned Andeved's face toward her, away from the other, calling the boy's name until his eyes found some measure of focus.

"I will need water."

"I know him. His name is Londy. He used to...we..."

"Water, Andeved. And a fire."

He nodded, prying loose Londy's fingers.

"Can you help him?" The need to ask and the fear of asking clouded his question.

Kendle's answer came quickly, before thought and with a breathlessness born of fear. "I hope I can."

She was grateful that was enough for Andeved for the moment. He rose and hurried to the task. Almost before she could begin to sort through the contents of the bag, an uncorked trail jug appeared, water sloshing just slightly as it was set down next to her. And then Andeved was gone again, leaving her to use the water, use the ointments, perhaps use other implements.

"How did you find us?" Someone knelt down on the other side of the injured man. When Kendle saw who it was she lost some small part of the tension across her shoulders.

"Orryn - oh, you are here - good, good, I am so glad. Here," Kendle made to pass over the open bag, "We - I - came to help if we can."

The gray-haired marchale nodded but gestured at her to keep the bag. "Help is what you will be, young lady. This is more than one aging field aide can manage. You wet down some bandages and sprinkle ravenscrown powder on them. Dab his face - it will numb the pain and clean the wound. I have to see to the woman we just pulled up, but I'll be back as soon as I can."

Orryn left at a run. Beside her, the Underion moaned. Her hands found strips of cloth, tipped out water from the jug, found the stoppered jar of ravenscrown and sprinkled the dried meshroon powder over the damp rags. And holding her breath for fear of causing more pain to the suffering man, dabbed his face, the dented side. Here. There. Wipe away blood. Wipe away dust. Soothe flesh. Oh, on bone. There. Here. Again.

Time stopped. All else faded. The terrible groans faded. His eyes drooped and closed. Almost dreamily, Kendle watched herself thread a needle, stitch here, there, a precise and hideous line of small x's. Watched as she uncapped the severille ointment and smeared it over the stitching. As she wrapped clean, dry bandages over the wounded places. As the pulse in the man's throat slowed and steadied...and stayed.

At last she heard only his breathing and hers. She closed her eyes, in relief, and was surprised that the lids lowered on tears, tears that followed an already used track down each side of her undented face.

Orryn was patting her shoulder, having returned from his other duties, though Kendle could not have said when.

"Well done, girl," he said, looking over her work. "I see your Grandfather Belsyn in those neat stitches. Well done."

Those words brought a quick smile to Kendle's face - a smile she ducked her head to hide, lest the pride that leaped to her heart showed. She had used the memories of her grandfather's skills, the ones she had watched and marveled at so often. And it seemed she had done a good job. At the same time she heard her grandmother's voice, as precise and painful as the needles that sewed through flesh, advising her not to bring grief on herself by aspiring to the skill, the reputation of Healer Belsyn. Not that Kendle was not smart, or skilled in other, useful ways - grandmother Ewena usually smiled, sometimes chuckled, as she said this - but no one matched her husband, the healer.

"Heigh the camp." From just beyond the farthest reaches of torchlight came the cry. Figures emerged from the dark. Underions, twenty or more - led by a light-bearing junior marchale. Mote.

"They came out looking for the cave in and found the...found me." Mote addressed his stammering report to the Lady Arrant who approached the group with an expression of surprise.

A short, broad-shouldered man stepped around Mote and toward Arrant. He was wearing a large pack slung low on his back. On his head was a hat with a very wide, stiff brim. All the other members of his group wore similar head-coverings. The brim was so wide that the man had to tilt his head sharply up to see more than just Arrant's feet.

"Head Mender Dawley here, lady, with menders to tend to the wounded and haulers to take them home." The man scrunched up his face, then loosed an explosive sneeze. "Sorry, 'scuse me." Dawley pulled a large, crumpled rag from his jacket and mopped his nose. "It's these plants and...things," he snuffled. "Makes me....well, not important. The important thing is that Lord Paell sent us, with his compliments as he said, to retrieve our own."

On Arrant's face the expression of surprise changed to indulgence and then to a cold blankness.

"I see," Arrant spoke carefully, coldly. "Your own. Well, I understand your concern. Had you come sooner, there might have been something for you to do. As it is, all those on the up side of the cave-in have been pulled out. There is nothing to do now but wait for first light. Moving wounded in the dark is, as I am sure you will agree, unwise."

The Underions shifted uneasily in their ranks. Mender Dawley shook his head slowly.

"Yes, unwise. Certainly. Except..." The obviously perturbed Underion pulled his ridiculous hat further down on his head. "Except we...those from Under...find the outsideness to be - challenging. It may not do the wounded good if they are staring up at the..." he glanced up at the night sky and immediately looked downward again, shivering, "...at that." He waved his arms vaguely upward.

Suddenly the ludicrous hats made sense to Arrant. While there were some Overites who found the open sky unsettling, it seemed many Underions were actually terrified. This had never been discussed in the visits made back and forth between the two demesnes during the betrothal negotiations. What stubbornness and need it must have taken to keep that secret. But they revealed this weakness tonight under the duress of the disaster, worried about their own because they knew what they would fear.

"Of course," the Lady's voice softened with the new knowledge. "And we can help with that. If you have more cloth - blankets, sheeting of any kind - we have ropes. Providing a shelter over the wounded, over us all, is a good idea. Just until dawn. Do you think?"

Dawley swiped his nose with his rag once again and then nodded so vigorously that his hat brim jiggled. "Yes, that could be of help. Yes, we have brought materials for making litters. They could..." He turned around to his group and began directing them to unload packs and pull out all the blankets and coverings they had.

From the corner of her eye, Arrant saw young Andeved kneeling by one of the wounded. He was nodding. It seemed in agreement, perhaps even relief. But behind the boy the peculiar Belwether person was motioning at her. Shaking his head. Mouthing the word 'no', scowling. What a fool. He could not see the rightness of what she was doing. Fool.

Arrant turned and walked closer to the edge of the void, reaching down to grab one of the staked-down ropes that had been used to pull up the wounded. Tents over the Underions, injured and non-injured alike. That would get them through 'til dawn. Our ropes and their...

Under her feet, the uneasy edge began to let loose. Arrant began to fall, faster than belief. Down, into darkness, choking on dirt. Clutching the rope, the life line, jerking violently as the rope played out. Hold. Hold. Slipping hands. Hold. Slipping.

Chapter Four

Beneath the stone, within a chamber, released from others but not alone. Not alone ever again. Standing posed, poised before an amazement of sand-made-into-silver. He let his fingers so lightly brush the very edge of the room-high mirror, exceedingly careful to leave no trace. The surface had been washed and polished until it flawlessly reflected. No bit of dust, no dulling marks. The mirror's twin stood shining on the opposite wall. In them, Paell could see himself into forever, each of him clad in dark vestments, each of him wearing the one-sided, sometimes fluttering crown that was the flett. Each of him with a hand raised to bless. Which of his many selves had thought to do that, he wondered.

Then left the wondering to begin the speech again.

"My dearest ones, you whose care it is my joy to..." No. Mentioning joy would be distasteful given the circumstances. Better a more graceful sorrow with notes of strength. Yes. Better. Lord Paell worked to find the best appearance of indomitable spirit and genuine sorrow. He stood evenly upon his well-placed feet, one arm slightly bent and palm upward, the other arm still raised as before. The expression needed to cover his face was more difficult. There would be no mask of mourning - the flett could not bear the covering. It was up to him to be the mask so that the crowd might know his heart.

"My dearest ones, you whose sorrow is mine own, whose tears I have shed, in this dark hour we are not alone." That was much improved. Paell composed a slight, empathetic smile. It graced the face of each of his mirrored selves, diminishing in size but not in faultlessness.

"Seven lives have been taken from us. Seven souls no longer telling the turning of the hours, no longer dwelling within the surety of stone. The stone that shelters us, protects us, the stone that we betrayed and so called down upon ourselves the cruel, the brutal incursion of aboveness." Paell shivered with the horror of it, in spite of his masterful control. It was so wise to rehearse the elegy, to feel through the weight and dread of it in advance. The grief of others demanded his compassionate serenity.

A small coolness, a tremble of softness by his cheek. The willing god lifted a wing and, with its fluttering, tousled Paell's hair. From long habit, he reached up to smooth down the unkemptness. When his hand reached the stray locks, a still moving wing touched his fingers. Hmm…ah…

"Paell? Can you hear me?" Etcherelle could not get his attention and it made her throat tighten with fear. Approaching desperation, she tugged at his arm, pulling, hoping to move him out of wherever he was and back into the now.

Slowly, too slowly, he turned his head. Turned to look down where her fingers gripped his arm. Focused on the hand not his own. Then raised his head so that his eyes should have seen her face.

"My lord? There is news from above. Can you hear me?"

Paell closed his eyes and smiled a smile that raised the hair on the back of the chief advisor's neck.

"Yes. We hear you." His voice sounded from afar in a way that did not involve distance. "She has fallen, has she not?"

Etcherelle frowned, confused. "She? Who do you mean?"

Paell pulled his arm from her grasp. "My Intended, of course. Fallen. See my face, hear my voice and know that we know."

"Yes, the Lady Arrant fell, over the edge of the cave-in, into our Under. She has been brought down for care as she is gravely injured." There was a hesitation before she could say the next words. "How did you know? You have been alone in...here..." she motioned to the mirrored chamber surrounding them, "for so long a time."

The darkly clad ruler of Under looked back into the mirror in front of them. "Gravely injured. You are correct. She will not live the night." He sighed deeply. "No morning for Arrant. Mourning for Arrant."

With steps more like a stately dance, Paell circled the chamber and glided out through the doorway. Etcherelle had no choice but to follow. She did so, but with great trepidation.

x • x • x

Andeved paced the hallway in front of the mender's chamber, but Kendle stood motionless, propped against the wall. They really shouldn't have let the menders shoo them out. Being kept from Arrant and her care was driving Kendle into a state of anger that only partly disguised her fear.

Both of them jumped when the metal door to the healing room squeaked open. Belwether's noticeable nose appeared, followed by the rest of himself. Andeved nearly leaped on him with his questions.

"How are you? What's happening?" from Andeved.

"Will I be able to see her now? Is she...is she...?" from Kendle.

Belwether held up his hands to halt the deluge. And the motion did stop the two, for both his hands were swathed in bandages. Parts of those bandages stained a telltale red. Evidence of the roughness of Overite rope and the damage the Oni suffered to pull Arrant up from the hole, the void.

"Kendle, your cousin," the Oni began in his low, dense voice, "she has not awakened."

Kendle caught her breath, her hands tightening into fists.

"The menders have tried all they know. But all they know now is to wait, to see..."

Tonn, tonn, tonn – the deep rolling voice of a bell careered down the stone passageway, speaking to all in Under: News. Sorrow and news. Come. Gather. Attend. It is the Hour of Remembering. Attend. Attend.

Andeved blanched. "It is time - Lord Paell is calling Under together," he said, more to himself, but also to Kendle who would not know this sound. "All must gather to tell the names of the dead and grieve."

"Surely I would not be required to attend," Kendle's voice was hoarse with strain. "I must stay here – with my cousin. In case..."

The bell stopped its deep ringing. Andeved held up his hand to signal that they must listen. "Now the bell will ring once for each lost." Another beat of silence. Then a slow, even toll.

One.

Two.

Three.

Tears rolled down the boy's face. "There will be seven, for Londy and for the others...."

Four.

Five.

Six.

Seven.

And then, eight.

The Oni rocked back on his heels. Andeved shook his head in confusion. Through the door to the healing chamber came Mender Dawley. He approached Kendle with a somber expression that looked unhappily practiced.

"She is gone, Kendle. The Lady Arrant is no more." The mender's face was pale, his hands moving aimlessly. "We did everything we could, but she never did wake." Dawley put one of his pointlessly motioning hands to use, laying it over his heart in the traditional gesture of condolence. "Our hearts to your heart, lady of Over." With that, the mender retreated once again into the healing chamber.

"No." And again, "No." Kendle leaned against the cold stone wall. "What will we do?" She reached up to touch her cheeks. "Where are my tears? There should be tears, because...because...." She looked up at Andeved and Belwether.

The boy swiped his own tears, striving to stand taller, to be stronger. It surprised him how much he needed to be of comfort to this no-longer-a-stranger. His upbringing had not taught him the ways of comfort, so he did what came first into his head – reached out and put his hand on Kendle's arm and said, "We care about you. I mean, we will care for you, help arrange...the...oh, Kendle, I am so grieved for you."

The Oni touched both of them, gently for their sake and for the sake of his ruined hands. "I am sorry for you both," his rumbling voice had an edge to it, "but there is no time for grief as yet. Did you not hear? The eighth bell tolled. Seven killed in the cave in. The eighth must be the Lady Arrant." Belwether's eyes shut and he began to shake his head. "You see. They knew already. Before the menders cried the time of leaving, someone knew."

Comprehension struggled to break through the heaviness of the moment. Kendle could not move. Andeved frowned, trying to understand. Finally, the young woman shaped words.

"If they knew...it might mean..." she shuddered, "it might mean they...helped it become true?"

"They?" Andeved sputtered his question. "Who are *they*? Not any of our people. What are you saying?"

"I am saying," Belwether gently responded, "that it would be well for Over to insist that the Lady be taken home. There are those in Over who have learned to tell the reasons for a body's betrayal. If some agent other than the terrible fall killed Arrant, they may be able to discover what it is and, from that, who."

Both the young people stared at the Oni in horror and disbelief. But slowly, and with great reluctance for the conclusions that might come, both found reasons to agree with that hideous plan.

Kendle brought herself upright, grasping at a duty to perform, anything to distract from the loss of family. Even this duty.

"I will go find those of the party come to Under. First I will send marchales to guard the…body. Then we will make the arrangements to take my cousin home. Chief Advisor Voeller will be instructed to demand this from Lord Paell."

She started to leave but turned again. Hesitant, looking younger than she had the moment before, she asked them for a favor, a boon. "Will you guard…Arrant…until my people can be sent?"

This attention Andeved knew he could provide.

"Of course we will. Do what you need and we will be here."

It was not possible for Kendle to speak at that. She could only turn again to her task of distraction. Underion and Oni watched her walk away, toward duty and the need to know.

Belwether cleared his throat and that, to Andeved, sounded like hesitation, unusual for his Attached.

"We should go into the mender's chamber to stand guard." The Oni ahemed again. "And we should accompany the Lady to her home."

"Well, yes," the boy agreed, "to see what…if…" He could not voice such suspicions in the echoing stone passageway.

Belwether shook his head slowly and sadly. He took the boy's arm with his bandaged hand. "Let us go into the chamber and stand watch."

X • X • X

Almost in the same moment that the Overite marchales arrived to relieve Andeved of his watch over what had been the Lady Arrant, a messenger found him. The winded courier had to catch her breath before she could speak more than two words together.

"I have had to look everywhere for you. No one knew where you were - again." The young woman paused to wipe a bead of sweat that trickled from underneath her herald's mask. She shook her head to clear it. "The message was sent with urgency, so be told: The Lord Paell requires you to come to him. Immediately. At the water clock."

"Why? What could he need me for?" The boy could not help the question.

The messenger stared at him through the eye-holes of the mask of office. Unblinking. Then shook her head.

"We do not ask why." In a lowered voice: "Though it is hard not to ask." And she left, her office performed.

The summons made Andeved uneasy. He took great pains to keep himself out of the line of authoritative sight. It was a source of great frustration that his efforts often brought him instead into sharper focus. Nor could he see why that was so. When caught stealing away or hiding among workers and crafters, he had found, however, that the best route to take was admission of the deed and silence under the tirade of whichever adult he had currently offended. Look seriously contrite, perform the penance and escape again.

"I suppose I should get there right away?" Andeved spoke this out loud, knowing that Belwether was no more than a few paces away. There was no confirmation of his supposition, however. It seemed that his constant shadow was back to being the passive Observer that Attached Oni were held by long tradition to be. With no more pause, the boy set out down the passageway, toward the Chamber of Ceremony in which the water clock and his cousin awaited him.

It was not too very far to the huge chamber, not too many stairs, turns, inclines or declines. But it was at the farthest edge of the burnished light from the chamber's tunnel mirrors, behind the steady drip of the water clock, beneath the lowest balcony, buried in shadow that he had to go to find Paell. Andeved would not have found him at all had he not heard hissing from the darkness, a whispering telling him to make the Oni stay away. Far away.

"Is he gone, enough gone?" Paell's voice leaked from the shadows. "Are you alone?"

Andeved looked over his shoulder to see whether Belwether had gone, caught sight of the Oni moving well away to the furthest wall. He turned back to reply and startled. Lord Paell was no more than a hand's width in front of him. Smiling, but in a way the boy hoped not to see again.

"They are asking strange and devious boons, little cousin. We mistrust them now more than ever. Intentions lie beneath their maskless faces, under their skin, but not in the ways of Under." Paell's breath was hot on Andeved's face and smelled of distant spice or something rare eaten a yesterday ago. "Have you heard what they require?"

"No, cousin-friend, I have not heard. But then, who am I to hear?"

"Yes, who are you indeed?" Paell leaned back but a bit and studied the boy's face with sudden intensity. "Who...to have grown a second shadow? What possesses Oni to attach to one but not another?" He leaned in closer again, swaying from side to side to see the whole of the young visage so close to him. "You are no one now, but we cannot see what you will be. And that may tell it all."

Andeved's heartbeats were turning rapid and harsh. Disquiet built with each hammer stroke.

Paell took in a breath and let it out slowly. "They ask for gesh, boy. Not just to take the emptiness that was Arrant back. They want gesh as well. Why? They say it is to hollow a burial chamber in the nearest rise of the mountains. It may truly be done, but there is more than that to their need. We cannot fathom the deeper why and it needs to be known." The dark vestments Paell wore swirled as he swung away from Andeved, turning in a circle part in light and part in shadow. "You will go with them. Yes. Yes. Our eyes cannot see what is hidden. You go. Take that Oni with you, or..." and here he stopped whirling for a beat, "or leave it - him - with me, if you like?"

Even the eerie maunderings of his cousin could not stay the boy's reply. "No. I mean of course I will go, but Oni are attached to one life for the length of that life. You know I could not leave him behind even if I wanted."

Paell said nothing, but slid again into the fullness of the dark. From those shadows he spoke a last direction.

"Go on my behalf, then. Tell your father and mother you are being sent. Come back knowing more. Much more."

"I will, cousin." Andeved found it easy to promise what he had already intended to do. But the promise was given to emptiness, for Paell was gone.

All that remained in the huge hollowness of the Chamber of Ceremony was disturbed air, a young boy becoming older, a usually-near Oni against a far wall and the relentlessly measured drip, drip, drip of the water clock. When, eventually, the boy and his Oni shadow left and the air chilled to quiet, it was only time then that moved through the hall.

It was time that Andeved dreaded, walking more slowly to his home chamber than his youth usually allowed. Telling his parents he was going out, outside, upside - it was the right thing to do. But not easy. No, not at all. When even his dragging steps could not prevent his arrival, he entered to see both his father and mother awaiting him. His father standing rigid with anger. His mother sniffling in her customary wash of sentiment.

"Oh, my dear," Glitter raised her heft from the blanket draped chair and came toward Andeved with the downturned mouth and upraised arms that announced a maternal embrace in the offing. "You made me so worried. Why do you do that? They said you were..." she glanced furtively at her husband, "*upside*," that word almost whispered, "by the terrible place where the horrible thing happened. And with those others."

Mother hugged son, her arms limply around him, her hands damply patting his shoulder blades.

"Enough, wife. The boy deserves no welcome when his absence was malicious." Sere's voice was as unyielding as his posture. "He has been told, clearly and often, to stay within the bounds of common space. To behave in a way that brings honor, not shame. But he will not. I begin to think he is not capable of it. And now, he is being sent away." His father stiffly moved toward Andeved.

The boy held his stance, his own anger building wordlessly in parallel.

"Sent away by your lord cousin, who is too lenient by far. Too kind even after the unkindness done to him." Sere took another step toward the boy. "I asked the Lord Paell for the right of punishment as is mete for a parent. But he would not." He took hold of Andeved's arm with a grip made painful by sinew and shame. "There were other words he spoke I did not comprehend, shadows of Paell's suffering it seemed. But the end of it all was that your wickedness has made you an exile, to travel with strangers of hidden intentions until such time that you have learned what it is to be a right acting man."

Sere released Andeved's arm and turned deliberately, slowly until his face could no longer see his son.

"Oh, well, dear," Glitter took up a traveling bag and rough-nubbed cloak from behind her chair. "It isn't that bad, really. You will have an adventure, you see. And they say the Overites are being given gesh to take along - that Paell agreed to let them have the beasties, though why I could not say as they are disgusting. The gesh, I mean." She handed her still mute son the bulging pack. "So here is a change of underlinens and something to eat better than the slickery meshroons those others go on about. There are some firesticks and a drawing you made when you were only four which I wrapped in a warm coverup so it wouldn't get smudged. And... well, here. Put the cloak on first, then the bag can be over your shoulder, see how that is?"

Andeved allowed his mother to drape the cloak around him and took the traveling bag without a glance inside it. He turned and started for the doorway - motion that caused his mother to sigh, loudly and long.

The boy, who grew older in that moment, stopped his outward steps one last time and spoke to his parents.

"Thank you for the provisions and the advice. I am sorry that who I am distresses you. Lord Paell has told me to go and I will do that. He has also told me to return. I hope I can find a way to do that, too."

He did not look back for a farewell picture to fix in his mind, for the father and mother he loved, but did not like in the least bit, had fixed themselves within him all too well.

CHAPTER FIVE

The massive doors of Under had not been opened this wide since the day of their creation. Teams of haulers strained and sweated to push the gates open, groaning with effort, though not as loudly as the huge hinges groaned with unaccustomed use. Debris left by lifetimes of wind and rain had to be cleared from the arc of opening. And all the while, the increasing brightness of outside crawled farther and farther inside as the entrance widened. Though it could not truly be called an entrance on this day, for the sole purpose of the unprecedented exertion was to make an exit.

From the now gaping maw emerged the once welcomed. First the most senior of Over's marchales emerged, walking on either side of a sadly repurposed camp wagon that held the body being taken home. Next followed Chief Advisor Voeller and a flock of clan leaders in somber garb. Kendle was the last of that cluster, having been told to be with the leading party as she was family, but advised to be unobtrusive so as not to offend the Underions. Why the sight of her might be offensive had not quite been explained.

What followed then, into the vastness of the morning, was another unprecedented sight. Six carts, each of which carried a cage. Each cage covered by heavy cloths so that no light of day passed through. From each draped contrivance came hissing, clicking, hideously rank odors that, even without a sight of them, made unmistakable the presence of gesh. One monster to a carted cage, each with an Overite marchale as guard. The six selected for this important duty by their training, their bravery, their picking of the short straw.

At the very end of the exodus, behind the last of the luggage carts and the few trailing cooks, tailors and camp aides, came newly promoted marchale Mote. It might be supposed that he would be walking proudly given his recent elevation. But the no longer junior marchale - it was only a very small promotion - could hardly be glimpsed through the clouds of dust roiled up by the long procession preceding him.

It was to find a breath of ungrimed air that made Mote step to the side of the road and wait for a bit. He'd been tasked with bringing up the rear, theoretically guarding against being snuck up on from behind. But once again who would be sneaking up and what they might want had not been detailed. Or even hinted at. Nor had he been briefed on how to accomplish this task precisely. Was he to look over his shoulder - a lot? Walk backwards, perhaps? Maybe step to the roadside, as he had just done, wait for the dust to settle and scan the road already traveled?

Well, no matter. The train of people and possessions had barely made the crest of the first hill. Not even out of sight of Under yet. Though the great doors were already closing. Closing more quickly than they had opened. Even as Mote watched, the massive gates lurched inward until they altogether shut with a metallic boom, a noise that should have echoed but fell hard. The graceless, unresonant sound made him shiver.

Likely it was because he had stopped to breathe and to watch Under closing itself away that Mote caught the movement. A figure stepped out from a shadowed spot that looked out on the road and the great, metal gates and began to work its way down toward the road.

"Well, mercy on my head," Mote muttered to himself. "Do I think I have already found a sneaking-up-from-behind problem?" Yet the figure did not trouble to hide. Just kept coming toward the road, and the place where the marchale stood. And now that he noticed, the gait of this whoever seemed familiar.

Nearer, then nearer. And then there he was, not really having snuck up and having his hands in his pockets like anybody would.

"Hey, Mote."

"Hey, Andeved."

An awkward pause. Mote shuffled his feet. Andeved raised his hand to shade his eyes, squinting nonetheless.

"So..." Said in unison by both, which was somewhat of a surprise to each.

Another noisy silence and a bit more pointless looking off into the distance.

"So, I was thinking that you," Andeved nodded at the Overite marchale, "well, I mean you" he swung an arm in the general direction of the departing people, wagons and carts, "could use someone who knew something about gesh. As in when they need to be milked and how to keep them cool enough but not too cold, how often they need to be fed. Things like that."

Mote nodded with what he hoped was a thoughtful expression, one that said he was carefully and maturely weighing the boy's suggestion. It had occurred to him that the type of information Andeved possessed was exactly what his people did not. And precisely what he, in all likelihood, would be ordered to attend to in the very near future. At tonight's camp site, if experience with the upper echelons was any indication.

"So you know all about gesh herding?" Mote's voice rose in the hopeful direction.

Andeved shrugged. "Not everything. Actually, just what I've learned hanging around the pens and listening to the geshherders. But it is more than...."

"More than I know, for a fact." Mote shrugged. "More than anyone that walked past you just now. And they seem to be dead certain...oh, unfortunate choice of words - my apologies...they are positively convinced that having these gesh is very, very important. It's just that...well..." Mote had a terrible feeling he should stop talking right about now, but could not seem to manage it. "It's just that we were told, quite sternly, that no...others...were to come near the..." now he waved vaguely toward the lumbering procession, "near that."

"We wouldn't get near *that*." Both young men startled at the rumbling voice that pronounced the promise. Somehow, once again, Belwether was there, peering over Andeved's shoulder. "I believe the lady Kendle would vouch for him."

"How does he do that?" Mote inquired of the boy behind whom an Oni with a fully packed travel bag stood.

"I don't really know," Andeved replied. "Never have figured it out. I find it part reassuring and part irritating. Mostly irritating."

"I can well imagine."

Belwether, in his usual manner, smiled benignly and seemed to take a step or two away, though he did not move at all.

Which left the two young men to decide what to do next. Andeved decided to stay silent, look helpful and hope for an invitation to tag after the gesh carts. Mote decided to both heed the warnings and take a small, surely well-intentioned initiative.

"I suppose you can come along for a while. I - we - could use the help with those ugly, smelly things. But you better stay well back of the main group and try not to be noticed by those at the head of the procession or we will all be in a great deal of trouble." Mote tried to deliver his decision in stern tones, basing his delivery on that of a grandfather who had embraced discipline more often than grandchildren.

"Of course, we will stay at the very edges and just help when needed and not draw attention to ourselves." Andeved stumbled a bit on the last part of the promise. It wasn't that he intended to cause an incident or entangle Mote, to whom he had taken a liking from the first, in any unfortunateness. It was just that such mishaps tended to happen in his vicinity. Often.

But for now, promises remained kept and intentions stayed well. In that spirit, the three began to walk toward the crest of the hill and the roadway beyond.

X • X • X

Kendle thanked herself, once again, for bringing sensible shoes. Going to Under, they had all ridden in carts drawn by the strong, uncomplaining mollucks. Now the understandably skittish mollucks were drawing those same carts loaded with gesh and the esteemed company walked home. It had always been hoped for, planned so. But evidently the others did not truly believe it would happen to them.

Yet here they were, the first night camp set up and, but for the well booted marchales and herself, groans and aches and poultices and foot rubbing abounded. Even the mollucks, used to hauling over hard-packed roads, lowed in weary protest until they were tethered far from the circle of carts it had been their lot to pull this whole long day.

In fact, by common though unspoken consensus, the gesh carts were circled at a fair remove from the general camp. Far enough that the disgusting clickings and squishings might not be heard through the night. And they were down wind. It almost put the beasts out of mind until that young marchale, the newly promoted Mote, distributed night soil pots with the reminder they would be collected in the morning. Breakfast for the gesh.

It rankled Kendle, all this fleshly fussing. Oh, the wagon with her cousin's...with her cousin...was said to have been put in a place of honor. There it was, on a small rise, just alone and, it felt, a bit removed. Sentries had been posted around the whole of the camp, but the honor guard of the day had not been replaced around the wagon for night. In the space designated for the marchales, a fire had been lit. Talking, some laughing around the fire. Evidences of snoring from bedrolls already undone in the more comforting darkness of night.

She spread her own blanket close to the burdened wagon. For good or for ill, her chosen place looked out on the camp entire. Kendle tried not to see the clan leaders huddling together, talking so low they could not be heard past their own backsides. Or Minister Voeller drawing a small coterie near, privately conferring on who knew what. So serious, so smug. All the habitual secrecy of home but without trees.

Home. The word gave Kendle pause. Messengers had already reached Aunt Zearia and Uncle Pember with the terrible news. What would their grief look like? Her own seemed to float just beyond reach. But parents. Surely their mourning would take clearer form. Perhaps a grief ravaged visage, a sadness so intense that it could not be looked upon without being moved. As she had done in the hallway outside the healing chamber in Under, Kendle wondered at her own lack of tears. And felt a weighty guilt at that lack.

It took forever, or so it seemed, for the camp to quiet, the fires to be banked, the rustlings and stirrings of tired folk to settle. Darkness cooled the air. An errant breeze brought a hint of damp. An hour passed, the kind of time observed so closely by the time-ridden Underions. A tap. Then tap, tap, tap. If Kendle had not, as yet, tears to shed, the night did. It began to rain.

So Kendle pulled her bedding under the very wagon that held her cousin, well and truly aware of the irony of that shelter. To even attempt sleep, she turned away from the camp and filled her hearing with the night's weeping.

At some point she must have fallen asleep, because right now she was coming awake. Slowly. Not to morning light but the color-leaching gray that came before it.

"Kendle. Wake up." The voice was familiar. Familiar but unsettling. Her eyes took their own time to open and find the face that produced that voice.

"Golion? Uh...Senior Healer Golion?"

"Wake up, girl, and come out from under there. I cannot talk with you this way. Move. Now." The lanky man resembled wrinkled laundry, his limbs all folded in the wrong places in his effort to peer under the wagon. His inconvenience was a small, savory satisfaction.

Kendle wriggled out from under the wagon. As she and Golion straightened, she ran her fingers through sleep-fuzzed hair and tried to clear her throat of newly-wakened croakiness so she could speak.

"I didn't know...ahem...you were coming to meet us, sir. I..."

Having regained his full height, which was considerable, Golion looked down on Kendle.

"What you thought is of no matter. And I must insist you keep your voice low. Get us inside before you wake the entire camp."

Golion grabbed her arm, pulling her to the side of the wagon that held the door.

"You have a key, I am told. Use it." As always, the senior healer's excellent social skills intensified Kendle's irritation. So much so, that she was quite pleased to announce that the key was in her cloak which was spread over her bedroll which was - she tried for a straight face - under the wagon.

"It will only take me a moment," Kendle assured the healer, whose face was fast turning from pre-dawn gray to sunset red. "I promise to be especially quiet, though." And she was, all the while as she stooped under the wagon and felt through the pockets of her cloak until the key was found and then crawled back out. Quiet, but rather slow.

"Give me that." Golion took the key from her hand and unlocked the narrow door, opened it and pulled down the wooden step. "Get yourself inside, young lady. This business is part yours. A matter that demands a more respectful response than you are wont to give." With that he pushed her up the step and into the wagon. Then followed her in and, with a deliberate show of quietness, shut the door.

Kendle was thankful for the immediate darkness inside the wagon. It hid her shame of being so disrespectful to someone who had come for serious work. Necessary and unhappy work for which she, herself, had begged. And begged to be kept quiet. Kept secret.

Scratch. The smell of sulphur and a tiny flame. Then more light as Golion put firestarter to oil lamp. He slid his travel bag from his shoulder and took from it a length of bark paper, tiny stoppered vials, several stumpy brushes and a long, thin knife that glinted in the lamplight. He set them on the end of the long planks that held the shrouded and terribly still body.

"All right, Kendle. Did you obtain what I need to make the determination? Or do I need to try for it myself?" He reached toward the sliver of a knife.

"No. I mean yes, I did get what you need." The thought of what the healer might need to do with that knife made Kendle's stomach turn. Shaking, she opened a wall mounted cabinet, took out a small jar and held it out to him. "It was taken soon after they said she was gone. No one saw except...no one from Under saw. It was soon enough that it still flowed."

And in that moment, knowing what had been done and why, what was at stake and for whom, tears came, silently released, flowing faster than the blood taken from Arrant.

Golion took the jar and set it down next to his supplies. Turning back to her, he took from an inner pocket a square of cloth and held it out to her.

"You did well, Kendle. Arrant could not be hurt by it. Only helped. That..." he gestured at the white wrapped body, "is now a placeholder for memories, a physical evidence that she is gone and we must find out how she is gone. If we can."

Kendle took the cloth and tried to wipe away the weeping, but still it came. Still more as Golion opened the jar and, with one of the brushes, smeared Arrant's blood down the middle of the bark paper. He opened one small vial after another, brushing the contents of each across the smear of blood.

Then Golion waited. And watched the places where the brush strokes crossed. Time and tears moved through the dimly lit wagon until at last, the senior healer allowed himself a small sigh and an even smaller smile.

"None of the indicators turned colors. It means there was nothing deadly in her blood. The Lady died of the wounds from the fall, died in the service others. This is what I have found and we may know."

It was so unexpected to hear compassion in Golion's voice, to find release and reassurance from this long-legged vexation. Had Kendle missed that possibility all this time? How often since her grandfather's passing had she silently watched the healer, albeit from a distance, as he mended the sick and injured. Brusque, focused, never flinching even when the wound was horrific, the illness grotesque. This is what she had always thought she saw. Perhaps too much watching of techniques and too little observation of a man's way with those he mended was her problem.

Already the senior healer was folding the stained page and replacing all his vials and brushes in his travel bag. Slinging the bag over his shoulder, he moved to the door and opened it. Pale morning light waited outside. Golion stepped down into it, pausing only to hold the door for Kendle. She also stepped into the early morning, now trying to find words of thanks. But the healer turned and walked away toward the road going home. As quiet as he had asked her to be. He was out of sight before she could say a word.

It was while she was staring after Golion that her eyes focused on another set of eyes. That were staring at her. It took a moment for her to realize who the hidden watcher was. Belwether.

He raised his shoulders and tilted his head. Kendle knew immediately the question he was asking. She put her hand to her head and kept it there. He would know it meant that only the fall had taken Arrant, the fall witnessed by so many as the accident it truly was.

Belwether stood still for a long moment. No expression on his face. Then he slipped from sight without a sound.

X · X · X

No one was unmoved when, in late daylight, the boulders and brambles gave way to the leading edge of the forest. Trees: tall, leafy, whispering in the lightest wind. Soon so many trees that they overspread above the road, inclining gracefully from each side to protect the dolorous procession. An hour more and they reached Outer Camp and the place where the roads crossed. So close to home now that the air smelled of it, the ground gave with it.

All this day's travel, Kendle had walked next to the camp wagon. Voeller had directed an honor guard for the day as well, but the guards let her walk with them. Nor did the High Minister object. Once truly away from Under, the strained vigilance of being in foreign surroundings altered to become the well observed hierarchy of secrecy. Kendle knew her place in the ranking - she was fully trusted to do things only if directed. Between directives, she remained invisible to everyone else, made so by what her parents, who had both died of canchous fever when she was still small, had done.

The procession came to a halt. Lost in her thoughts, Kendle almost banged into the marchale in front of her. She looked up to find that her cousin's parents, and those of suitable rank, were standing in the crossing of the roads. Dressed in garments of darkest gray, the small company stood silent, all eyes on the wooden camp wagon.

Uncle Pember. Aunt Zearia. Arrant's father and mother who were also Kendle's foster parents. Their faces did not show the signs of grief in ways Kendle had imagined. Grim, set, pale, dry-eyed, they seemed made of the stone so mercilessly common in Under.

With measured steps they moved to the wagon. Zearia turned her head from the dingy conveyance, but reached out to touch the splintery wood of the side wall, as if she could feel her daughter within. Pember pulled his wife's hand away, but gently. In so doing, he chanced to meet Kendle's eyes. The coldness, the accusation of his stare took all the breath from Kendle. Blood pounded in her ears but could not block out what her uncle said.

"We sent you with her for safety's sake, asking just this one thing of you. How could you allow her to die?" His words, each a fiery brand, seared.

Aunt Zearia found voice as well. "The gesh were gotten. At least our people have that. But at the price of Arrant's life?" Her aunt turned away from Kendle. "We can no longer manage to see you daily in the home that once held our daughter. It would be too painful." And here the grief of a mother did show itself - sobs began, brutal and staggering. Pember caught his wife in his arms and guided her toward the wayfarer's shelter at the edge of Outer Camp.

Leaving Kendle speechless, bereft. She ran. Away from the eyes and the whisperings and the wagon. Not knowing where, only toward the darkest forest shadows she could find.

X · X · X

From the far side of the gesh carts, Andeved could not clearly see or hear what had happened. But he could tell it was terrible. He could tell that Kendle had been harmed in some way. And he could see that she ran. Away from the dying day. Into the forest deeps.

Without another thought, Andeved grabbed his travel bag and, keeping to the edges of the camp, headed toward the place where

Kendle had left the roadway and entered the woods. Running became hard, almost impossible, in the tangle of undergrowth. He tripped and lurched through the brush, trying to find the smallest bit of pathway or open ground. A brief nostalgia for stone floors came and went.

Eventually, the undergrowth thinned, as the trees grew taller and wider. Moss, much like jinncar but not glowing, covered almost everything. There - that looked like a long straight line of pathway. He made for it only to see that it was a very old fallen tree, laid low long ago, rotting into the semblance of direction.

Andeved stopped, catching his breath and trying to figure out where, in all this green gloom, Kendle had passed.

"Good you stopped. We can get our bearings."

Andeved started and turned around to find Mote, hardly winded and not nearly as sweaty.

"How did you..."

"Shush. If we want to track Kendle, you need to be quiet. All this bashing around isn't helping." Mote gestured for silence. "Listen."

At first Andeved could hear nothing. Then he could only hear his raspy breath and the sound of the blood tides from his heart.

"There! That way. Did you hear that?" Mote pointed in a new direction.

Andeved caught his breath, willed the tides to wait for just a moment, and listened. And heard. Sounds that could only mean that something ahead was moving through the woods in haste.

"If you've caught your breath and found a direction," Belwether's deep tones sank into the forest moss, "then perhaps we should follow."

Though once again Andeved experienced the irritation of being surprised, it was more reassuring to find the Oni with him now. In this place. And the look of astonishment on Mote's face was rather gratifying. Altogether, it felt a bit like being given a fine tool for an important task. Taller, and surer. That's what is made him feel.

"Indeed, let's follow the sounds." Andeved heard his own voice as deeper somehow. "But it might not be Kendle. We don't know."

"That is true," Mote added. "The way it goes with our folk, an outlier is always sought after and...well...they're sought." What the marchale would or could not say left a dark uncertainty.

Belwether stepped over a fallen branch, cocking his ear toward the rustling ahead of them. The Oni's face reflected back the gray-green light falling through the dense leaves. Oddly enough, the effect made him blend into the surroundings. Which took Andeved by surprise as his constant companion had always seemed nearer to a stone-gray, a perfect tone for slying through Under. A fleeting wonder of how Belwether truly looked, or looked when in his own part of the land, passed through the boy's mind.

"We need to find her, before others do." Mote drew himself up and began to walk ahead. A few steps forward and he turned back, a shy expression of hope on his face, to see if the other two would consent to follow.

They did - the young marchale pathmaking for the earnest blundering of the cave dweller and slow but near invisible progress of the followtail. What was fortunate for the unlikely trackers was that whatever traveled ahead of them made enough noise to cover their sounds. What was unfortunate was what, soon enough, they discovered also thrashing through the trees. A squad of marchales, walking a long line, poking and prying into every hollow trunk, every shadowed cranny. Stirring up twigs, leaves, mice, meshroon spores and a deeply offended mosstode that managed to hop between the thudding boots of the marchales and disappear.

"Over here." The squad's forward scout called back to the line walkers. "The trail goes this way."

Andeved sank lower behind the huge log that hid the three of them. "They've found her trail and they will find her." A picture of shadow-hidden Kendle being turned out and taken made him wince.

"Mmm. Perhaps." Mote frowned. "She might know ways. Maybe we hurry ahead and lay a false trail?" His glance at the other two showed what he thought of that idea's likelihood of success. "Well, since they have her trail, at least we can follow and try to help when she's caught." But he sounded dubious and did not move to lead out again even as the noise of the marchales moved away from them.

"There is water here." Belwether's voice came from somewhere behind them. "And something else that is interesting."

Both Mote and Andeved headed in the direction from which the Oni's voice had come. It was only a few steps past the bulk of a tree trunk that they found him standing beside a brooklet so tiny it hardly made a sound as it wove its way along the forest floor.

Andeved knelt down to fill the water bag. And saw the footprint imprinted on the other side of the little stream. A fresh print, still filled with water seeped up from the mossy streamside.

CHAPTER SIX

It was the dream woke him. So flowing strange at first, like a heard-about place seen through a thin, warm veil.

He was walking knee-deep in color – yellows and greens with rose reds and soft blues, a garden run rampant. No stone-gray, no stone. Under open sky. Beside him a lady dressed all in white with long, thin, floating ribbons around each wrist.

There came a troubling wind that required answering. "I am Paell, Lord of Under," he spoke into the disturbance. And said it again, and again as if to carve the words into the uneasy air. "I am Paell, Lord of Under." No stillness came in confirmation. He heard that the lady, too, was answering. "Still I am Arrant, though I am no more," was what the lady said. And said again, for no calm came at this either.

Then ahead of them rose the great doors of Under. He turned to the lady and told her with his mind that she could find comfort within the stonehold. "I will bring you there. I am lord of that place." He held out his hand. But the lady fell upward into the emptiness of open air. Far upward, her ribbons fluttering behind her, until nothing was with him anymore.

In the dream, he wept. In the dream. Needing to return to his own self place, he sought to open the mighty doors. But they were covered over with flowering vines, pendants of berry clusters glistening ripe, thorn-guarded twisted branches thick as his arm and dark as a tree shadow.

He stood, expectant of welcome. A wind blew. Petals dropped. Vines closed around keyholes, berries dropped in red ruptures, thorns turned inward piercing metal.

"I am Paell," he cried at the doors, "Lord of Under." But of his words there was not even an echo.

Behind him another rustling, this an even harsher sound. He turned to see a large dome-headed bird flying toward him and alight on the ground in front of him. Huge and darkly brown was this creature, with feathers glinting sharply, a curved beak that looked made to crush, and cruelly barbed talons. But the eyes, oh the eyes. Ember red they were. Unblinking. And the searing gaze was to him.

He could not move, could not cry out as the great bird slowly spread its wings and took a single downward stroke. Launching itself closer, reaching out with weaponed talons. Seizing the flett, ripping it away. Dark wings beating upward, outward flight, blood trailing from the clutched prize like long, thin, floating ribbons.

Agony. Blood. Loss.

He awoke then and found himself curled tightly beside the water clock in the Hall of Ceremony. Remembering the dream so much more clearly, he found himself feeling his clothes for blood. None. Wiping his cheek – wiping nothing. Reaching back, behind his ear, to see if his little god was still in place. Gently, reverently touching. Just a touch for comfort, reassurance, even for the pleasure it gave. But for the first time, the flett gave him pain. Exquisite, unparalleled pain.

X · X · X

Surely it had to be close by now. She had not come this way often, and only on the bridgeway, never clabbering around in the unpredictable dirt. If not the place itself, at least the old bridgeway must be near - though Kendle could not say for certain if that was true or only a need, a fervent wish. Most likely it was a false hope, one of the many she had been too blind to see for the lies they were. Lies behind secrets behind...

She had to stop. The way before her had blurred so badly Kendle could not walk on. Crying would not help. Not now. Get to the hiding place first. Then mewl like an infant. But not now. No time.

Behind the dim-glinting tears came a terrible remembrance of Under's relentless water clock, drop by drop marking the death of the now. The now that would never be again.

Kendle roughly wiped her cheeks, rubbed her eyes until they hurt. Willing herself to get on, pushing down what needed grieving, covering over the deep dark of it with a more useful anger.

Not more than a dozen steps and there it was, lengths of faded wood lashed together, hung between stanchions an arm's reach above the forest floor. The bridgeway. It was old, here and there missing a plank with signs of rotting lashings, but it would do and it led where she needed most to go.

As usual, getting up on the walkway in mid-span was a bit of a clamber. But once up, Kendle quickly found balance, her legs remembering the sway of the bridgeway, the careful placement of slat-to-slat steps. And no hidden rivulets to surprise one with rising damp. It was comforting, in a fleshly way, to be back upon the wood.

This wooden path was flawed, uneven, randomly intermittent, requiring more vigilance than the well-used 'ways did. Which quickly became tiring, only adding to the fatigue from the flight and hunt Kendle had already endured. Now and again she slipped, stumbled, had to jump gaps or pull herself along the thick, bristly ropes strung as handrails.

The day's light, what diminished part of it filtered through the dense canopy, was nearly gone when Kendle finally saw her goal. Almost completely hidden from the bridgeway by what had been a deliberately encouraged profusion of green, the abandoned observation post hung from a mid-high branch. Almost completely hidden unless one knew where to look. It was already old when her parents had first brought her with them to use it for what it had been built to do - hiding observers from what was being observed and sheltering them when the looking was done.

She descended from the bridgeway and worked her way over to the post's hometree. Kendle found that once she had grasped the first of the handholds, her body retained enough memory of the climb to make it almost easy. With relief, Kendle clambered up onto the creaking platform, stooped to remove her sensible but now mucky shoes, and entered the hut. On her previous trips she had brought a few supplies, so first thing she checked the storage chest to see if they were still there and in useable condition. It was, she thought, a sign of the shatterings so recent to her, that untouched food stuffs could be so moving. The raincatcher was full as well. A drink of cool water, a splash of it against her face was what she needed.

Refreshed just enough, Kendle suddenly found herself without a plan. She had gotten this far, had known this hidden sanctuary was where she would be safest. But now the enormity of becoming an outlier threatened to break against her. Unlike the always working, always helping, always understanding person she had been, this Kendle could not find in the desolation of her heart any task to which she might set her hand, any other person she might bolster, errand to be done. The consolation of busyness not being possible, Kendle sank down on the rough sleeping pallet. Using the last of her strength, she wrenched her heart away from what had happened, found a muted, numb state in which to take cover and fell hard into distracting sleep.

In that sad sleep, some tattered remnant of woe must have found its way outward, for a tear slid across Kendle's face. From above, through tightly twined branches that served as roof, came one exquisitely tiny creature, winged, possessed of its own light, to hover above that face. With a suggestion of tenderness, it drank softly of the tear. And then flew away as quietly as it had come.

x • x • x

"Here it is," Mote called. Though it had been quite a while since they had heard or seen the hunters of Over, it was imprudent to trumpet their location. "I mean," he lowered his voice, "this way. She walked here."

Loud rustling in the brush and the crack of trodden branches announced Andeved. How like an Underion to bash about through the trees. Mote's irritation came swift but left soon, because he could see Andeved struggling to understand and adapt to the complexity of forest, of the outside. That was a part of Andeved, a part not like others of Under, Mote had come so quickly to observe and respect.

"Excellent work, young man." Belwether's voice rumbled softly nearby. As usual, it startled Mote and made him want to use some of the more indelicate phrases employed by veteran marchales. He was the expert here, but it felt like the Oni was showing off, and showing him up, by his lurking ways. Mote tried to feel more grateful for Belwether's just-in-time help and unflagging support. Tried. Kept trying.

The three, now together, stooped to look at the discovered footprint. It amazed Andeved that such a small thing could be found in such overwhelmingly abundant surroundings. Nothing in the rigid corridors of Under had prepared him for this kind of... well...he really felt it was an adventure. Beneath the apprehension, the fear of what the hunters might do if they caught Kendle, or what might be done to him, underneath that was a bright ember of excitement. What he was seeing, doing, learning, coming to know - it was burning away the restive spirit that had been his burden.

Andeved stood up, easing his travel bag to the other shoulder. "How did you ever find that little footprint in all of this?" He gestured widely. "When there is a chance, some time, could you teach me how you do that?"

Mote flushed a bit from the admiration of his forest skills. "Well, surely. Yes. We could."

"When there is time." Belwether turned in the direction the footprint indicated. "Later." Almost there was heat in those few words. Andeved and Mote glanced at one another, seeking perhaps a confirmation of what they thought they heard. But the Oni was already many steps ahead of them and it would be all they could do to keep up.

When they did catch up, Belwether was standing quite still, looking ahead at a strange, hanging structure of ropes and planks. Without turning around, he asked the approaching Mote, "Is this one of your bridgeways?"

"Yes. Yes, it is." Mote frowned. "But I know all our regular 'ways and this is not one of them. I mean, look at it." He huffed out his chest just a small bit. "We keep our bridgeways in excellent repair. So this one must not have been made by waybuilders. And it certainly isn't on their maintenance patrol."

Belwether pointed at muddy smudges on several of the nearest planks. "Nevertheless, signs of recent use are there." He turned to Mote. "Might you examine the indications and give us your opinion?"

"I was just going to do that." Mote rankled at what seemed to be over-politeness from the Oni. In his experience, such deference often masked other, less happy attitudes. But he clambered up onto the rotting walkway all the same. As always, there was a sense of appropriateness at being over. Even upon such a derelict 'way. And, of course, the smudges clearly were muddy shoeprints.

When it was obvious that the signs pointed in a certain direction, Andeved rushed to climb up onto the walkway suspended well above his head. He had heard of these curious structures, as well as speculation as to why they existed, but he had never actually seen one. If Kendle had been there, he would have thanked her for leading them this way. Well, might have thanked her once he got his feet under him. The whole section of hanging planks swayed something fierce just by the three of them trying to get their balance on the fool thing.

"Be careful of the missing parts," Mote called over his shoulder. "And hang on to the rope rails." He stepped over a gap in the boards, pulling himself along slowly so he might still track the shoeprints as they grew fainter, and demonstrate bridgewalking to the others.

That three of them were struggling to slog along only increased the dip and swing of the hanging walkway. Had Andeved eaten anything recently, it might have left him abruptly as the uneven swaying unbalanced his stomach. He had to keep his eyes on the planks, or lack of planks, just ahead of each step. Between the boards the forest floor he could glimpse rose into rocky points and fell into narrow, deep ravines. All the while the ill-made bridgeway tilted and swung mercilessly. Not only did his gorge rise, but he was getting dizzy. He tried, by will alone, to calm his gut and unspin his head. The difference that made was marginal. What was left was to put one foot in front of the other, suffering the misery as best he could. The effort so consumed his awareness that he only barely heard the cry and felt the jerk that came from behind him.

Clutching the rope rails for balance, Andeved turned and looked back. To see nothing. No Belwether on the bridgeway. One of the planks showed a splintered glimpse of new wood against the dull outer stains. Andeved fought to move toward the gap. It took hideous moments for the walkway to stop lurching so he could see what lay below on the forest floor.

Belwether. Unmoving. And there was blood. And more blood, pooling around the Oni's head like a dark crown.

Andeved tore his gaze from the rocks below and frantically tried to figure how to get down to the stony ravine. But the ground was too far down, the walkway strung as it was between two high points. Cut rope from the handrails? Tie it on a bottom plank and climb down? He tried to gauge the distance to the ground. And caught sight of someone moving toward Belwether, someone with his head down, reaching for...

The man looked up. It was Mote.

"Go to the next stanchion and climb down there." The marchale pointed overward. "Hurry. I can hear the Oni breathing."

Breathing. Belwether was alive still. That possibility tremored Andeved with a frisson of hope. He turned in the direction Mote had pointed, pulling himself along the handrails, nearly blinded by relief and fear. Somehow he managed to crawl to the stanchion and climb down the ladder pegs. Stumbling in haste across the uneven ground, sliding downhill at the last.

Belwether had landed face up in the narrow base of the ravine. Most of him lay akimbo in the soggy, forgiving clutter of the forest floor. But his head - that rested on an outcropping of stone. On a bloody rock Andeved hated on sight. He was of Under. He knew both the surety of stone and the cruelty of rock. He did not realize his hand had reached Belwether's head until he found he had turned that head ever so gently to one side. And could see the terrible gash, the oozing of darkening scarlet against a sliver of bone white.

"We need to get him up out of here." Mote was digging though his travel pack. "Cannot treat him here." He drew out a woven cap and, moving Andeved's hand away with a jerk, put the cap on the Oni. When the boy started to protest, Mote silenced him with a look. "The cap holds...everything...in place while we move him to higher ground."

The marchale dug into his pack again and brought out a length of rope, thinner and smoother than the type used on the walkways. Then, frustration on his face, he emptied out the pack altogether.

"Help me put this under his shoulders. It's all we have to keep his neck steady. In case..." But Mote was already trying to shove the pack under Belwether. With Mote on one side and Andeved on the other, the struggle was waged to slide the stiff-backed pack under the Oni's substantial shoulders and secure it with the rope. Haste and weight brought both of them to a sweaty, shaky state all too soon.

Finally, with Belwether's head and neck as protected as they could manage, Mote made a huge loop from the remaining rope, spread open the loop and gave one side of it to Andeved. Taking another side for himself, they began to pull.

Progress was slow, doubtlessly for Belwether painfully slow. But the Oni still did not open his eyes or make any sound. Andeved's muscles became shaky with the effort and once he groaned as if on Belwether's behalf. Mote kept up a stream of encouragements. "That's it." "We got him over that one." "Just a bit more." "Careful there. Good." It was impossible to know who, exactly, he was encouraging. All the while, the thin light that filtered through the high trees faded and dimmed as this vile day came to its end.

It was full dark when Mote called a stop. By some bit of grace, they had managed to get the Oni to dry, level ground. Mote reached in his pockets and retrieved his small oil lamp. In moments it flickered into light, though what it illuminated was not reassuring. Belwether had begun to shiver and twitch.

"Is he cold or...?" Andeved's voice cracked with the strain of the question.

"I think his body is reacting to the injuries. We need to keep him warm. I guess." The certainty that had marked Mote's actions from rescue to here had suddenly fled.

"A fire, that's it. That's what he needs." Andeved forced himself into motion once again. He turned toward the darkness, groping for fallen branches. Bringing back one armful. Going out again. Heedless of twisting roots, slapping branches, in his haste sometimes grabbing things that were definitely not kindling.

"Andeved." Mote was calling. "Come back."

The boy turned toward the sound and saw the dim edges of lamp light. He made for them in as much haste as walking in darkness afforded. Slowly he realized the circle of light was bigger than it had been. There was another person. Holding a larger, brighter lantern.

The glare of it hid the person's face and for a terrible, heart snaring moment Andeved thought that the Overite marchales had found them.

But then the lantern was set on a nearby stump and the newcomer was revealed.

"I heard you coming," Kendle took off the long cloak she wore and laid it over Belwether. "And then I heard the bridge break and saw him fall." She tucked a corner of the cloak around the Oni's feet and looked up. Worry and fear had joined to wrench Kendle's face into a grim mask.

"We were looking for you..."

"He's really hurt. What...."

The young men talked over each other in relief and urgency.

"Shush!" Kendle's command was harsh though the word was soft. "The traces of your path can be erased. But sounds cannot. You know too well, Mote, the hunt dogs have keen ears."

The young marchale grimaced in embarrassment. "Yes, keen ears. It's just that..." he motioned toward the Oni.

"Sorry, Kendle," Andeved spoke barely above a whisper. "We meant to give help, not need it."

"I know," she sighed and picked up her lantern again. "If you can pull Belwether but a little way more, there is a shelter with some healing supplies within."

"Aye," was the muted reply. Chafed hands once more picked up the loop of rope and pulled the burden that was not a burden.

Kendle led by her light and, as she had promised, it was only a short distance to where she motioned them to stop. Quietly, she pointed to a long pallet on the ground with a length of rope at each corner. The ropes disappeared upward, into a dark mass of leaves and branches. With gestures she indicated they should move Belwether onto it. Wearily, but gently, they did so and then looked to Kendle for direction. She had disappeared.

"Up here!" Her voice floated down from the tree above, followed by a sliver of light through the leaves. "The boles on the trunk make a ladder. Put out your lamp, Mote. It's easier to feel the right handholds than see them."

Mote pulled Andeved closer to the tree and then extinguished his little oil lamp. He felt around the tree trunk and, just about waist high, found a long broken branch that would hold. He grabbed Andeved's hand and placed it on the branch.

"Try not to overly think about the next handhold. Just pull up and feel for it. It will be there." And it was.

It took both forever and not long to reach the platform. Kendle held open a trapdoor through which they came. Amazingly, the lantern showed a large room with several sleeping pads, shelves, raincatcher, a table with chairs. The young men gasped in surprise, fairly much in unison.

But Kendle was already at the far side of the room unlatching a section of wall.

"You will have to help me pull him up." She reached into the dark beyond the wall and retrieved a length of rope that wrapped over a sort of wheel. "It's a pulley. They used to bring up supplies with it. It should still work."

Kendle threw the rope's end to them and then leaned out beyond the wall, tugging and straining at branches and intertwined clusters of leaves. "It has overgrown without use, but I think we can still get him through it."

Closing their gaping mouths, Andeved and Mote grabbed the pulley line and began to pull. The first tug was easy. Then it became difficult as the slack in the ropes caught up and the pallet suspended with Belwether's full weight on it. Still they strained to bring the Oni upward. Kendle nearly fell forward into the darkness as she struggled to clear a way through the dense growth of the huge tree that surrounded the shelter.

Bit by exhausting bit the pallet drew closer, until at last Kendle could pull it into the room and they could lower it safely onto a sleeping pad.

They had done it. Belwether was brought to a place where care could be given. And Kendle had been found alive and well hidden. In relief, Mote wiped sweat from his face, only to discover his palms were so abraded they were bleeding. He looked over and saw his own condition mirrored in the Underion. They had done it. They had. Both sank into chairs in a daze of fatigue.

Kendle moved with purpose through the room, latching the section of wall back into place, gathering medicine bottles and bandages, bowls of water, pouches of herbs. She knelt by the motionless Oni and carefully peeled back the cap that covered the worst of the damage. And tried not to gasp at what she saw, tried to keep calm, to remember what needed to be remembered. First cleaning the wound, yes. Bowls of water brought clear and taken away deep red. Again and again until finally she could see that the bone was but slightly fractured, though the skin had been brutally sliced. It would take a long time and many fine stitches to pull it together again.

It was as Kendle slipped thread through needle that the sound came. All three of them heard it. And it stopped their breath, stopped their hearts.

From far away, a long, deep howl carried through the forest. Somewhere a hunt dog claimed a scent.

CHAPTER SEVEN

Though Under and Over are exceeding different, inhabitants of each place consider their own environment to be both enormously silent and, simultaneously, filled with sound. In Under, the stone is eternally still, yet there echoes continuously the dripping of the water clock, the soughing of wind through passageways, the tinkling of bells as corridored mirrors are turned to catch light and, beneath all, the beating of hearts and taking of breath.

The forests of Over are hugely and agedly silent. But even the ears of grossfolk can hear the dripping of rain from leaf to leaf, the rustle of branches from overhead breezes, the creaking of bridgeways under the weight of use and, beneath all, the beating of hearts and taking of breath.

It is also true that what exists may be seen as good if benevolently intended or wickedness if malevolently inclined. In this way silence may be either a calm sanctuary or a terrible hush in which the hard breathing of prey cannot be hid. Protection might come, instead, with the thrumming of rain on countless leaves.

Night and storm have descended on Over. In a long abandoned observation post, the sound of heavy rain is loud enough that the beating of hearts, especially one that beats but faintly, is drowned out. Wind stirs the higher canopy so that the washing water of the forest sluices down here and there, carrying away signs and scents. The slight glow of a traveler's oil lamp is well contained. It illuminates the travelers. Two are sleepers whose bandaged-wrapped hands lie at rest after much work. There is another one who lies as if in sleep. He is propped on his side to preserve the delicate stitchwork joining flesh over bone.

Only one is awake, turning over and over in her mind the possible mornings. The rain is a boon. It washes away most of the scent and sign while covering sounds they may have made. But they cannot hear, either, should someone be coming closer. The darkness is a boon. It helps to hide and makes walking the 'ways or, if needed, the forest floor much chancier. But it will not last and the coming of light will not be help for them. Stillness by the injured one helps keep them from detection, but it does not bode well for healing.

Kendle stood, stretching stiff limbs, feeling the need for small comforts. Outside the rain still fell - a small fire under a pot of water would do no harm. No more harm than what exists already. Wearily rifling through the stores box, she found the particular pouch she wanted, took out a bit of the dried leaves and 'shroons mixture inside, bundled it in a small cloth - and looked away from the pot. Then smiled at herself. 'Watched water never boils.' Silly what a person does without thought.

Soon, no doubt because unwatched, the water was hot and the cloth bundle seeped until a deep, earthy aroma meandered through the room. Kendle ladled out a bowl of the broth and, leaving spoons still snugged in the stores box, sipped goodness from the rim. The warmth found her belly, worked outward to her hands and feet and lastly, as it always did, made her nose warm and in need of a wipe. 'Thaw you inside and out' is what her mother used to say. Said here, in this very room, what seemed so very long ago.

Kendle sipped and remembered the three of them sitting at the small, square table that used to be here. Her mother gesturing with her fork, dripping little bits of breakfast here and there, talking ardently about her work. And father, having cooked the eggs and 'shroons with just a touch of herbs, eating tidily, though he talked every bit as much. On the other side of the table, small in a large chair, her younger self earnestly approaching her meal, trying to eat neatly, trying to understand the complexities of the conversations that excited others. It was not her fault she wasn't old enough to be part of the ebb and flow of words and ideas.

Even now, Kendle can feel the loneliness of being with her parents. Yes, she did love them, and they loved her in their own way. But their vocation, an avocation as well, took up so much of life, waking and dreaming, that even a small, very good girl could barely find a place to be. Then, when she did find a place that mattered for them, it was too late.

A ragged breath, a groan, brought her back to the now. Belwether had made a sound. She went to his side bringing fear and hope with her. This was the critical moment. He would wake to either say his last words or emerge to the mending battle.

"Belwether?" His eyes opened slowly, hesitantly. For the longest moment there appeared no awareness; then, like an ember stirred by wind, recognition flamed again.

Kendle's knees nearly gave way, her relief was so great and sudden. The Oni that was Belwether still resided in that thick skull. In fact, he tried to move, but she put her hand on his shoulder to keep him from turning onto the wound. He calmed under her hand, and yet continued to look at her. She did not see confusion in his eyes. Pain, yes. But something else, too.

"I fell...before..." Belwether's usually deep rumble was thin and cracked, "...and it changed...it all. They didn't tell you, did they?" He closed his eyes and breathed in and out, the easy breathing of sleep. Healing sleep.

Pulling the blanket up over the Oni's bulk, Kendle muttered to herself in relief, letting a bit of anger build to ease the breath-holding fear she had endured these last terrible hours. How like Belwether to utter something cryptic and then stop on the brink of making sense. And those...those boys, really. Did they not think to tell her

Belwether had fallen before? It might have made a difference, could have been important. But no, not a jot of thought between them.

It came as a surprise that tears were tracing down her cheeks. Kendle stopped her muttering, hearing the release of worry that it was, and barely made it to her sleeping pallet before she sagged completely with strain and fatigue. Belwether was going to heal. Andeved and Mote would be almost themselves after a night's rest. The storm had washed away their trail and overridden their sounds from the marchales and their hounds. They were safe for now.

Still Kendle could not make the tears stop. Turning away from the sleepers, she quit fighting the outpouring of her distress. The others would heal, would go back. She would not. Could not. For outliers, home was a place that used to be.

Sometime in the night the storm passed, the rain ceased, the wind left to stir other places, and Kendle fell into a vast, empty sleep.

X · X · X

She did not quite come fully awake, but she could hear snatches of their talk.

"Catch the rope when I throw it up to you." Mote's voice sounded faintly.

"Shush, you'll wake them." Andeved was nearer.

"Shush?" There was humor in the rebuke. "My, my, what a veteran forester you've become."

"And aren't you the prickly fish before breakfast?"

Whoosh. Pause. Rustle.

"I said catch it when I throw it up to you."

"Get it within catching distance and I will."

"If you think you could do better..."

"Well, I can aim a sweetround with accuracy at 100 paces. You couldn't hit the ground with a rock."

Whoosh.

"Got it."

"Finally."

Their voices and the sounds of their movements faded into a just-before-waking dream, the kind that blends what is real and what is not and what may yet be. In the dream, Kendle saw herself spinning thread from dried meshroon netting, letting the filament twist through her fingers until it became so thin it was almost invisible. Andeved stood in the place, too, juggling sweetround fruit. In the dream she understood that he was trying to keep the fruit in the air so they could ripen. His face was furrowed with concentration. Between the spinning wheel and the juggler stood Belwether. He was laughing. It seemed very wrong and very right. And all around were little lights, shimmering, dancing, flitting, growing brighter and brighter.

Bright light. Morning still, but dawn long past if the brightness of the light shafting on her face was any indication. Time to awaken fully. Which Kendle did, to find Mote and Andeved seated cross-legged on the floor, sorting through their travel packs, congenial, smiling. Next to the sleeping Belwether.

Andeved glanced over and saw Kendle had awakened.

"Good morning. We thought you were going to sleep all day."

"No, I could not do that with you two flailing around shushing one another. I did hear you earlier, you know."

Mote elbowed Andeved good naturedly.

"You were right, sharp ears. Should have been quieter, eh? Except how would we have been able," and here Mote got up and went to the traveler's stove that still radiated heat, "to get fresh meshroons. And pleybird eggs." He brought over a plate with a hearty serving of breakfast and presented it, and a spoon, with a triumphant flourish.

Kendle sat up on her pallet and received the savory smelling offering with a smile. "This looks very good." She looked up at the marchale who puffed up just a bit.

"Yes, well, have to keep strong. Fill up." He went back to his seat next to Andeved and began again to sort through what items they still had from their packs.

Kendle made herself more comfortable on the pallet and dug into the eggs, which proved to be quite as tasty as they looked. It felt good to have the most elementary stuff of life: rest, food, companionship, shelter. And safety, if only for a time. For this moment, it was enough.

"Kendle?" Andeved's voice was strained thin. The boy's eyes were huge, his body tense. He was staring at Belwether.

Around the Oni's wounded head, tiny points of light were gathering. More and more they came, each so minute no detail could be seen. In numbers, a crown of moving brightnesses.

"What is that...are they?" Andeved again. On the point of action. "They must not hurt him."

"Stay where you are." Kendle made no sudden movement, hoping no one else did either. "Be still. They will help."

"No! We found out about them. They DO hurt. Even though these are smaller, much smaller, they are made to hurt." Andeved's desperation was painful to hear. Next to him, Mote sat frozen in wonderment.

"I promise you, Andeved, these will do no harm. These will help the healing. It is one thing my parents came to know, for a surety, from their studies. I have seen it myself. Watch. Trust me, please. For Belwether's sake."

Kendle watched Andeved strain against his fear, speechlessly plead with her for certainty.

"Unbandage and hold out your hands, Andeved. Slowly. Let them come nearer. It won't hurt you. I promise. It will help. You'll see."

For many heartbeats the boy fought with what he believed and who he believed. Then, beside him, the no longer junior marchale cautiously unbandaged and held out his hands, palms up. Andeved abruptly decided, jerking his hands forward. The suddenness of the movement caused the tiny lights to swirl away as if frightened.

Kendle caught her breath. *Please stay, they won't hurt you, please.* The unfledged could not hear her thoughts, she knew that. She just could not help but repeat the voiceless plea, the silent desire. *Stay. Please. Stay and help us.*

A tentative few, only a few of the now scattered lights, came closer to the four scraped and scored hands. Closer. Then one and three and then more ever so lightly touched down on the proffered wounds. Andeved felt each of the touches, like the flick of the tiniest of feathers. It did not seem so at first, but as he watched he found the cuts and scrapes were...taken away. There was no other explanation. Carried away by healers so small he could only see their light.

In the same way, the lightlettes eddied and curled around the Oni's head. Swirled and dipped to touch the wound, each lifting such a tiny bit of blood, such a trifling measure of illness that no one mote could have effected a change. Yet the rivulet of brightness bore away with it the dark stains, the ragged edges of flesh that could not be saved, the possibility of wound illness. Most of the tiny flitterings, burdened with the harm done to Belwether, drifted upward again, finding their way out, taking their light with them. But a few stayed, landing along the Oni's wound, illuminating the stitched line. Slowly, at dream-like speed, the illuminating sparks crawled onto the wound, a dotted ribbon across a bloodied slash.

Andeved moaned: "What have we done?"

"Wait for a while more." Kendle felt the anxiety of hope seep into her voice. "Be patient and watch. You will see."

Time passed in the shadowed room, passed in time to Belwether's steady and Andeved's ragged breathing. Mote put his arm around the distressed boy, knowing there was more to his companion's distress than was understood just now. But the marchale believed in the waiting. Believed in what they would see.

"There!" Kendle's cry came so loudly that Andeved and Mote flinched. For the first time since the lights had come, Kendle moved toward Belwether, pointing toward the wound. Pointing to where very dim, barely discernable gleams, like tiny, pale moons rose up. Not quickly as they once had, but slowly. Not as brightly as before, but diminished. Drifting outward until they disappeared into the Over.

Belwether sat up, reaching one hand to gingerly touch the back of his head. He made an attempt to get up, but it was not successful.

"You all seem to be staring at me," the Oni's voice was as rumblingly resonant as ever. "Perhaps, if you would be so kind, one of you might bring me some water. And good lady if you have any ranciple powder, I seem to have an ache in my head. Actually, most everywhere."

While Andeved did nothing but stare, Mote got up to fetch a tumbler of water. Kendle laughed with relief and went to search the shelves for a pouch of ranciple. When Belwether had drunk water, three trips made to fill the tumbler before he was satisfied, he turned his attention to the still staring Andeved.

"We each are made to blink now and again. You might want to try that, Andeved. Andeved?"

The young man brought himself around with several blinks and a determined throat clearing.

"Yes, well, yes. I was just so surprised to see you so...well. I mean...feeling well. After the fall...I thought...we thought you were really hurt. And then those things came and got into your head."

If Belwether had been endowed with expressive eyebrows, they would have shot upward. "Things? On my head? Explain yourself."

"It is mine to explain, and yet I am afraid to begin." Kendle sat down cross-legged on the floor. "What I know for certain is both good and bad. What I do not know for certain, that which I can only surmise, may be best and worst of all."

She took in a breath, readying for words but keeping her eyes fixed on her hands which were fisted in her lap.

"My parents built this observation post and then studied here for many seasons. Their special interest was in creatures that existed in benefit to growing things. Most especially when the contagion spread."

"Kendle?" Mote indicated Andeved and the Oni to her. "Should you be telling them about that?" He sounded rather marchale-like with the question.

"Why should this be secret, like everything else that matters? Did keeping the secret provide anything of use? Of what value was secrecy among the leaders of Over to those who suffered and died? How did secrets restore the deep forest meshroons that could have saved many? It was stupid, senseless secrecy to keep the healing gifts of unfledged fletts concealed until it was too late. Too late for my own parents - the ones who discovered it and were fools enough to...."

Kendle's voice broke from fierceness and grief. "Yes, I should be telling *them* about *that*."

There was a silence built in respect of Kendle's outpouring. But behind the pause, within each of the four, conflicts of known and unknown clamored and clashed. It was Andeved who broke into the outer quiet.

"You know, Mote, it is time for you to decide. If you stay with us I think, from what I do know of Over, you will also be exiled. Kendle had no choice, Belwether is an exile, so to speak, by nature, and I have always considered myself apart. But you - you can choose. Though it had better be now, before any more is said."

Mote looked down at his hands which were clenched together, white-knuckled. He frowned and tried to loosen the grip his hands had on themselves. As if they were strangers, they resisted the command to undo, resisted and then grudgingly complied. He could look up then, at the three who were near him, and say what he meant.

"For a long time I hoped that there might come a time, a chance to find out more true things, the how and why of things. You are my chance."

Mote smiled, shyly but with a well-defined hope.

"Good. Good. So then," came Belwether's bass rumble, "might we return for just a moment to the things, which I now gather are fletts, and what they were doing in my head? Because Andeved and I were shown evidence of a nature far, far different from benevolent."

Kendle's face reddened and she shifted uncomfortably on the hard floor. Clearly there was something that was guilt-provoking in what she knew. The other three, having so recently heard her opinion of keeping secrets, settled in to listen.

X · X · X

If the man would only sit down, the conversation would be much more productive. And the house would not sway quite so much. It made Zearia unsettled to see Voeller pace so furiously. The smile she had installed on her face for this occasion had begun to tighten. Besides, it was inappropriate for Over's high minister to evidence unease, especially in front of her and Pember. Once again she entertained the idea that Voeller's stay in Under had, in some way, rattled him. Shaken what should have been rock solid. Now that was not amusing. *Rock solid*, indeed. How irritating that even she was using images from Under. The place that had killed their daughter.

Zearia took a spiced heznut from the serving tray. How many times she had used this little trick. Even now the strong flavor kept her from thinking of much else. Her smile loosened somewhat though a careful observer, she knew, would see a tiny heznut-sized bulge in her cheek. But worth it. Much calmer now. If only the man would sit down.

"We called back the marchales, as you directed." Voeller spoke as he reached the far side of the room and turned to pace back again. "But it made no sense to do so. We knew where she was headed. They could have found her and taken care of it all. That was, as you had informed me, the plan after all." His voice strained just to the point of a whine.

In all the years Pember and Zearia had ruled Over, Voeller had been useful and appropriate. Most of the time. Unless he felt excluded from any planning, any discussion, any decisions. It did not benefit the high minister to be petulant when a few, only a very few, secrets were not given to him. Did the man not understand his place?

Pember looked over at his wife, the only other person in Over who shared all the secrets he knew. She had that bump in her cheek. Voeller's whining had obviously distressed her.

"Minister," Pember grabbed Voeller's tunic as he paced by. "Sit down. Contain yourself. You are making the house swing more than usual."

Attempting some semblance of dignity, Voeller folded his boney frame into a chair.

"Now then," Pember rallied what patience remained to him, "it is abundantly clear to us that you did all you were asked to do. You were invaluable in planning, excellent in the execution of your duties as envoy to Under. We have gesh of our own, for which you deserve credit and thanks."

Voeller received the positive words with a narrowing of his eyes and an ever so slight tilt of his head. In the chair behind him, where he could not see her, Zearia rolled her eyes and crunched down on the nut she had been savoring. Pember, who heard that, knew better than to smile.

"But you must admit that, while you were there in that wretched Under, the…well…unexpected actions of certain members of the party required new strategies. We had to make decisions without you. Not our choice. But necessary. Surely you see that?"

"I understand that," Voeller leaned forward in the chair. "It is the reason for letting Kendle get away that eludes me. The clan leaders already talk amongst themselves, wondering in whispers why an outlier such as she is not hunted to conclusion. An outlier who, it is said, dawdled about with Underions even as the Lady Arrant fell to her death."

Pember knew, from long practice, that the wrath rising within him was not reflected in any way on his face. Much later, when appropriate, it would emerge. And there would be consequences. But for now, no fire lit his expression. The useful part of the rage informed his words, however.

"Did any of the clan leaders presume to grieve a father's grief, a mother's sorrow? Do the whisperers say we did not love our daughter enough to fully avenge ourselves on she who allowed her cousin to die? There is no trust, then, in us - in the heart of who we are and what we do for the sake of Over, for Over above all?"

His mouth tightened into a grim line. Voeller said nothing.

Pember abruptly rose from his chair and walked to the door. He put his hand on the latch, but spoke before he drew it open.

"Yes, the marchales were called back. What you were not yet told is that one hunter is tasked with the managing of our Kendle problem. A single, especially skilled hunter. Tell the clan leaders that the once-niece needs but one to manage her. And counsel yourself to more patience. Next time we meet, wait until we have shared our minds first before you make the house sway."

Now Pember opened the door. Voeller unfolded himself and left without another word. When the door was shut once again, both Pember and Zearia felt the house settle into a better balanced state.

"He is useful, you know." Zearia shook her head.

"A useful idiot." Pember drew the latch tight, went to his wife and embraced her. No words could be spoken about their parental grief for fear too many tears, feeble rationales, anger and guilt would break loose. Secrets and sorrow held them and they held each other.

X · X · X

The storm had left signs of itself. Greens were brighter, browns shown with late lying mist, even the moss-spider's web was dotted with the clearest crystals and the air smelled of damp soil. Here and there meshroons poked their unexpected and welcomed heads above ground. Not far into the Season of Sweeping Rain and already the moldering reminders of a stunted Gathering Season had been washed away. With the possession of their own gesh, all the past disappointments would soon be gone. At least this was what the people of Over saw, inhaled, remembered and hoped as they assembled to honor the life of the Lady Arrant.

No house or hall could hold the many who came to give tribute. Nor was there a bridgeway capable of sustaining the weight of such a gathering. Long, long ago a place had been made for disposing of the dead - a place that could not be seen from the houses or well-used 'ways, one that had been cleared of trees and the richness they lent to the soil with their own deaths. To enter that place required stepping from the higher walks onto barren ground that only took and did not give back.

Pember and Zearia, as the grieving parents, were closest to the new-made burial mound. All others arranged themselves along the muddy paths winding between hummocks already shrunken by time and inattention. There was a clan responsible for this sort of occasion, but its leader was only newly inherited of the duties. When the untried clan leader stepped forward to begin the ceremony, she held up her arms for silence a goodly while before quiet was accomplished. Too many of the attendees were still elbowing their way toward a better view. Others simply could not finish the whispers they felt compelled to share.

Pember was acutely aware of his people's motive forces because, as he admitted to himself in the darker moments, they were his own as well. He was here to finish the journey of his daughter's body, to be of support to Zearia, to observe who was here and in what state so that friends and not-friends might be counted, to extract from the whispers what might help and what might harm, to try to ignore the inevitability of his own death and to hold those secrets safe that ensured he held sway in Over.

Zearia winced as the fledgling clan leader stumbled through the ritual. How like the young to be so arrogant, to believe they could take on the managing of so much with so little experience. Arrant had been like that. Too impulsive, stubbornly insisting on what she felt was right. As if emotions were accurate predictors of ascendancy. At least there was the satisfaction of knowing her daughter's mission had been, in large part, a success. But the nearness of freshly turned dirt was too terrible for mother Zearia. She filched a heznut from her pocket and slipped it into her mouth.

Finally the ceremony came to an end. Both the clan leader and the crowd were relieved. It was Pember's cue to make the speech he had rehearsed with his wife into the late hours of the night.

"In usual times, as Head Secretholders, Zearia and I would now speak a few words on behalf of the greater body of Over in the loss of one of its own. We have done this many times, weeping with the left who loved, remembering together the rhythms and significance of a life lived among us. How can we now be both those who weep and those who comfort?"

Pember looked from one side of the crowd to the other, letting all see the well-practiced expression of sorrow and duty displayed on his face, drawing sustenance from the sighs that rose from all around.

Beside him, Zearia nodded solemnly, one side of her face hidden in the shadow of his shoulder. This speech was important as the clans were unsettled, there was a need to enlist more hearts to the direction of her mind. And Pember's mind, of course. Still, the sooner this was done, the sooner she could meet with Nomic and loose the hunter. Just the thought of that comforted Zearia so she could endure as Pember ended his address with the words they had chosen so carefully.

"The gesh are ours. The forest floor will once again repay us with abundance in the season of that name. This is comfort for you, and for Zearia and for me. In this we can be one. Thank you, Arrant. Thank you all."

Zearia bit down on the soggy heznut and looked up. She picked Nomic out of the crowd and marked his attendance.

X · X · X

Nomic seriously considered his beard. Not everyone viewed decorative facial hair favorably, though he did not understand why anyone would not. Granted he had an increasing number of gray hairs amongst the dark. But the contrast of silver with rich wood brown was rather fine. Perhaps he should visit his fellow Overites and survey the matter. He was, after all, Over's pre-eminent researcher.

But the thought of conversing with the unreasoning masses gave him pause. So very few even approached his level of thought, it was difficult to find kindred minds. With a sigh, he gave his beard a bit of a comb and went back to his workbench. When Zearia arrived she would expect progress and he still had a few ragged ends to smooth before this creature would be ready.

Nomic ran his fingers along the line of small glass cases crowding the shelves to the side of his work table. No movements in this one. Slight flickerings in this one. This one empty, the sides dimmed by smudges. Another just cleaned and polished, ready for new occupants. It was fascinating the number of subjects needed to complete research large enough to bring satisfactory results.

The brightest result of his recent study lived in the largest of the containers. A bit of hair, twisted in a ragged piece of cloth, lay close by on the shelf. Nomic picked it up and, prying the lid just the slightest awry, dropped the twined hair and cloth into the glass case. As usual, it did not immediately attract the creature's attention. But very soon the hair had been scented and circled and the small hunter, no more than the length of a finger, dropped onto the material. The researcher watched as the flett sought to bond with the item. The futile attempts to do this during the training period often made Nomic laugh out loud.

A knocking on his front door startled him. So few came to see him. It must be Zearia. With a sense of anticipation he never felt for the intrusion of others, he gave his beard a last fluffing and fairly ran to open the door.

There she was.

"Greetings, Head Researcher. I hope I'm not intruding. May I come in?"

Without a doubt you may enter is what he wanted to say. But Nomic, the rational, mumbled something incomprehensible and motioned awkwardly for Zearia to step in.

As she crossed the threshold, Zearia reached up and ruffled Nomic's beard. "That lovely beard just gets better every time I see you. And look, this time no bits of lint or lunch. What a rogue you are."

Nomic followed her in and closed the door behind them.

X · X · X

Drop by drop by drop the Hour of Mid-Dark came and went. So did the Lord of Under come and go, the slightest slap-slap of his steps on the unfeeling stone the only marking of his passage. He had wrapped himself in dark colors, not arrayed in garments so much as in swaths of berry-dyed cloth that billowed with his forward motion and trailed behind him collecting dust, dirt and the small bits lives left behind in the hours of light.

Paell stationed himself beside the water clock, eagerly awaiting the drowsy Ceremonialist to call out the arrival of night's exact middle.

"Dark half come, dark half gone,

In Under there is time to sleep,

To rest, to drop into the deep

Of quiet. To prepare the people

For the coming dreams.

No turning now,

Turning will come again."

Having finished the proscribed phrases, the Ceremonialist removed her mask of office and placed it on the ledge above the pool made by the water clock's spent time. The day was finally over and a soft bed called to her weariness. But Lord Paell's appearance these last few nights troubled her. He did not speak, was not dressed properly and took odd postures. Extending a leg, toe pointed and raising his arms until they reached a line straight out from his shoulders. Slowly turning side to side, the cloth that made his coverings fluttering and swaying. Most unsettling of all, Lord Paell hovered so perilously close to the water clock she feared his strange gestures might cause him to interrupt the drops that kept the time.

So each night she asked him, "May I assist you in any way, Lord Paell?" And each night he said nothing, but gathered his drapes and folds and walked away. She did not mention to anyone else this apparition-like attendance to her nightly ritual. To talk of it would be an admission of the uneasiness it brought her. After all, it was his right to attend, his duty to ensure that duty was done by one and by all. As long as the Hours were said and the water clock remained uninterrupted - that was all that mattered.

Unlike the other nights, this time Lord Paell answered her question.

"You are the present ending of a line of yourselves. Tellers of Time through time, taking on the mask and then giving it to the next. Does this make you more or less the 'you' you believe yourself to be?"

The Ceremonialist frowned, trying to concentrate on the Lord's twist of thoughts. Her fatigue was painful by now and this only made it worse. But she knew she should not leave until he left and the water clock's dependability was assured.

"I am the Ceremonialist, true. And I am also Iogene, daughter of Cowl and Merseeah. Is that what you mean?"

No sign of comprehension crossed Paell's face. Instead, he bent down and put a finger into the dark pool and brought it up to his lips, wetting them with spent time. Without another word, he left as silently as he had come.

With the water clock seemingly safe once more, the Ceremonialist began a weary and uneasy walk toward waiting sleep.

Paell did not walk toward sleep. In the silent corridors he shivered his way here and there, sweeping past low-growth jinncar that briefly fluoresced in the eddies of air. Though he seemed not to need the dim greenish light, or any light for that matter, to illuminate his way. Some other awareness saw, if seeing is what was being done, the nooks, alcoves, rooms, halls and stairways. That sight-like attribute led him, always by the Hour of Dreaming, to the rubble strewn site of the accident. The event. The misfortune.

Oh, his people had worked hard to clear what they could. Ceremonies of Remembrance had been said for those already buried in the tumbled rocks. Like random shrines, the largest boulders were still there - waiting for the dissolution that gesh bile would provide. But for now, they stood or leaned or laid and Paell stroked each one seven times. And kissed each once, never even feeling the coldness of the stone. Seven times, once for each Underion lost. A kiss for the Lady.

This night, when the reverences were done, Paell did not resume his haunting of the hallways. This night he stood at attention, his head tilted to catch the whispers of another voice. *Come, this way,* it said. In the reaches of his heart the echo came: *This way, come.* So rare an agreement made him almost giddy with happiness.

With no other thought but to go as the harmonies directed, Paell shed most of the cloth that wound around him. He kept only a single blanket of deepest red, wearing it like a cloak of state. Then he began to climb, one hand over the other, up boulder, tree root and hard-dried soil. Upward farther and farther, then through the gaping hole that let the darkness of outer night bleed into the darkness of Under. Fingers bleeding, knees abraded, the Lord of Under clambered up the debris until he stood erect in not-Under.

This way.

There was no stumbling about, no considering the route. Such confidence the voices gave him. He rarely stopped or even slowed. But now and again, once he reached the beginning of the scrub brush, he broke off likely twigs and leaves and arranged them in his hair. On the side of his head not already inhabited. And walked on. Over land.

CHAPTER EIGHT

Truth be told, Mote enjoyed getting down from the bridgeways in his quest for meshroons and other foodstuffs. No doubt a legacy of his dirtwalker upbringing in Ressa. Still, if he found 'shroons to eat and bits of greens to add for flavor, it felt good. When he came across plants he did not know, or knew to be rarely seen, there was a pleasure he smiled to feel. Nor would he ever tire of hearing the whir-beat of wings as birds rose from sun-speckled clearings into the cool safety of high branches. Creatures that hunted or were hunted looked out slyly or shyly, from hollow logs or brushy cover. One could be, in the same moment, the taker or the taken. What moved and grew, lived and died, ate or was eaten in the forest made sense to him.

It was people that confused him. Why did they make things so needlessly complicated? Like what Kendle told them last night about her parents, how they just wanted to study fletts and how that good thing got twisted into darker secrets. Finding that unfledged fletts could heal wounds, that they were good for the meshroons, so good that 'shroons could not be healthy without them, should have been a happy discovery of benefit to all.

Grossfolk, unlike the creatures of the woods, sometimes killed more than they could eat and ate more than they needed. And evidently someone who had heard of the research - Kendle did not know who and, in Over's strict protection of secrets, despaired of finding out - ate more secrets than they needed, captured so many of the flittering lights that they were overused, overwhelmed. When the contagion came, the meshroon type that offered healing for fevers had already been decimated. All by a sudden dearth of the tiny flyers.

The laid-down log on which Mote had been resting suddenly became too hard and too cold for comfort. He put himself into motion again. If breakfast was going to happen, he needed to find a few more eggs. It had been easy to find 'shrooms these last few days. All sorts and types flourished near the flett colonies. And where they grew in numbers, others things thrived: graywings, eldarhounds, coneys, wild mollucks. Even the ancient trees added season rings in their massive trunks, seeming loftier, prouder than the ones that bent to hold bridgeways or houses.

There. The telltale profusion of twigs and moss in a varithorn bush meant a pleybird nest. He moved closer and peered through the spiked branches. Yes, there were the usual five brown speckled eggs. With one hand he lifted up the outermost prickly branch, holding it aside while he reached very carefully in with the other hand. It was a stickery business and Mote often found he was holding his breath through the whole process.

Only one, slight scratch this time and he came away with the two eggs he needed. Back to the observation post with his gatherings. He hoped, rather fiercely, that the stove would be hot and the teebark had been simmered. Maybe a little honey in it?

X · X · X

"But you know what they say about fletts - the bigger ones, I mean." Andeved's brow furrowed in earnestness. "They are rarely seen and less often bond with grossfolk. But when they do, it is a good thing, that the person who receives the flett is happier, lives a better life. Yet what we saw in the Archives - the way they must bore into the head, steal nourishment from the host. How can that be good?"

Neither Kendle nor Andeved could keep still, so Kendle had adjourned the debate to the forest floor. They were well into indenting a new trail with all their walking and talking. These were terrifying matters they discussed and yet, in some earlier formed part of Kendle, she found it was also a pleasure, this back and forth with words.

"Think of it this way, Andeved, if the youngling fletts do good to both folk and forest, then how is it they change so markedly just by getting older? What they are is what they are, no matter what season."

"I can imagine change well enough. Who has not seen a harmless infant grow into cruelness, a bright child become deadly dull? Or, as is my case," Andeved could not refrain from the smallest of grins, "go from corrigible to incorrigible with the passage of time."

"A good point, that." Kendle smiled at the young man's expression of both humility and pride, but the moment sank under the weight of the subject. "Yet, children cannot devise the deeper harms that those with more years create."

"The argument goes both ways, does it not?" Belwether's rumble came from beside them. He had seated himself under a maladryn tree, regarding the pacing debaters from a more comfortable position. "From virtuous to wicked, yes, but also from profligate to provident, lazy to industrious, debased to noble. It is the reason we..." It looked as if the Oni had startled himself into silence.

The Overite and Underion both stopped short and stared at Belwether, though it was Andeved who felt the breath knocked from him. For he knew more deeply and from long experience why the Oni might silence himself. Oni never revealed, they only observed. How desperately he wanted to know *why* the Fool did what he did.

"It is the reason you..?" Andeved struggled to sound encouraging but not demanding. How hard to wait for the answer.

In the distance a brook rattled and splashed, a little wind stirred leaves and whoooed into hollows. From above came the long, mournful cry of a graywing. Somewhere, hidden in muddy dampness, a mosstode carrumped. And coming closer and closer, a rustle and crackling that announced an arrival. Kendle and Andeved turned to see the one they expected.

Brandishing a bulging provisions sack, Mote high-stepped over a clump of mollucktail plants. "Please tell me the stove is hot and the teebark simmered?"

"Shush, Mote." At Kendle's tone Mote's smile faded. "Can't you see we are in the middle of something more important than eating?"

Andeved gestured toward the maladryn tree behind him. "He was just going to--"

"He who?" Mote's puzzlement made the other two turn around.

"Ahhhgg," The Underion stamped his foot in frustration. "How does he disappear? I *hate* that."

"Well, he can't have gone far. Probably up there." Kendle looked at the observation post perched just above them. "Let's try there first."

Mote followed the other two upward, his sack of edibles slung over his back, hope for a hot meal still held close. It was, perhaps, this vision of breakfast that distracted him and caused him to bump his head on Andeved's boot. Could the boy not climb any faster? The marchale craned to see what was making the delay. And saw Belwether leaning out of the shelter's doorway, gesturing for silence and stillness with an expression of near panic. Andeved had frozen in place, clutching the handholds, white-knuckled, breath coming shallow and swift. Kendle, too, hugged close to the tree, taking the Oni's unprecedented alarm seriously. So Mote froze as well, but not before he saw a bright globe of light streak out from the shelter and fly with the swiftness of thought round and round the tree. Like an arrow it pierced the air, so bright it burned a trail on the eye. Zizz. It was suddenly near Mote's head. Hovering, as if seeking. Then zizz. Away and back, faster and brighter.

Upward the not-tiny flett streaked, this time making dizzying circles above Belwether's head, pausing near the still healing wound. As if drawn to it. But skittering away and circling lower, away and back, then swiftly toward Kendle. Like straight aimed lightning. It hovered beside her. Staying there. Moving closer.

Kendle let loose one hand and tried to capture the imminent, winged light. And in doing so lost her hold altogether, falling past Andeved and Mote, landing on the forgiving cushion of the mollucktail plants. Only the wind knocked out of her. Except the flett had followed. It did not pause again. As Kendle struggled to catch her breath, the bright worm plunged the last little way into the one it had been seeking.

X • X • X

His feet were bloodied, his belly empty and his throat dry. But for the little god ministering to him, he would surely be in greater affliction. Almost he was tempted to ask why, why any pain at all. But even as Paell considered it, the idea slipped away, unable to take hold in the bright softness of his mind.

There were still satisfactions: the deep scarlet of his royal robe, his opulent crown made half of gold and half of living divinity, sunlight falling from up above in long, warm slants, furry mosses, songs of birds for which he had no name and yet loved. It was not his Under. It was Arrant's Over. Nay, both were his now. The lordship of this amalgam, born in hope and sorrow, was his burden alone. Yet it was one he gladly carried. He would not fail his people, any of the many of his people.

Rousing himself, Paell discovered he was curled up beneath a tree of some sort, wrapped for warmth in dark red cloth. He worked at parting his dry lips. It was midday, if he correctly gauged the quality and angle of light in a place where illumination fell from above and did not reflect its way from out to in. Still, he missed the jingle-jangle of bells along the mirror ropes, or the steady drip-drip that told the hours.

But there, did he hear a water clock? It could not be, and yet his heart yearned for it. He begged his wondrous companion to heal his feet just enough that he could find it. Standing up, it was plain the companion had other tasks of more importance. Nonetheless, Lord Paell took one, then two, then more steps toward the comforting sound, praising himself, as no one else seemed ready to do it, for his bravery.

Not far, treading in dirt, stumbling over roots and rocks, not far and his forward progress was rewarded by a pool, hardly more than a puddle. The tiniest of rivulets tentatively wound through mosses and twigs, tumbling down into the pond with a liquid murmur. Almost as if it might call out the hours. Almost.

Bliss, without measure, to bring up in a cupped hand spring water. Cool on his cracked lips, soothing to a roughened throat. Paell brought himself fully into the entirely ordinary, presently remarkable act of drinking water. Thirst finally slaked, he dipped a corner of the red cloth into the pool. His face must show the stains of this strange travel. Surely, though, a sovereign must be well groomed. And there, the pool had settled again. The surface might provide a reflection for his ablutions.

Over the silvered pool he leaned, his breath making slight ripples. He waited for them to soften away that he might see himself clearly. And he did. He saw the grime of the journey. He saw, not gold, but sprigs and leaves jutting this way and that. He saw, not a small god, but an ailing creature, wings limp and torn, no longer shining but dull and veined. In shock, he reached up to touch the thing, watching himself move in the stillness of the waters. Fingers on the being brought a spasm of agony. His scream tore the forest into pieces, shattered the light, terrified the pleybirds into scattered flight. Just the one, tormented cry and the sovereign, Lord Paell, was flung into darkness.

$$X \cdot X \cdot X$$

If Quist plonked a steptie on his fingers once more, Neeli knew he would blow. Oh, and then that fumbly bottomed root-rat would feel his wrath. Why, in the name of all that is good, did they assign the clumsiest, slowest, dreariest bridgeworker apprentice to him? What had he done that was so terrible it warranted this dense, this...

The 'way bucked and swayed as Quist hunkered down at the edge, dangling his feet over the newly mended stepties.

"Time. See?" The blocky apprentice pointed up at the barely angled lightbeams. "Mid-work break. That's what the rules say." Satisfied he was abiding by regulations, Quist pulled an enormous bundle of food from his tool pack and began to unwrap endless bits of edibles. Some of which looked very, very good.

Neeli forced himself to turn away from the carnage Quist was making of what surely was an overly solicitous mother's idea of 'a little something for my boy'. He needed, in fact, to look down at the last of the knots he had to make to secure the replacement steptie. Well, he would see the plank snug and safe. And when the meal break was over, a certain apprentice was going to get some serious training. 'Rules say' indeed. Why--

A howl, painful and hideous, assaulted the air. Neeli shuddered violently, clutching the bridge ropes. Then the awful sound cut off. That seemed worse. Quist ducked, as if the cry had flown at him. His lovely food fell to the dirt below.

"What...what was that?" The ruddiness of a 'wayworker apprentice no longer showed in Quist's face. It had drained away.

Neeli wanted to be able to explain the sound, identify it, make it knowable. But he could not.

"I don't know. It didn't sound like...like anything that..." Neeli stopped talking and the silence that followed seemed desperate to break. But it did not. No ruffling breeze, no flightwing beats, no creak of trees bending. No...nothing of that other, harrowing sound.

The two men reached their bravest decisions in almost the same moment so that words were unnecessary. They put away their tools, walked to the nearest stanchion and climbed down to the ground. Something in that cry spoke of suffering no forest creature could ever know. A man had made that sound and that man must be helped. It was that simple. And that terrifying.

They headed in the direction that had seared itself in their minds. It took very little time at all to find the small pool and the still man beside it.

"Is...is he dead?" The apprentice's voice trembled with the question.

Neeli moved closer to the figure on the ground, knelt and touched the man's neck to feel for the tide of life. And found that the man lived. Barely. And that what the 'wayworker had, at first, taken to be a bedraggled and grotesque adornment was a flett.

Neeli and Quist, though far from the loci of secrets and power, knew enough to take the man toward help. They knew enough, in fact, to realize the man they carried the long and difficult way back toward the center of Over was Lord Paell.

X·X·X

"Kendle. Kendle!" Andeved's heart bashed in his chest, fear narrowed his vision until he could only see her head and the wicked thing that had bored into it. There was blood on her neck, her eyes were turning milky. The delicate, varicolored wings of the abomination folded over the ear of its acquired host, a satisfied beast. No words came from Kendle's throat. Only groans of pain and fear. She clutched his arm so tightly he could feel the tearing of his skin even as he angrily dismissed his pain as nothing. Nothing.

While he watched, the creature wriggled itself deeper into Kendle's skull. The gorge rose in Andeved's throat as his hand reached toward the beast. To take it out, to cast it away, to crush it, to kill it for what it was doing.

A strong hand grabbed his wrist.

"No!" Mote yanked on his arm. "You can't pull it out. You'll kill her. Do not touch it. Stop."

But Andeved could not work out the meaning of Mote's warning. In his terror words lost hold, only blood and death spoke. He would do this.

More hands caught him, held him back with stronger, Oni force. Pulled him back, farther back, then wrapped arms around him, kept him from that...from...

Unable to move in Belwether's grip, the boy slowly regained authority over himself. Now he could see the whole of Kendle, understand that his impulse would have worsened what was already terrible, could feel tears of helplessness course down his face.

"Then what can we do? There must be something. Look at her."

They did look. But Kendle could not look back, for her eyes were now the color of the whitest clouds, so featureless that it must surely mean she was blind. Her mouth worked to make words, and though the guttural noises that came from her throat retained the cadence of speech, there was no meaning. Gibberish.

Belwether loosed his grip on Andeved and moved to take Kendle's arm to let her know they were here, close by. Mote went to her other side and took her hand in his. With caution and hope, they helped her sit up and then, as she seemed able, to rise to her feet. She was shaky to the point that her three caretakers lowered the pallet that had not so long ago brought Belwether up into the observation post. Having carefully raised her up into the shelter, they laid her on a sleeping pad and brought blankets to her, though the day was still warm. It was a gesture each felt driven to make. Andeved, fighting against helplessness, put the kettle on.

It was while trying to tell Kendle that a mug of tee was ready for her that they discovered she also could not understand their speech. Though each of the three realized it in the same moment, no one spoke of this added hardship. Instead, there began a discussion of what to do now.

Andeved paced the narrow room in agitation. "It needs to be removed. But safely, I know. Kendle wouldn't want to go back to her home, but the people there know about the adult fletts. They had one that went to my cousin. There must be some knowledge, some skill that will help."

Mote, stolidly reluctant, made his worries known. "I am in no hurry, either, to go back. We have been hunted, in case you forgot. To bring an outlier back for help - well, it is hard to imagine a welcome. If we came in the open, in front of all of the folk, it might be different. Surely her uncle and aunt, her own foster parents, would not turn her away under such...." He gestured toward Kendle, unable to put a name to her condition. "Yet marchale patrols would be everywhere. With secret orders from secret sources - orders they would execute--" The young marchale frowned. "A poor choice of words. I apologize." He looked at Andeved. "Still..."

Andeved abruptly stopped his pacing and sank down on one of the wooden stools. "You are right. We would likely face a dangerous reception. It is just that my whole being craves boldness and brave words. My head speaks reason, even while my fists," he looked down at his tight-clenched hands, "demand a target."

"In developing strategies," Belwether had not moved from Kendle's side, still holding her hand, "it is often useful to look where you are for the most immediate help."

The Oni's calming rumble fell into the room like much-needed rain, freshening and settling what swirled and eddied. It brought a momentary silence that, until it happened, was not known to have been needed. A silence that held for a beat, then another, until it was amended by motion from Kendle.

Extracting her hand from Belwether's comforting hold, she held her arms above her head and made her fingers flutter in a downward motion that ended near but definitely not touching, the intruder that curled around her ear. She repeated the gesture, this time adding words that only she could understand but which gave unmistakable determination to the gesture.

"What is she trying to say, do you think?" Andeved followed Kendle's gesturing with puzzlement.

"Here! The help that is here." Mote jumped, literally in excitement and to his conclusion. "The little fletts. Maybe they will come and make her better. Like they did us. She is showing the little lights coming down and fixing this. They fix hurts." Mote's desire for it to be true was fierce. "That's what she is trying to say. You think?"

Andeved's agreement came slowly at first, a lingering disgust at the terrible exhibit in the archives of Under still fresh for him. "Yes, I think so. Help closest at hand. What say you, Belwether?" In asking the Oni so directly for an opinion, Andeved surprised himself.

"Well, her motions certainly suggest that is her desire. As it does not appear she is in pain any longer, it cannot bring harm to rest here for the night. If the unfledgelings come, then so much the better." So saying, the Oni took hold of Kendle's hands and raised her arms. Then, his fingers interwoven with hers, he mimicked her gesture once, twice. And was rewarded with a sudden smile and nod from Kendle.

Everyone, it seemed, agreed. Everyone turned to find the angle of light in the trees, trying to anticipate the arrival of night and the healing they hoped it would bring. Only three saw the dimming daylight. One could only feel the lessening warmth of the late day on the uninhabited side of her face.

It was an act of bravery for each to wait until darkness, to wait through the darkness, with such hope and such fear. They were braver still when dawn inevitably came and the unfledged had not. Wordlessly, but unambiguously, Kendle pleaded for another night, her face stretched taut with a determination that put an end to discussion.

A very long day and an even longer night passed in terrible anticipation. Passed and left. Not even the tiniest of fletts answered the deep, unspoken pleas. Even Kendle's stubborn hope faded into the prospect of endurance. Just before the third dawn, the sound of a friend's muffled weeping turned talk again to devising a plan, a direction, some action that might bring answers. Or, at least, mask the sour taste of futility.

Andeved once again posited the return to Over, but his proposal lacked confidence and he withdrew it without argument. Mote had no other plan or insight, used to being ordered as he was. His only offering was to put on the kettle and simmer the last of the teebark.

It was Belwether who astonished them with his strategy.

"It is knowledge we lack. Do we heal the flett and thus Kendle? Or do we remove the flett and heal Kendle? In this time and in the understandings of Under and Over there seems no answer." A rare frown creased his forehead. "It may be time for me to return to my home. I...we...that is, there may be old familiarities in the chronicles. History is meticulously recorded and kept in the Chronicle Houses of On. The House from which I was sent..." But here the Oni's words ran down to a stop.

Kendle spoke some nonsensical syllables and held out her empty mug. Belwether went over and gently took it from her and headed for the still simmering kettle.

"So, we have a plan." Andeved, hit nearly breathless with the Oni's unprecedented disclosure, clutched at the action it suggested. "Seek travel provisions today. With Belwether to On tomorrow."

The Oni looked up with real alarm. But Mote thumped his shoulder in a marchale salute. "So it is said, so it will be done." He grinned, having found good direction and the prospect of walking into the unknown.

Belwether spilled most of the now filled mug. "No, that was not the plan. I must go alone."

"Of course," Andeved mimicked the marchale's salute - and his grin. "Naturally, alone. No other way. Right, Mote?"

"No other way."

X · X · X

By the time they had reached the work camp, Neeli had reluctantly but surely come to a better appreciation of his hulking partner. He had watched Quist place gentling hands on the precipitously declining wanderer from Under. Though Lord Paell moaned with almost every breath, could not walk unguided, when lowered to sit and rest wept until his tears were dust, Quist unfailingly coaxed, tended, comforted and surprisingly, for a long portion of the journey, sang. Sang small songs of childhood, simple tunes carried by a clear voice that brought the only visible signs of relief to Paell's pain ravaged body.

Even with the unexpected skill Quist brought to bear on their guest, progress was pathetically slow. It was all they could do to make it to a work camp lately sprung up outside the home settlement. At least a healer would be at the camp, and shelter. And Neeli had decided early on that someone else needed to take on this difficult guest, someone higher up, who knew more than he did about...well...about most everything. It was not, he told himself, for lack of compassion he determined this so quickly. It would be best for the ailing visitor as well. Who but a secretholder might have the knowledge of what to do and the power to see it done?

They were met at the far edge of the work camp by marchales who had observed their slow approach. A healer, too, came with a pallet and bearers. Quist stayed close to Paell as he was carried toward an aid tent, still singing even with so many listeners, no sign of embarrassment on his wide face. Neeli trailed behind the group, finding himself pulled farther back by the marchales. Herded toward the tent that, by its size and placement, must belong to the camp's manager.

A guard pulled open the door flap of the large tent and Neeli bent to enter. Behind a campaign table littered with maps and directives sat a woman, graying hair frizzled out in short bursts, cool eyes raised in appraisal, most clearly in charge of the site.

"This particular camp is off limits to all but the workers assigned to it." The manager's voice crinkled and cracked as she spoke. It reminded Neeli of paper being crumpled. "You are not assigned here. So why have you come?"

"We, my work partner and I, were assigned to repair stepties down the bridgeway." Neeli felt his anxiety lessen as he gave his story. Soon it would not be his burden to carry. "We heard a scream and found the man. He was too wounded to go any farther without being seen by a healer. And he is, you could say, a singular visitor. From Under, that is, and what with the flett that looks sick as well..."

The manager's gaze tightened so sharply that Neeli could almost feel it pierce his flesh.

"From Under, you say, and with a flett?" She got up so abruptly that her chair flew backwards, making the tent billow out behind her. "What sort of idiot are you to bring such a one to our gesh camp? Fool! Come on."

The manager stormed past Neeli, who now felt the fool he had been called. Meekly, but quickly, he followed her outside and past guards that closed in behind him. All of them following the camp's leader to the healer's tent. She motioned for the sentries to stay outside, but grabbed Neeli by the arm and dragged him in. She shoved him onto a stool and hissed at him not to move, even breathe, unless she told him he could. Then she turned toward the pallet and the patient it held.

"Ah, Head Marchale Shawen, I see you were informed of the arrival." The healer barely looked up from his ministrations as he removed a musty smelling cloth from the patient's face, a face that now looked to be deep in sleep.

Neeli's heart sank. The woman wasn't just a camp manager, she was a clan leader. Of the marchales, no less. And she was furious at him. This did not bode well. From the far corner of the tent he heard a low, melodious humming. It was Quist, stuck in the shadows but still trying to soothe with sound.

"Indeed, I have come to see just who it is we have been brought." Shawen leaned in toward the pallet, took in a long breath, and then straightened. "Can we, *with all certainty*, determine who this person is, Healer Roust?"

The healer moved toward his patient's legs and began to remove the makeshift bandages Quist had wound over bleeding feet. "There are some indicators here. Though I take it," and here he looked over at the head marchale, "we cannot determine with all certainty the stranger's identity. That would be the purview of others?"

"The purview of others, yes. Precisely." Shawen nodded in agreement. "All attempts to heal at this outpost will, of necessity, be minimal but helpful enough to allow the patient to travel on. Yes?"

"Yes, of course."

"As for these two unassigned workers," Shawen looked for the first time at Quist, then over at a despairing Neeli, "I can simply assign them to this camp. No longer in violation, their mistake is no longer a problem. I'm sure they will enjoy learning, as we all are, the intricacies of working with gesh."

The head marchale pointed at the far corner of the tent.

"You, the big one over there, come. Now."

Quist rose, his head brushing the canvas ceiling, and lumbered toward the entrance. When Shawen indicated, Neeli also followed her outside into the waiting circle of guards.

"Take them to the supplies officer and get them on the ledger. See they are put on milking detail."

Her authority flapping about her like a flag, Clan Leader Shawen strode away from the newly assigned workers and their escort. Inside the circle of sentries, Quist stopped humming.

X · X · X

His face no longer pleased him. He had seen it. Scratched and gaunt, stubbled and wild-eyed. The vanity of that previous life tore the garments of his soul in shame. The little god was no such thing. He had seen it. It was but a small, ruptured, darkening beast, shrieking with Paell's own voice, refusing to die.

The long borne illness of his mind. He had seen it. How had it taken him? When had he first obeyed the twisting whispers that made of his thoughts a hideous maze? Was there any grace that could let him forgive himself, knowing the illness had taken him long before the little beast.

Somehow he had left the mirroring rain-wallow, was moving though he could not imagine where. Only a simple, sweet succession of melodies kept him upright. That, and two hands of which each gentle finger was a measure of balm. There was someone who walked beside him without judgment, without the scorn that made of souls a blasted waste. Paell had not been of that gracious sort. He knew that now and wept, both for the wickedness of former mockeries and the present relief of unaffected care.

There were other hands on him, he began to understand, pulling him in their own directions. Like fleeting glimpses caught in lightning, faces or trees or boots burned on his eyes only to cause a paroxysm by the little beast, a flagellation of its attaching member within his skull. For the screams it tore from him, he felt no shame.

So they, whoever they might be, brought him to another place with other hands and faces and trees and boots. He only screamed as necessary. Still, those who heard did not seem to comprehend the reason for the sound. He was laid on a pallet, his head turned so that the creature, the flett as he remembered to name it, could be seen. Perhaps tended to. This hope, weak and dim, was of some comfort. Until a dank and musty smell forced its way into his nose and throat. Down he sank into the bitter darkness he feared, down and down, into the maelstrom of merciless nightmares.

X · X · X

It was as if the pelting rain, so harsh as it fell, had apologized afterward by restoring the green of leaves and grasses, the deep brown-black of dampened soil, the cheerful glints of blue above the tree canopy and the colorless cleanness of freshened air. Zearia leaned into the bright day that could bring such pleasure, took a deep breath and stepped out of her front door and surveyed the town of Lodenbye as it hung, homes and halls and bridgeways swaying ever so slightly with the movement of its residents.

To this gemlike day was added another nice thing - meeting with friends over a midday meal. Her stomach rumbled with anticipation because this day it was Senty's turn to host. And he was just about the best cook ever known. If he served the breast of pleybird in herb sauce she wouldn't mind one bit. Naturally the platter would be passed to her first, before any of the less prestigious guests put their noses too near the savory dish.

Zearia shivered with a delicious memory of the time when knife-beaked Parcee had actually gotten cream sauce on the tip of her nose. Too amusing, too humiliating. It brought a lightness to her step and a sway to her hips that made the swing of the bridgeway even more pronounced. Perhaps today would produce another story-worthy incident. Hopefully, it would wait until Pember, adjudicating a minor but tedious community complaint, joined them. It was always more enjoyable if her husband arrived in time for a tasty transgression and the final sweets and cheese course.

A terrible shriek. So horrific it made her stumble. So piercing she felt her ears must be bleeding. The silence that followed that swift suffering was almost worse. It demanded to know who or what could have produced that sound, and why. When she righted herself and found balance again, Zearia could see doors opening, people emerging, looking here and there, hoping to identify the noise and thus tame it, while fearing that the noise might be untamable.

At the very edge of the hold emerged a group that was walking, not on the ordained bridgeway, but on dirt. Onlookers muttered their confusion at this ill-seeming departure from protocol. As they came closer, Zearia, and the many that had gathered on, above and beside 'ways, looked down on marchales carrying a pallet upon which lay a man. He was wrapped in blankets and tied with ropes so that he could move only his head. Which bore a creature residing on one side of that head, a creature Zearia could, with knowledge to which she was privy, recognize even in its diseased state as a flett.

Before anyone of the many arrayed around and above the marchaled group could speak or move, the man on the pallet opened his eyes for the briefest of moments. Opened to see hanging bridgeways lined with folk who did not know and wanted to find out. But the eyes slammed shut, the tiny beast writhed, the man took in clear, rain-washed air. And screamed again.

Some flinched, some gasped, here and there some began to weep. This one yelled in fright and that one turned away, overcome. Talking began. Questions. Then shouting. Zearia felt the verbal distress of her people pound against already bruised ears. Her throat constricted with grief, not from the confusion of her people, but from one of the most powerful of secrets that lay tied to a pallet in plain sight. Because as this secret was now being revealed, so the ascendancy she and Pember had attained was being diminished.

Zearia realized that the marchales had seen her and were looking to her for direction. This small shred of pride she could still salvage.

"This way. Follow me." Her voice was still hers to command and so it commanded others. The marchales hefted their burden again and, ignoring the calls and queries from onlookers, followed a leader. Who led them, across the usually untrod dirt, toward a dwelling at a remove from the rest. She did not look back because she knew what was coming.

Nomic must have heard the commotion, even from this distance, because he was waiting at his front door for the macabre procession. He kept his eyes on what lay on the pallet, for which Zearia was grateful. Let him be the clear-headed puzzle-solver of public appearances and not the disagreeably lustful creature of private moments.

As soon as the marchales had hoisted their burden up and into Nomic's front room, one of them began a report.

"Lady Zearia, we were sent by Head Marchale Shawen from the work camp. This man was found wandering in our protectorate and Healer Roust, having minimal supplies--"

"That's enough." Zearia stopped the report as soon as she knew enough. "You have done your duty. Return immediately to the work camp and let Shawen and Roust know that I will see the man gets the care he requires. And be it known that this matter is of no value except as discretion is applied to it. Do you understand?"

The marchale captain, veteran of making reports to secretholders of various ranks, nodded her understanding. Past experience told her that to even verbally acknowledge comprehension was to break the silence that had just been demanded. Only a brief and pointed account to the work camp manager was left to her. That and a long walk back.

Zearia waited, impatiently, until no marchales remained within. Then her fear covered itself in anger and lashed out at Nomic.

"Look at that thing, that parody of a flett. What did you do to it? You promised me an instrument of pleasure, of control and it is become--" she sputtered in search of words to describe the oozing, bloated abomination that clung to Paell's head.

The researcher licked his lips, his fingers fumbling at the string of keys around his neck.

"I do not know what has happened, lady. I...I may have substances that, when used on the creature, might be of some help."

"Too late for helping. Or do your eyes not see what mine see? The beast is dying. And it looks to be taking Paell with it. Fool, fool, seven times a fool!"

Nomic flinched, then startled as the front door flew open. Pember stumbled in, slamming the door shut behind him.

"Do you know what they are saying out there? Have you any idea how mortally serious..."

He stopped talking. His wife's fury and its underlying terror were all too plain. What surprised him, however, was the fearful, guilty cowering of the usually arrogant Head Researcher. In an unexpected surge of desperate hope, Lord Pember saw possibilities ahead of him. He turned and leaned over the twitching mumbling Underion, then looked at his wife.

"Oh my dear lady wife, what a tragedy is here."

"Well, yes." Zearia squinted at her husband, wondering what he was working toward in his mind. "A tragedy. Of course."

"If Lord Paell passes beyond from the pain that is so unfortunately his, we will be saddened by loss again. How will we bear it? First our daughter, then an almost son." Pember reached out his hand and poked the blighted flett. His finger came away with red-green ichor, which he wiped absently on his tunic. Paell moaned. The color fled from Nomic's face. Zearia found she could make tears and made sure Nomic saw them.

Pember straightened up. He turned his gaze fully on the head researcher, paused to slowly shake his head, then moved toward him and took him gently by the shoulders.

"We had faith in you. You rose above others by the confidences we shared with you. It was you we told what the entirety of Under refused to acknowledge - that their Lord was afflicted in his mind. It was with you we made a plan that we so deeply, fervently hoped would make that affliction no longer an impediment to our daughter's marriage or Under's tranquility. It was you who promised to breed a flett of unparalleled healing powers, one that could even make a twisted mind straight."

Pember's hold on Nomic tightened.

"And we believed you could do that. We trusted you."

Now it was Nomic who moaned. And shook so badly he might have fallen to his knees had not Pember held him fast.

"I can still help." The researcher scrabbled to find some tiniest bit of hope. "I can remove this flett - and there are others. I could put one in its place that could--"

"No." Zearia's voice was loud and strong for one whose face was streaked by tears. "You have done enough. More than enough."

Pember inclined his head toward his wife. "You are right, my dear. It is clear there is nothing more to be done but ease Lord Paell's way from this terrible pain he is so bravely enduring. It will be difficult for us but we owe him that much, do we not?"

"We do, we do." Zearia nodded her complete support of what she now understood to be her husband's grasping toward the possibility that their ascendancy could be snatched from the fire. "Yes, and Nomic, here, has many beneficial concoctions that will aid us...Lord Paell. Fetch something that will end the flett. Get it. Now."

Nomic gaped at the object of his former adoration. As shaken as he was, he understood what he was being asked to do. It was now the only course if he was to keep his stupidity, his culpability hidden. He turned toward the door to his laboratory, but found he could hardly manage to put one foot in front of the other. And yet he managed. Somehow, he managed.

CHAPTER NINE

In what she now thought of as her previous life, Kendle had not appreciated the mosstode. Not that she had given the biliously green, warty, mud-loving creatures much consideration. But here, sitting on a log, waiting for others to bring her food and water, the sound of a mosstode's buhroking was unexpectedly comforting. Alone in the mossy crook of a small stream, a living creature sent out sound in search of another of its kind. A noise, not words, but understandable just the same.

Kendle closed her eyes. She still tried so hard to penetrate the white-gray cloudiness that swirled in her eyes she often forgot to blink. Dry eyes burned, sighted or not. At first she had determined to just keep them shut, but always found them open again. Eventually she gave up and only closed her eyes in sleep. Though the grayish eddies stayed on the inside of her closed lids all night long.

"Gelen, flah yind cu...mar."

The words were nonsense. Worse, they were different nonsense every time so nothing could be learned by repetition. But because she recognized Andeved's gait, heard him walking toward her, she knew he would likely say her name and then, because he took her hand and put a bowl on it, would tell her supper was ready. So she nodded her thanks, and smiled in what she hoped was his direction.

By taste Kendle knew that Mote had gathered and cooked tonight. He had a deft hand with the provender of the forest. Yes, more savory when Mote cooked. And she was grateful the Ressan marchale had spent so much time walking the dirt. By necessity they could not walk the bridgeways. Without sight, she could not seem to balance. Besides, the risk of being seen was too dangerous by far. So they were reduced to treading over every rock, stump, puddle, fallen branch, rising root. Being brushed by weaver webs, leafy limbs and errant insects.

Supper was done. Kendle heard the sound of utensils being cleaned. The air had turned cooler. It must be dusk. She dreaded dusk, had kept her mind occupied with words that only made sense when left unuttered. But no use putting it off. The sooner done, the sooner to sleep. So she carefully stood up and made the agreed upon gesture. For a mercy it was Belwether who took her hands and led her beyond a cluster of bushes. He gave her a wad of leaves and then she heard him moving off a way, though not too far. With a sigh of resignation, she managed her clothes.

X • X • X

Mote and Andeved moved around the camp, the evening's chores having become routine by now. Seven days gone since they left the observation post. Seven days of avoiding bridgeways, treading the trackless dirt, talking in low tones the few times it seemed reasonably safe to do so. The making and breaking of camp, taking watches, devising routes that safely bypassed habitations, hearing far away baying and slogging endlessly through stream beds to cover their scent, everything served to take them closer to Oni territory and to one another.

"Do you think she'll last the whole way?" Andeved stuffed the bowls and spoons into his travel pack.

Mote straightened up from the campfire he had been carefully dousing. "If you mean will her legs take her the whole way, then yes." He poked the remaining cinders with the toe of his boot. "If you mean will it let her last, will she stay steady or shatter, then I don't know."

Andeved tried to find something positive to say, but his growing fear for Kendle had made him uncharacteristically solemn. Besides, he had a burden of guilt to carry along with a heavy pack. Because this trip, no matter how fraught with danger, was actually exciting. He felt stronger and more competent, it made him feel proud. And pride was so completely inappropriate under the circumstances. Though they did not talk about this to one another, he was sure Mote felt the same way.

"Belwether thinks that, going this slowly, it will take another two days, maybe three, to get to the nearest Chronicle House. And he isn't sure the knowledge that will help Kendle is even at that house."

Mote looked thoughtful for a moment. "Yes, though we'll be in Oni territory sooner, I think. I've noticed the trees thinning out a bit and other plants becoming more numerous."

The two glanced at one another and each began to grin.

"Belwether's home," Andeved chuckled. "Worth the walk, I hope."

Mote nodded his agreement. "We're going to get a close look at places and things hardly anyone else has seen. It better be more than dusty books and reading chairs."

Rustling from the bushes nearby alerted them that Belwether was leading Kendle back from the business of the evening. Even though she could not see them, they replaced their grins with more decorous concern. Silly to do it really, just as silly as not talking about her when she was within earshot. Though perhaps it was more respect than irrational response.

"I believe I heard comments about books and chairs." Belwether helped Kendle get comfortable on her blanket and then began to spread out his own. "Please do not worry. The Oni have chairs designed for even the most," he frowned, searching for the best word, "for the most reluctant reader. Small spikes are placed in the seat back so that dozing is never an option."

Andeved pretended to faint onto his blanket. "Water, Mote, I am overcome with Oni wit."

Mote, always the helpful companion, dashed the bit of water left in his fire-dousing cup on Andeved's face.

Once the tiny attempt at comaraderie was exhausted, then so were the travelers. It did not take long for sleep to quietly arrive. Those on watch took turns shaking Belwether so that his occasional sonorous snoring did not wake every creature within a three day's walk. Even Kendle took a watch, for her hearing had become sharper with each passing day. And poking the Oni in the ribs did not, after all, take language.

At first the rest of the party had refused Kendle's unspoken but obvious offer to stand watch. They reasoned that walking took much more strength from her. Being at the mercy of others for daily needs was exhausting. And it was evident that the wound where the flett had bored into her head caused great agony whenever the creature was touched. There were two factors that eventually led them to give the first watch to Kendle. First of all, she would not take no for an answer, a situation that was abundantly clear, words or not. And secondly, what she must endure during sleep was more than they could take. Restless, she sometimes accidentally brushed the flett and then woke with a cry of pain, gasping for breath. Even when her sleep came in longer doses, there were murmurs and moans from what must surely be night terrors.

So they stumbled through days, were grateful for the care of others at day's end, endured the nights. All the while the forest retreated behind them until it was no more. Ahead and all around were rolling, rock strewn hills, gray clouds covered the sky more often than not, dense brush huddled in crevices and crannies against cold, gusty winds that reddened cheeks and buffeted cloaks.

There was an unending supply of small, icy streams and clutches of brown, squawking birds that possessed wings but could fly only a hand's breadth upward. Belwether called them kwall and described them as tasty when you could catch more than one. In that he proved correct. One kwall was only a bite or two and, though tasty as promised, not nearly enough for sustenance. It took a lot of catching to make a meal.

It was interesting to watch the changes in Belwether as he led them farther into On. At first he was almost expansive, pointing out features of the changing landscape, commenting on the bracing weather that he said was sometimes quite warm. Not just now, however. Clearly.

If questioned about their destination, the Oni began his answers with a frown and then said something like: "This Chronicle House is different from the others. It is a sort of first step into On. You'll see." They could get no more from him. And then he spoke less and less, becoming more like the shadow he had been in Under. While his brief span of relatively lengthy conversations had left them speechless, this return to the taciturn was eerie.

The gently rolling hills they had first encountered now became steep and treacherous. Andeved's long experience of Under's stairs helped him with the ups and downs, but the unyielding openness unnerved him more than he care to admit.

Mote, meanwhile, cursed the scarped knolls. Even the forest floor had some softness to it, the bridgeways a pleasant roll. Not here. He put on a marchale pose during a day's trudging, but at evening he nursed blisters on his aching feet. This was the longest march he had ever taken, and no doubt the most demanding. Though every time he thought to complain, he caught sight of Kendle and just rubbed his toes in silence.

Kendle made use of the childhood that came after her parent's death. She called on her facility to bury emotion, to tend to the task at hand, to endure what must be endured as a measure of fitness to exist. The more she quashed her fear, pain, anger and hurt, the thicker her defenses became. Once again she could be measured, competent, tearless. The white-gray cloudiness in front of her eyes slowly changed to a gray blankness rimmed with darkness that whispered of ruin. With an imposed determination, she chose to ignore that change. And walked, up and down, toward what she did not know.

At last, one midday, they reached the crest of a high hill and Belwether stopped them. Deep below spread a valley, long and narrow, sheltered and green. Dotted here and there were stone-built dwellings from which ribbons of smoke uncurled, plowed fields contained by stacked-rock fences, barns with stone walls and roofs that looked to be made of woven brush. Against the far wall of the valley stood a high, wide structure to which all pathways below led. It could be no other than the Chronicle House.

There was only one trail leading down into the vale. It was narrow but well maintained, winding back and forth to manage the slope. Belwether took the lead, followed by Kendle with her hand on his shoulder, feeling the tension there. Andeved came next, and then Mote.

Descent took a very long time. Not once in that twisting way was there sign of sentries. Nor, when at last the trail eased onto the valley floor, was their arrival the subject of curiosity or surprise from the dwellers in the glen. Oni glanced at them, then went back to whatever task was at hand. Only once was there a deviation from the marked lack of interest in what was assuredly an odd party. A small number of children played in a field, kicking a ball between them and laughing as children do. Mote, who had nieces and nephews of whom he was excessively fond, waved at the group. One girl, her hair tied back by a kerchief and her boots muddied by the exuberant play, lifted a hand and waved back. It was the only sign of welcome they saw the entire way to their destination.

It was a destination that grew in size the closer they drew. From the valley's outer crest, the massiveness of the Chronicle House could not be measured. Now, standing in front of it, the only way to see the roofline was to lean far backward. The doors to the place, in Andeved's mind, were even larger than the gates of Under. And more shut, if that could be determined by simply looking at the carvings and fretwork that covered them. Mote estimated the building to be as wide as a first-grown tree was high. It made his chest feel tight. Only Kendle remained unmoved since the sight was unseen, though surely she heard the more labored breaths that Mote took, or the tiny creak of Andeved's pack as he craned to take in the entirety of the frontiswall.

Belwether had said not one word along the turning path, pulling his silence around him like a cloak. Now he gestured for them to stay at the bottom of the wide steps leading to the massive doors, while he alone went up and pulled down on a long rope. There was a distant sound of a deep throated bell. Then nothing for what felt like forever.

Hidden within the massive doors there appeared a smaller door that could only be seen when it opened, which it did to reveal a woman whose tunic was covered in dust. She wore grimy gloves and a cloth tied around her face, covering her nose and mouth. When the door was halfway open, she paused, pulled the kerchief down and stared at Belwether only. Her expression was neither friendly nor hostile. The neutrality was so perfect it mostly certainly had been cultivated.

Andeved and Mote shifted and squirmed watching the door-woman's unemotional gaze. Then Belwether made a strange gesture, putting his hands flat together in front of him, fingers pointed toward the woman, then spread his hands outward. He inclined his head toward the darkness beyond the half opened door and said, quietly: "I am Belwether, out of Third House, on attachment and in need."

Silence. The stare continued. Finally, the keeper stepped back and motioned for Belwether to enter. With a finality that echoed within, she shut the door and turned a lockbolt with a loud bang. Mote startled at the sound. But Andeved helped Kendle sit down on the steps because they felt a long, long wait coming on and they were tired. With no instructions to do otherwise, Mote rummaged in his supplies and found a few edibles which made, for the three of them, a cold supper.

X · X · X

Vety said nothing to Belwether as she led him down the central corridor, moving past row after row of shelves so long they stretched on each side far into the darkness. Stairs to the upper floor or below ground would be at the far wall. It was that way in each House.

Not until there had been one turn and more rows and the front door could not possibly be seen did Vety wave the light orbs into their warm, ivory lambency. Two more turnings and the waiting place appeared ahead, a high desk facing a few empty benches. Belwether had hoped the desk would have been occupied, but it was not. Vety had already disappeared down one of the rows, light orbs popping on to mark her progress, so he made for one of the benches and sat down. The House Registrar would most certainly let him stew on the hard bench for just a bit longer than prescribed. Perhaps quite a bit today. In spite of the cool, dry air that filled the House, a bead of sweat started its way down Belwether's back.

Knowing that they had been observed from the moment they entered On, he reviewed his behavior. Deviations from protocols were noted with strong disapproval. Already his place at the head of the party would have been clearly evident. And he'd brought an Attached with him. Not only that but Kendle, who now required the help he sought, had been passed over through no fault of her own. His own clumsy fault. Of that he had always been too well aware. How many Code transgressions before entry was denied? Before they were turned out, or he was sanctioned?

And those were only his easily observable errors. Belwether pulled tightly around himself the visible dispassion his position demanded. Beneath that veneer, however, emotions forbidden to one of his calling shone light into the grayness of life that had been his. First, affection for his Attached, the boy-becoming-man that was the gangly, rebellious, intelligent though not yet wise Andeved. Then pity that quickly became respect for Kendle, she who had almost been his Attached if not for the accident. Her heart beat strong against terrible blows of loss, rejection and pain. And of course Mote, intuitive and practical, out of his element but endearingly determined. All of that must be well hidden if any chronicle boxes were to be opened.

Belwether was still rehearsing his arguments when the sough of soft soled boots on old wooden stairs, the muffled click of heels on stone, gave signal to the approach of more House staff than expected. A single Registrar was the usual response to a declaration of need. This could not bode well. He rose from the bench as courtesy required.

Orbs made a circle of glaring light on and around the waiting area. An elder woman, bent with age and wrinkled with decades of gathering, referencing, cross-referencing and knowledge maintenance, ascended the few stairs to the Registrar's desk platform with effort. The gray of her robe of office washed out under the massed illumination, but not her hawk-like eyes.

A grizzle-bearded man in a red robe and a mid-span woman robed in green took seats to the Registrar's left. Belwether had trouble catching his breath. These were Quadrant Deans for this House, the man of Under Quadrant, the woman heading the Over Quad. To the right, the blue-robed young woman heading On Quadrant appeared and finally, a hugely rotund man whose rolling gait would have rocked the bridgeways of Over beyond endurance. He was draped in a massive robe that dragged on one side, then the other, as he lurched to the rightside bench and lowered himself heavily onto it. With surprisingly long and deft fingers, he arranged the folds of his black robe, then took in a rasping breath, coughed into his sleeve and folded his arms across the wide expanse of his belly. The Aeonimate Quadrant Dean of First House settled in to hear the proceedings.

"Belwether of the Third House presents today with a declaration of need." The Registrar's voice was thin and sharp, like a fine blade. "Let him explain to us the need that brought him to us."

Taking a step forward, Belwether took in a breath and began to state his case. "I am come to request information only. The subject matter is the structure and function of fletts."

The Registrar hissed him to silence. "Untrue. You have brought your Attached and two others. If your request was for information only, then you would have stayed with your Attached as is proper and sent a written request. Again we ask you to state the need."

So his hope that a simple research request would gain them entry had failed. Belwether calmed himself and tried again.

"I come to request information concerning fletts so that repairs to Lord Paell of Under and Kendle of Over might be made. Both of whom are Pivotal Pieces."

This time the Quadrant deans conferred in whispers, glancing at the Registrar when the conferences were done.

The old woman eyed Belwether with half closed eyes, though her gaze was still piercing. "Fletts are a natural manifestation of life. Lord Paell and Kendle have encountered this life type in the way of things. Pivotal Pieces are to be observed. They are never to be interfered with. Request denied."

"I formally appeal this decision on the basis that," here Belwether took another step forward, leaning in toward the Quadrant deans, "on the basis that neither the fletts encountered nor the circumstances of those encounters were natural effects of life and thus require the adjustment of a Keeper."

The appeal brought the huge Aeonimate leader to his feet in outrage.

"Who has ventured this breach? No reports note this, no connections have been made. How can we be sure an abomination has occurred?" The man came closer and closer with each word he spoke until the outer limits of his girth threatened to push Belwether backward.

"There is observable fact, but I found no couriers to relay this information," Belwether ventured. "So few have been sent over the years, I came to understand that the Council did not place much importance on my assignment. In this instance, I concluded that both my report and declaration of need must be taken to the proper authorities myself."

Belwether had not wanted to reveal his theory, and his statement that proof had been observed was true only as far as it went. But this inference that Council politics might have prevented the deans from getting all the tasty bits of information they spun and wove into prediction might be the turning point. At least that was his hope. He had no other arguments to bring. And outside on cold steps Kendle waited, sightless, confounded, inhabited.

All the deans now stood, the Registrar announcing that the appeal was of such a nature as to require deliberations. "You will stay within the House guest quarters," she added. And then, over her shoulder, as if it were an irritation, "and the three outside will be taken to Megrim's barn for shelter. Protocol requires that no one, most especially you, may speak with them until we return our decision."

When they had gone, the waiting area felt used and clammy. Belwether left it immediately, heading for guest quarters as instructed. Worry knotted itself between his shoulders. And, though previously he would not have thought it possible, he felt a growing need to apologize for how Oni treated outsiders. Then his stomach rumbled loudly, letting him know that a visit to the kitchens was necessary. Perhaps he could manage to acquire extra food and pack it away for the trip he hoped they would take.

X • X • X

The door flew open and banged loudly against the wall, partly flung by a rising wind and partly by an agitated Golion.

"Where is he?" The Senior Healer flung the question and like a hammer blow it hit Pember, staggering him with the audacity of the healer's intrusion and the dangerousness of his inquiry.

"Wh...what are you doing? You don't belong...belong here... now."

"There is a person in need of care here. Where else should Over's senior healer be? Now take me to him."

The demand was so compelling that, although he did not want to, Pember took a step toward the hallway. Thinking better of it, knowing what Golion would find behind the far closed door, he turned and made himself a barrier.

"Delicate procedures are going on that cannot be interrupted. No one else is of sufficient station to--"

"Come on, he's here," Golion stepped just outside the opened door and hefted his portable cabinet of potions and herbs, followed by his wide-eyed young apprentice who bore satchels of treatment supplies. The healer did not gently push by Pember, whose stance guarding the workroom hall was both indicative and pointless. He could hear the Senior Secretholder bang against the wall as he cleared a way through. Even in his rush, it was satisfying to hear and to have caused.

A second door was roughly opened, but the sight that assaulted the healer stopped him short, stunned, horrified. Lord Paell lay helpless, barely breathing, gray-faced, hands in fists so tight that, even in forced sleep, blood oozed from them. Above him, the head researcher of Over tipped a vial of liquid onto a cloth. A dark smell, like oily smoke off a burning carcass, unwound itself into eyes and throats. Golion knew that fetid odor.

"Stop, this isn't right." The healer reached out to hold Nomic's arm, but his own arm was grasped from behind, hard, and held. He had not seen Zearia at first, but now she hissed into his ear.

"We know what we are doing, bandage-maker, if you do not. The wounds of the people are what we are healing, and you," her fingers dug in like talons, "will not interfere."

"No more, lady, no more." Golion felt the banked coals of his customary restraint catch fire. "The only wounds our people have sustained are of your making. And that will be no more. Too many saw the flett-ridden Underion, heard his cries, felt his pain. They watched as you directed those you clearly despised as underlings to bring the Lord Paell here. Not to a healer or even to those who ease and honor passings. But here, to a researcher's laboratory. Did you think they would misunderstand the meaning of that?"

Nomic remained frozen, unmoving, his eyes wide and unblinking. But Zearia's hand gripped even harder. It was all the healer could do to retain hold of his potion box.

"Oh, you have reached above yourself, Golion. There is more here that must be done than you have the skill or stomach to do. Be grateful, you and those many out there, that I keep the secrets that matter, execute the plans that are needful."

"How fitting you use the word *execute*," Golion twisted to face the infuriated lady, "as I assume that is what is about to occur."

Nomic finally moved, taking a step backward, looking wildly from Zearia to Golion.

A pause. A silence. Waiting, hoping that something or someone would change.

Zearia let loose of the Senior Healer's arm. She sighed so deeply that it sounded torn from what depths she possessed.

"Of course. You are right. We thought Paell would not survive and we were only left to mitigate his terrible pain. But you should see him first. We might have been hasty. There may still be comfort you can bring the poor man."

Golion, who was watching Zearia's face as she spoke, saw only the chance he had so fiercely desired.

"Get out. And let my apprentice in. I need her and the supplies she carries."

"Naturally," Zearia stepped past him into the hallway and motioned for the apprentice to enter. "Whatever is needed to help. Nothing will be spared."

Zearia closed the laboratory door and went over to stand by her husband. Pember put his arm around his wife's shoulders. This difficult night was not yet over.

"I heard you back there," he whispered. "The healer will do his work, in the full knowledge of the people, yes?"

"Yes," his wife replied.

"I recognize the apprentice." Pember was thoughtful. "Hilly is her name, I believe. Golion has been working with her for a number of seasons. Since his short-lived attempt to recruit Kendle to his work."

Zearia leaned her head against her husband's shoulder. "You are right. Hilly has no doubt received most of the man's secrets, though she seems a bit young for such responsibility. Looking at it another way, Golion is a bit too old for burdensome duties. No doubt when he fails at this, he will feel very badly."

"Very badly, indeed. We'll have to help him."

ᛉ • ᛉ • ᛉ

The flett shuddered, sending a thick ooze of ichor on a slow crawl over Paell's cheek. Golion shivered, but kept on rummaging through satchel and box for anything, instrument or concoction, that might help. From the corner of his eye, he saw Hilly reach to take the poison from Nomic. But the man would not release it and in the struggle, the vial shattered, splattering the viscous potion on his arms, his sleeves.

Nomic gasped. "Look what you've done." He held out his stained hands.

Hilly was, indeed, staring at the researcher's hands. Nomic followed her gaze back down and saw gashes, saw a thinner, redder liquid begin to drip from his palms."no, No NO!" He lowered his arms, forcing more blood to run faster. "Fools." His voice was cracked, his face ashen.

Both Golion and Hilly tried to get hold of him and cleanse his hands. But with the strength of panic, he broke away and ran down the row of glass cases, stopping in front of one that, even in the farthest dark of the room, glowed with soft, fluttering light. He grabbed the case, his hands leaving red smears, and pulled it off the shelf. As it toppled, the cover fell off and a myriad of tiny lights burst from their containment.

"Here, here," Nomic yelled, waving his arms through the fluttering particles. "Hurry, before...here, here." The glimmers he knocked aside with his frantic motions fell to the floor, but some caught on his hands, on the wounds. He gave a sob of relief and watched, as did the stunned healer and apprentice, while the unfledged fletts knit together the bleeding slashes. More of the little lights paused over the dark poison next to the wounds. And drank of it. Then, one by one, their lights extinguished.

No gleams flew free. But the researcher's palms were no longer cut. He looked up at Golion, his face a picture of relief. Then a look of puzzlement replaced relief. Beads of sweat gathered on Nomic's brow and his body began to twitch and seize. Now he looked deeply sad, utterly defeated.

"Too late. The tocsin got in the blood. They didn't heal the cuts quickly enough. And they are not able to work in the blood." A brutal tremor rocked Nomic to the floor. The sweat of his brow turned red as blood. "I had plans to breed for blood fletts. You see..." He gasped as his fingers twisted cruelly into unnatural shapes. "You have murdered me, you two. Murdered me." All breath left the body that had held Over's head researcher. It did not return.

Golion and Hilly stood in stunned silence. What sense could they make of what they had just seen? Too much of import had assaulted them, and left a secretholder dead.

A deep groan brought the two healers back from their bewilderment. A patient was in need of care. Right now. No time to waste. Season after season of experience put Golion into action almost without thought. He barked orders at Hilly, who leaped into motion, clinging to what she knew to do.

Then the healer lost track of anything else. He had found the tools he hoped would work. He eased a clean cloth under Paell's neck and, unstopping a bottle, poured a blue-green liquid carefully at the base of the flett where it entered the head, grateful that the secretholders had at least put the Underion into a forced sleep.

Now Golion took up pincers with flat paddles at each end. Hilly was at his side with a basin and a tray of bores, knives, needles and thread. He also found that he was trembling. A deep breath, eyes shut for a moment and then opened. His hands began to move steadily now, sliding the bottom paddle under the flett, closing the pincers to grip the dying creature, and pulling. Up. Coming away. Until there was resistance at the base where Paell's bone had been drilled through.

Golion steadied himself for another pull. Still stuck. Another tug. Another. And then, as if a seal were broken, the two long tubes that had taken residence in Paell's head slid slowly up and out. From the holes in the bone came jets of black blood. The healer discarded the removed flett into the catch basin and grabbed more cloth to press against the wounds. He scanned his charge's body for effects and saw the Underion's fists jerk, then fall limply open. Did it mean pain had been taken away, or did it mean death?

Paell's chest still rose and fell with breath. Golion reached for the laverin again, pouring more over the bleeding holes. Now the blood ran more red than black. More laverin. And when there was a bright red surging with the tides of the heart, healer and apprentice began the frantic and necessary work of closing the wounded flesh.

They could not replace the bone. No one had ever had that secret to pass along.

Only after the stitching was done, after Lord Paell had been cleaned and bandaged, did Golion allow himself to see anything else beyond the face of need. He discovered himself splattered with red and black blood, red-green ichor and drenched in sweat. Carefully he moved away from the pallet, wary of the slippery floor. He and Hilly worked in silence to clean the area and themselves. It was a routine they did together every time, for their charges and for themselves. This time it also included removing the rest of the poison from the room and from Nomic's body. No one who would come to prepare him for finalities should be threatened by the tocsin that had taken him.

So it was done. Now they could only wait. And hope.

"Is it over?" Pember's voice startled the healers. They turned to find Over's leaders, husband and wife, blocking the doorway. "We heard noises, but we didn't want to interrupt you in your work."

Golion instinctively moved in front of Lord Paell. "Yes, all we can do has been done. You stayed outside long enough. There is a body for you to dispose of."

"Oh," from Pember.

"How sad," from Zearia," we have lost a great man."

"I did not know you considered Nomic a great man." Golion pointed at the far wall where Hilly stood near the lifeless body of the former head researcher. "But perhaps his studies were of value to you. I would like to examine his specimens and notes when there is time later, as I believe some had to do with healing."

But neither of the couple heard the healer's request, for they had finally grasped that it was not Paell but Nomic who had not survived.

"What happened?" Zearia's question came in a low, flat tone.

Hilly stepped forward and earnestly answered. "There was an accident. I was trying to take the vial and he gripped it so tightly that it broke in his hands - and cut him. He tried to get some of his specimens to heal him." She pointed to the shattered case and the small, dark specks scattered on the floor. "They did - heal the gashes at any rate. It was amazing. But he said they could not mend poison in the blood. It must be true, for he died quickly." The apprentice shook her head in wonder. "I have never seen such things as these tiny flettlings."

"Yes, well," Pember shifted from one foot to the other, "his studies were complicated, not yet very...useful."

"But the Underion," Zearia tried to get between Golion and his patient, "how is he? Now."

"The flett, which was next to death, was removed. Lord Paell lost a great deal of blood and has other injuries that appear to be from his journey from Under to here. We have done what we can. What happens now is difficult to predict as there are no records of this," he laid his hand gently on Paell's shoulder, "of this kind of procedure. Recovery is unknown. Time alone will conclude."

Zearia pulled at her husband's arm. "Of course. Understood. Best to keep the sick room quiet. Pember and I will arrange for caretakers to discreetly retrieve the researcher. He deserves gratitude for being so intensely involved in Lord Paell's condition. The people should know this. They will mourn. And await news of Lord Paell." She dragged Pember from the room and the door swung shut behind them.

Golion realized he was slack-jawed, a condition seldom known to inflict itself on him. A glance at Hilly told him she, too, suffered from incredulity.

"I believe those two live in another place, one that shares no common reality with Over. Can they truly believe what they say? Or--"

Golion's hand was grasped suddenly. He startled and turned to see that it was Lord Paell who held him, weakly, but amazingly for all that.

"Help me." The Underion's voice was thin and raw.

The healer leaned over to better hear and to calm the man.

"We have given you all the care in our power, Lord Paell. Rest and let your wounds heal."

Paell's fingers tightened on Golion's wrist.

"No, please help me go home. I have been...away...now and for a long time before. They need to hear, to know. There is..." he labored to take in a breath, "...there is atonement...mercy, let there be atonement." Panting with the effort to speak, Paell had to gather strength.

It was painful for the healer to see the man's anguish. He had heard of the mind sickness that had been the Underion leader's burden for long years. Now to be inflicted with a diseased flett and to bear the loss of his intended bride. Golion trembled with long-postponed grief. Arrant - gone. At least he could look Paell in the eye knowing that her death had been a true accident.

"We will take you home, Lord. But first you must rest or you will not survive the journey."

"Now. I must be taken now. I will live to see home again. I must." Tears slid quietly from eye to cheek. Paell's breath rattled in his chest. Still he found strength enough to pull Golion even closer to him.

"You are a good man, healer. In your eyes and the touch of your hands it shows. Give me the chance to be a better man. Promise you will see I am taken home. Swear to me, on your healer's secrets. I beg you."

Search as he could, Golion could not see madness in the man that lay before him. What he could see, what he could hear and what he felt from the desperate grip spoke more to the saving of the man than the saving of his life. When death came to claim broken bodies, broken lives cried out for redemption. Healers came to understand that this happened. It was a thing skill could not touch.

"Sleep for now, Lord. Gather your strength. On my healer's word your journey home starts on the morrow. This I swear to you."

Paell closed his eyes and let go his grasp of the healer's wrist. Already he was asleep, his chest rising and falling in a shallow, but steady rhythm.

Golion looked up to find the apprentice nearby, having heard all that had been said. "Hilly, here may not be the safest place to be, but..."

"It doesn't matter. I will stay with Lord Paell. You do what is needed."

Golion nodded with a deeper appreciation of Hilly's strength of character.

"For all our sakes, it is better, I believe, to make it known that Lord Paell still lives and that we must honor his wishes to be taken home. Fewer secrets, fewer accidents."

And with that, Golion strode from the room and out into the night and toward the curious crowd that had, unlike itself in the past, waited in the open for the telling of secrets.

CHAPTER TEN

The waiting was like a fever that would not break. It heated the cool dimness of the stacks, simmered a stew of aches and was an unwelcome sign of an underlying disease. At least that is what Belwether, in the third day of the confidential deliberations by the First House Quadrant Council, felt in his otherwise patient bones.

He was not allowed to leave the Chronicle House. Keys kept folks out - and in. Not even a message to the others was permitted, though he had been told blankets, food and water had been given to them. Enough to sustain they told him, though he imagined an ungenerous, or perhaps just unconcerned, undertone in the reassurance. It drove him to walk the stacks, pace the corridors, climb up and down the wood and metal stairs that gave just a bit when trod. Not as much as the bridgeways of Over. More than the stone steps of Under. His mother had taken Belwether for long rambles whenever she wished to talk with him of important things. Young men, she said, thought better when moving. Young women, she never failed to add, thought better. Period. His father had just amiably chuckled.

So to give better thought to some sort of plan, he walked. And that brought him, in the very early hours of the second morning, called the 'Mother's Hour' in Under's way of naming time, to the long, narrow room that housed the Locus Device.

Belwether hesitated to enter. Rules were as strong as locked doors and he was not allowed, by rule, to approach the Device. Exile was the price paid if caught. But there was information he needed to know that the Device might be able to tell him. Still, his training had been as an Attached, so he had never actually used this scholar's tool. And it was quite the overwhelming apparatus. Two floors high, almost as wide as the Chronicle House itself, the Device was divided into a massive grid seventy columns wide and forty rows high. Each grid square had a symbol on it that could be deciphered in a huge book atop a reading pedestal nearby. On the far wall were containers of large, perfectly round stones. As he understood it, a researcher used the book to find six symbols that related to the stored knowledge he wished to find. Using the ceiling tall ladder on a horizontal rolling track, the scholar placed a stone ball in each of the grid baskets with the appropriate symbol. Then the lever was pulled. Down and around, over and through, the stones rolled. Pulled one way by force of air, dropped another way in the manner of all falling things. Until, at last, the stones reached the bottom grid row. Each stone, at last resting in the indentations of the lowest row, was now dabbed by colored chalk, the colors indicating where the knowledge was stored. The first stone showed which site, the next the building, then the floor, then row, then shelf and the sixth stone denoted status.

If it was to be done, then this was the hour in which to do it. In his mind, Belwether saw Kendle's clouded eyes, regretted the unwarranted calluses on Andeved's heart, heard the bravery in Mote's offers of assistance. Beyond the three he also saw secrets, vanities and failings silently, like the keenest of blades, slice here, stab there, leaving behind wounded in the one and in the many. The many rise and fall in the same way they treat the few. So said his father.

Belwether stepped over to the book of signs. It was a struggle to decide on the attributes to be used in the location search, but in the end he settled on six: flett, breeding, detachment, hosts, healing, unfledged. It took longer to find the appropriate symbols, at least those he hoped were correct, and to note them on paper kept next to the book. There were four pages of listings for 'hosts' and it was difficult to wade through the variously nuanced definitions. But eventually he was able to deposit a stone ball in each of six baskets. He rolled the ladder back to one side and then reached up for the thick rope that hung from the top of the massive lever. Taller than he was, the lever looked impossible to pull down. And once pulled, the process could not be stopped. Finding the attributes and placing the stones had taken so long, morning and discovery were so very close now.

But, no choice. He leaned into the rope until the lever slowly tugged, then caught. A whiff of pale blue dust puffed out from the slot that housed the lever. Then the noise started. Clicks, clacks, tumbles, thuds, a whoosh, clank, movement mutterings, several hisses, one ding and too many bumps to count. Balls rolled. Tubes joined and shifted. Baskets flipped, held, jerked.

Until finally, six daubed stones came to rest in six indentations near the floor. Belwether realized he had held his breath through the whole process. Now he breathed. And noted on his paper the color or colors on each stone, in order. Back to the book of signs to decipher the results. He started with the last stone: status. It could be active, closed or archived. Yellow. Active. A good start.

The stone denoting shelf had two colors which translated to shelf 6, a reachable height since Oni counted them from the bottom up. Next row - with four colors that meant row 42. Each Chronicle House's arrangement was the same so it would be easy to find the stack. Floor: brown for underground floor. Building: Red for the Chronicle House itself, though some icons or collections lived in outbuildings. And now site.

Two colors. Green and blue. Impossible. A unique collection of knowledge was singular. It could not be in two places at once. Belwether turned the stone over, checking to see if one color was fainter than the other, perhaps left from a previous search. But no, both were vibrant, new.

Noise in the corridor. He grabbed the resetting cloth and wiped the chalk marks from each of the stones and put them back in the storage basket, checked that all the blue dust had disappeared, shook the cloth to blur its new colors and stuffed the paper with his notes into a deep pocket. Peeking through the entryway, he scanned for oncomers but found no one yet in the corridor. As the noise seemed to come from one direction, he turned the other. Above all the sounds of steps and hurry came the deep peal of a large bell.

X • X • X

Andeved found it odd, how this barn could seem so familiar when nothing in his upbringing looked, smelled or felt as this shelter did. It was not remotely like the gesh pens. The flat, curling horns of the four-legged mollucks were far different than the thumb-sized hearing appendages of the bulging six-legged gesh. Nor did the mollucks have an offensive odor. More like the mustiness of old barley sacks.

Hay, also, was a fairly recent acquaintance. Now he knew it could be feed for stock, packing for easily breakable items, floor covering that absorbed the more offensive molluck contributions, or piled up in a loft as a soft, fragrant, if rather pokey, bed. Which last function the three of them had tested to their satisfaction these nights past.

Three nights during which they slept deeply, recovering strength and distracting themselves from the tension that jittered through the endless hours of the day. Hours that were not named and marked as those of Under. Which made days seem even longer, though the younger boy Andeved had so recently been would have thought that impossible. Time was the same, yet he was irritated when it was too highly regimented or when, oppositely, it was too ill defined, unmeasured. This observation by himself about himself suddenly struck him as ironic. Being mature enough to appreciate irony pleased him. But his inner musings were interrupted by Mote. As was also becoming usual.

"You are to be commended, Kendle, for making such tidy work of packing this morning." Mote had taken up talking to Kendle in spite of her inability to decipher words. He had concluded she could tell much from the tone of a comment and what she knew of the speaker. It was a small act of hope, but it distracted him from the impulse to treat her as a fragile child, which she was not. Not before and not now. "Especially since Andeved has rolled half a mound of hay in his bedroll. Perhaps he is mooning over the kerchief girl we saw on our way here. Who knows but that Oni women consider his knobby knees and pointy elbows handsome. You think?"

Andeved looked down at his blanket and found that Mote was correct. How annoying.

"Yes, yes. The little kerchief girl?" Andeved shook out the blanket and started all over. With less hay. "Hardly possible. Not that her parents would approve as she appears to be slightly too young for me. Or you." He shot a glance at Mote. "Or anyone."

Nearby, Kendle had finished packing up and was sitting on the remains of last night's bed. She smiled, turning her face toward the sounds of her two companions. Each of these mornings fell into a pattern for them: wake with a start, rummage in the sparsely supplied food basket for sustenance, tidy themselves, pack belongings as if a long journey would begin at any moment, and then wait. Wait. At first with anticipation, then with impatience, then worry. Toward evening came fear - though each did their best to hide that from the others. The darkening hour, as the last light died, was the worst. Noises of a barn cooling and creaking, the restlessness of mollucks in the dusk, tiny creatures skittering toward nests, each sound promised to be Belwether come to bring news. So that when full darkness finally came, they were exhausted with expectation and turned desperately to sleep.

Until this moment came, with the ringing of a deep throated bell at the Chronicle House. Excitedly, Mote and Andeved peered through the barn's windows. The small door of the House opened and disgorged several people. Yes, they were coming this way. And didn't that fellow toward the end of the procession look like Belwether? Anticipation gave swiftness to their climb down from the loft to the wide barn floor. This smaller time of waiting passed in a shiver.

The first of the four Oni to enter the barn strode straight to the molluck stalls, pulled one from its pen and began to hitch it to a small wagon stored under the loft. In a matter of moments the thing was done. In all of this, not one word was spoken.

Next entered the woman who had opened the door for Belwether, still garbed in gray but appearing today ungrimed and authoritative. Behind her came - what relief it was to see him - Belwether. Last there came a man of stocky build and grim demeanor, dressed for the road. He had two full packs slung on his back, though their bulk did not seem to affect him.

The gray lady spoke, not as before, but with the cadence of ritual: "I am Vety, Registrar of the First House, sent to convey the judgments and directions of our Quadrant Deans. Their resolution is this: First, the continuity of the observation is prime. If the continuity is threatened, adjustments must be made based on a reading of the Reticulum. The Reticulum resides in The Second House. Therefore, the Attached Pair, that being Andeved and Belwether, go to the Second House.

"Second, the uninvited may not stay in On. Therefore, the two Overites will be escorted across the border of On and are forbidden from returning. As I have been told, I have said. As I have said, so will it be."

Immediately the grim man slipped one of the travel bags from his shoulder and dropped it into the wagon. He turned to Mote, looked him up and down in assessment. "Get her," pointing at Kendle, "ready."

Belwether, his face without expression the whole time, made his way to Andeved's side. In a voice that could be heard by the whole of the gathering, he said: "We are pledged to go the Second House and must leave now. No appeal will be brooked."

Andeved, stunned by the swift and impossible direction this had taken, stood rooted to the spot. He would not leave his friends. Kendle deserved better than this. How could Belwether pledge such a monstrous thing?

"I can't believe Oni are so cruel. We came in search of knowledge to help someone afflicted by," Andeved gestured toward Kendle, "by an abomination. And you turn her away. Refuse access to knowledge that could---"

Belwether grabbed Andeved by the arm and pulled him, relentlessly, toward the wagon. The large man took the boy's other arm in a grip that would surely leave deep and painful furrows. Together the two Oni, with the strength and inevitability inborn to them, set the protesting boy in the bed of the wagon. And bound him with ropes. Belwether climbed up, took the reins, and urged the molluck forward and out of the barn.

Though Mote had seen it all, he could believe none of it. Words had fled and all he could salvage was the continued presence of Kendle. The terrible sound of the pronouncements had caused her to hold onto Mote's arm. It was the only touch of the real that remained.

The other Oni, including the hateful Vety woman, left. All except the large and determined man. He retrieved the travel bags for Mote and Kendle, which he thrust at them roughly.

"We are leaving. You first. I follow." He pulled a coil of rope from a nearby molluck stall. "Unless....?"

Mote could think of no other choice. Kendle was not able to flee and he would not leave her. If he could walk slowly enough, perhaps he could devise a plan. Refusing to think about the loss of Andeved and the betrayal by Belwether, Mote gently pulled Kendle forward and eased into the measured walk that had been their way on the journey so far.

X • X • X

It shamed him that his lips tasted of salt. Andeved had tried hard to stoke his anger so that grief could not have its way. There was much to keep fury alive: the sudden betrayal, loss of Kendle and Mote, the humiliation of being bound, the bitterness of a gag. The molluck had lumbered only a short while when the Oni had stopped the cart and ungently stilled Andeved's heated torrent of rage with a ragged bit of cloth. "There must be no doubt at all," was all the now-enemy said before he climbed back on the wagon and drove forward again until dusk came on.

Now they sheltered next to walls of stone, a waystation for journeyers. Belwether had unhitched the molluck and tied it nearby. He had also tied the captive to a wheel of the cart. The Oni's eyes never met Andeved's, nor did he say why or how, express any remorse, give assurance or warning. When the gag was removed, it was only for a drink of water and scant spoonfuls of mush. Andeved tried to reason, plead, threaten, question, but Belwether would not hear. It was much worse than Kendle's inability, for this seemed deliberately chosen and cruelly maintained. The small cooking fire diminished itself even as did the day, until only darkness remained. Darkness and silence.

Morning light brought no warmth. Cold water and seed bread only to break the fast. Making waste at the end of a tether, the residue steaming with just-left body heat in the damp chill. Andeved suddenly wished for a gesh to clear his night soil and turn it into bile. He would use it to eat through the stones of the Oni house until they collapsed. Then the knowledge inside would be his and he would get it to Kendle and to his mad cousin.

But it was only himself and his traitorous captor in the biting cold of a merciless wind. At least the gag, which Belwether brusquely replaced, kept Andeved's teeth from chattering.

He treats the beast better than he does me. Andeved's thoughts were all the more bitter for not being spoken. The cloth in his mouth, now a sodden mess, had come to represent the calculated and personal calumny revealed in Belwether's duplicity. What a dullard he had been to equate the Oni's ever-presence with closeness. If his mother and, more improbably, his father had been more...had been less...well, the space in his heart that should have been filled by parents might never have been empty. *I should not have needed so much. I should have known better.*

But his chastisement of himself did not soothe the pain that gripped his chest. Nor did it cushion his backside from the jolts and thuds of the wagon. He had never felt so miserable. By the time the plodding molluck dragged the cart over the crest of a hill and the Second Chronicle House came into view, Andeved felt good and truly sorry for himself, for Kendle and for Mote. It did not hinder him from also feeling a determination to still be of aid to his friends and to avenge himself somehow on Belwether. These, he vowed, would be his only thoughts from now on.

The settlement that surrounded this House looked more actively inhabited to Andeved. More folks bustling here and there between larger stone-walled dwellings on cobble-paved streets. Broader fields and pastures spread out farther down the dell. Yet all roads and pathways led to the center. Even homes were arranged so that front doors looked toward the vast multi-tiered Chronicle House that rose high above the valley floor. That it looked livelier and more important bothered Andeved. If heartless pronouncements came from a lesser place, what might come of this greater one?

He found himself looking for this settlement's kerchief girl. Some small sign of welcome. A crack in the stone faces that might bring comfort. But there was nothing. Nothing to gird Andeved with the tiniest touch of fellow feeling.

Down into the vale they rode, met by no one but seen by all. Passing by folk who barely looked up but seemed to already know who was arriving and why. Until the wagon halted before the wide, already opened red and black doors of this Chronicle House and four stern-visaged elders met them with crow-cunning attention. And watched Andeved's humiliation as Belwether unbound him and lifted him up and out of the wagon like a bag of rags. No sooner had his feet hit ground than the four Oni, robed in varying colors, surrounded the two arrivals and herded them into the dark interior of the massive House.

The inside was chilled, dim and vast. Belwether walked beside him within the enclosing square of elders, but took continuous care to avoid any touch or connection of look. Still, it seemed to Andeved that the Oni was as much under guard as he was. That was a provocative, perhaps useful, idea.

They paced past rows and rows of shelves, exactly like those in the First House. But eventually the similarity ended and the building opened into a space that put Andeved in awe by the sheer reaches of the construction. Where the group had stopped there were chairs arranged before a raised table – clearly made to be a place of judgment. But beyond this initial arrangement was a copper-colored drapery so wide and so high that it looked to have its own wafting currents of air and play of light independent of the several scholars that passed in and out of a split in the middle of it. Andeved tried to find the top of the curtain, but it seemed to recede into the darker recesses of the rafters.

His amazement was cut short by the approach of a forbidding looking woman dressed in dark clothes much like those worn by the grim man who had taken Kendle and Mote from On. She made quick work of unbinding Andeved's hands and removing the sopping gag. Her proximity did not encourage speech, however. She turned him toward the dais and stood with her hand firmly on his shoulder.

The quadrant leaders arrayed themselves behind the long, heavy table. From behind the immense curtain came a dozen scholars, by the look of them. Each was dressed in a brown tunic belted by a length of rope on which large wooden beads, the size of an infant's head, were strung. They made an odd clacking sound when the scholars moved and when they sat down in the chairs behind Andeved and Belwether.

When all was quiet again, Belwether took a step forward and began to speak. But the black robed quadrant leader silenced him with a gesture. Then that leader, a woman of girth and wild-arrayed dark hair, spoke.

"We know why you are here. Your progress from First to Second House was noted and reported. A reading of the Reticulum is required. To make the reading, however, questions must be asked. Answers must be true. Falsehoods willfully given are cause for death."

Andeved felt the statement like a fist in his stomach.

"Belwether," the woman began, "you brought your Attached and two other outsiders to On. You stated that it was to report aberrant activities by Overites and to correct a consequence of these activities, namely the inhabiting of an Overite girl by a modified flett. Is this a true account of your actions?"

Belwether took in a breath and answered without hesitation: "Yes, that is a true account."

"You are dismissed. You will await the results of the reading in the antechamber."

For a moment only Belwether seemed unable to move, as if his limbs would not obey direction. But then he nodded, turned and walked away. Now Andeved was alone, abandoned and the terrible attention of the judging elders turned upon him.

A tall, angular man robed in blue stood and leaned over the table.

"Do you, boy, understand the penalty for willful falsehood?"

"Yes. I heard what was said." Andeved's anxiety left him breathless.

"Then answer these questions. First, will you leave immediately of your own accord and return to your home in Under?"

Andeved clenched his fists until his palms hurt, tried to take in a deep breath because he knew the answer and wanted to say it loudly enough that the impossibly high rafters would echo with it.

"No. I have to find my companions, wherever they have been sent by you. Though Oni are indifferent to the pain of others, I am not. I gave them my word."

His answer did not change the questioner's expression one bit. Instead, with no inflection or warmth, he asked: "Will you willingly take Belwether back with you in the way of the Attached?"

"No. I should only rejoice if I were never to see the false Belwether again."

A very slight flicker of some emotion, too briefly felt before being hidden again, lit the eyes of the blue robed leader. But he did not let it keep him from the final question.

"Lastly, do you still desire to meet the demand of your cousin, Lord Paell, and report to him observations you have made on his behalf concerning the secrets of Over?"

Andeved startled. How could they know about Paell's demand? It had been made only to him in the deserted hall of the water clock. No one else was there, except, perhaps, in the shadows?

"No to this question as well." Andeved reached deep to steady his voice. "I cannot bring any matters to my cousin as he is mad and may infect the whole of Under with his madness. These are my answers. Each is true - not a thought of falsehood in any one. Not now. Not ever."

The leader's brow, that had been furrowed, cleared. "Then let the Reticulum be readied and read."

Straightening, the man pointed at one, then another, then a third scholar waiting, it now appeared, for just this moment. Scurrying like upright insects, the scholars disappeared into the curtained beyond, each carrying in their mandibular hands one of the large, wooden beads. Sound barely breached the hanging wall of cloth. Szssz...clack....a muffled word...thap...szssz. It made no sense to Andeved. No experience in his life 'til now could put a process or apparatus to the uncanny sounds, or the bends and ripples of the immense drapery. The utter strangeness of it replaced fear and anger for a rather long time. Until the noises stopped and one woman, holding a folded document, emerged from the opening in the huge curtain. She made her way to the red robed quadrant dean who had been, until now, seated in silence with only a slight tapping of his forefinger on the tabletop to indicate awareness of all that had preceded this moment. He took the parchment, opened it, read it, put it down on the table, paused. Into that pause came the voice of the blue robed leader: "Fetch Belwether. The Reticulum has indicated."

It was only a very few moments before the messenger returned with Belwether. To Andeved it felt endless. And then it was almost beyond enduring to be forced to stand with the traitor.

The man robed in red did not rise, nor did he focus on Andeved or Belwether. Indeed, his eyes seem to stare far away, beyond the room, beyond the instant. When at last he spoke, his voice came to the air as a dreamer's might.

"This nexus and that, beaded differently now, strung and restrung, told and retold. It is changed, this tomorrow we had once seen." He sighed a shallow, swift exhalation. "You, boy, once were a Pivotal Piece. Today you are nothing. Where once the web found Andeved in a plotted point, now his bead is fallen from sight. No need to Attach to nothing. So, too, the Observer is dismissed. No longer of value when the observed is valueless."

Now the red-robed man languidly rose. He took up the parchment, folded it once again and, closing his eyes, declared:

"Andeved of Under will be taken to the border of On. He may go where he will from there as he is of no interest to Oni henceforth. Let Belwether, previously Attached and recently seditious, return to the Third House, the point of his origin."

The leader did open his eyes now, and rested his gaze on Belwether. "Let the proctors at your House take up your reconstruction." He turned, and over his shoulder as he departed the room, said: "You may leave." It was not clear who all he meant by the dismissal.

CHAPTER ELEVEN

It was not difficult to know when they re-entered Over. Kendle could hear it coming - the soughing of breeze-ruffled leaves, the creaks and sighs of trees nodding agreeably. Even the streams sounded more industrious, better natured as they chuckled over rocks and roots. Not like the narrowly restrained, painfully cold waters of On. Or the unchecked wind that could scrape cheeks raw. No, it was very good to have left the confusingly hostile On.

So it seemed to Kendle as she sat warming her toes near the remains of the morning fire, her face in a small pool of daylight she could feel but not see. Her eyes still saw nothing but unrelieved grayness. Awake or asleep, no difference. The only way to avoid the panic, the madness of that hideous blankness was to concentrate on what could be touched or heard or smelled. A mug of hot soup. The clinks and thups of Mote packing up camp. Wood smoke.

If only the others were here. Kendle still could not puzzle out what had happened that morning in the Oni barn. Weren't they there to get help? Why then did Belwether, who had led them to On, suddenly shut himself off from them? Though the words spoken by the Oni made no sense to her, the taut and hostile tone was unmistakable. How had the friend of yesterday become the enemy of today? And she had heard Andeved's struggle against this wounding dismissal. The pain underneath his shouting cut Kendle so deeply it was as agonizing as a touch to the flett that curled around her ear.

Even after the terrible leaving of Belwether with Andeved, Kendle missed them both so deeply it amazed her. Andeved, yes, it was a loss. Yet somewhere in her flett-invaded head there was a conviction she would see him again. Without reason this stuck firmly with her. That she missed Belwether, even after the pain and betrayal, astonished her. Mixed with the ache of desertion was a second conviction – that she would never see Belwether again.

Kendle gave a sudden, short laugh. *See* Belwether. See *anything* anymore. Mote was doing a better job of finding ways to adapt to her blindness than she. Who knew that even the choice of common phrases would be affected by her new state of affairs?

The brief laugh changed to welling eyes with the sound, not too far away, of song sung in a husky but agreeable voice. More and more she came to appreciate Mote's ways. When he had to go off to hunt for food, he began to hum or sing as he returned to camp. He didn't want her to be anxious about unseeable rustlings and footsteps. They were still near On and they were still unwelcome in Over. But he made the noise anyway for her sake - though Kendle guessed Mote had scouted the area near them thoroughly enough to be confident they were safe and the sound would not give them away.

This morning Mote had pulled an old children's ditty from his memory. Though his words came to her ears as nonsense, the simple song had been one her mother sang to her long ago. She remembered it well:

> Little stones that skip the water top,
>
> Little leaves that catch a water drop,
>
> All the ways that rivulets grow,
>
> All the ways we come to know.
>
> Bigger stones that make a waterfall,

Bigger trees that reach so very tall,

All the ways that forests grow,

All the ways we come to know.

By the time Mote reached camp, Kendle was humming along with him. Both knew the words so there was no need to sing them out loud and endure that dissonance. Kendle even managed a bit of harmony in the last little chorus. She hoped her face showed Mote how much that brief, unfettered connection meant to her.

Then they busied themselves with dousing the fire and setting out again. This part of Over was not familiar to them, but after much drawing on the palm of Kendle's hand by Mote and drawing in the dirt by Kendle for Mote, there was agreement reached on the ultimate destination. With care to be undiscovered, they meant to return to the old observation post. It was shelter, could be made even safer than it had been, and was known by Andeved. If he was to find them, this seemed the best place to wait.

The deeper into Over they walked, the more difficult ground travel became. Though Mote took exceeding care with obstacles that might cause her a misstep, Kendle bore scratches from errant brambles, bruises from stones that hid themselves until too late. Halfway through the third day Kendle caught her foot under an exposed root and took a bad fall. On the way down to the hard ground, a branch whipped back and snapped a welt across Kendle's cheek, catching the flett a stinging blow on the way. Pain struck like a hundred hot, jagged knives. The scream was inevitable. It bounced from tree to tree, a ball-lightning of anguish. For a time, she could not later say how long, Kendle was lost in the agony. Slowly, very slowly she came back up to awareness. The air was cooling tears that had dampened her cheeks. The foot that had caught under the root was free. She was shaking, yes, but someone had put a cloak around her shoulders and was holding her so that the flett was not being touched by anything. Someone.

Kendle carefully reached out, feeling upward from Mote's shoulder to his face. His cheeks, too, were wet with salt tears. His hand closed over hers and brought it to his mouth, his lips moving against her fingers: *I am so sorry. My fault.* But that would not do, not at all, so Kendle pressed her fingers against the words that had been deeply felt but silently spoken, stopping them from any repetition. And then shook her head just enough that it did not worsen the ache but still wordlessly said: *Not your fault. Never your fault.*

It was not until later, when camp had been made and both were much recovered, that they realized Kendle had understood the words Mote had mouthed. It was one of the astonishing discoveries of that day.

X • X • X

Somewhere between the fourth and fifth scrubbing, Neeli began to believe the guards were serious. It might just be that he and Quist were being freed from duty in the gesh pens. By the time they had been issued clean clothes, fairly new boots and travel satchels he was sure. No one got barely used boots for no good reason.

The only worm in the 'shroon was that it had been only Quist they wanted. Surprisingly, the big 'prentice insisted he would not leave unless Neeli left with him. Looking back, it did not appear to Neeli that he had treated his 'way partner well enough to have earned that sort of loyalty. It might call for some gratitude on his part, and that made him feel awkward. Nevertheless, when the smell of the gesh pens had finally been removed and the gates of the encampment opened, Neeli found he did not feel so awkward that he could not walk out close alongside the moveable stump that was Quist.

Doubt returned momentarily when the accompanying guards stopped at the nearby bridgeway access stanchion. But it was clear from the way the marchales kept looking upway that they were waiting for someone, not waiting to drag him back to those hideous beasts. Yes, there was something coming. Neeli's practiced eye could tell the span ropes were vibrating with oncoming walkers. More than one walker, actually many if the forward sway was any indicator. But still they waited. And waited. In all his years he had never seen such slow progress. What was this? Who were they, these oncomers?

At last Neeli sighted, far up, a long string of folk spaced along the bridgeway. As they drew closer, he could see that the group included bearers carrying a pallet, the kind made for transporting the badly injured, or taking the dead to their last rest. He had a very uneasy feeling about this. Pulled from the gesh pens and pushed into a burial detail. Aside from the newish boots, this was not going very well. He wished, with all his being, that the travel pack he'd been given was filled to the top with jugs of brew, the more potent the better. He shook the satchel, hoping to hear sloshing. No, just the clank of what sounded like tools. Too sad.

The procession on the bridgeway had drawn up to where they stood. Now it was clear that the one being carried was Lord Paell, back again but going homeward this time. Evidently, Paell still lived, though Neeli was amazed to see it true, having witnessed firsthand the man's mortal condition. Near the pallet was Golion, Over's senior healer. Neither Neeli nor Quist had ever laid eyes on the man. But the robe and shoulder badge of his distinction identified who was coming down the access ladder. Toward them.

Lost in his nervous observations, Neeli nearly jumped out of his skin when Quist abruptly began to sing. What did that stump-blunder think he was doing? Even worse, the 'prentice strode past Golion and, taking the stanchion steps two at a time, shouldered his way to a place just beside Lord Paell. Oh, he would be punished for that breach of protocol for certain.

"You are Neeli, I believe." Golion seemed to loom over him and the marchales beside him.

"Yes. Sir." Despair made Neeli sputter. He just knew Golion was going to dismiss him back to the gesh pens. They only wanted Quist's soothing songs, the ones that had brought the flett-infected Underion so far before.

"Well met, then, Neeli. Lord Paell has requested to speak with you. I wonder if you would be kind enough to come with me?"

He was wanted? *He* was? By a high born, a lord? The whole notion briefly paralyzed Neeli. Though it might not have been that brief, for Golion pointedly cleared his throat, that ubiquitous attention-getting device of the more unsubtle communicators. It did the trick.

"Why, yes. Yes, of course. Naturally. A request. Well, uh," he gestured stiffly toward the bridgeway, "after you. Sir. There."

He followed close behind the healer until they reached the pallet on which the Lord of Under lay. And, mercy, the state of the man they had found and carried. Neeli knew he should not show the shock he felt, but it was hard not to flinch. Though the space around Paell's ear was empty of the rotting flett, the bandages were soaked with red. Tight lines of pain creased bloodless cheeks. Darkness the color of cold ash surrounded fever bright eyes. Truly this man was dying, and not gently. Yet he managed a small nod and smile in welcome. The bravery it must have taken to do so made Neeli's eyes burn.

More amazingly, the man gestured, albeit with a feeble pass of his hand, for Neeli to come closer. He seemed to want to tell him something. The only response thinkable was to lean in and listen.

"You helped me." Paell's voice was thin, weak. "My thanks for that."

"Um. Yes. Well."

"Would you help me now return home? I only ask. I am done with commands and they are done with me."

Something there was in the eyes, in the voice of this man. Something compelling and sad...and good. It had set Quist to sing the soothing. It now set Neeli forward, to the head of the line, beyond it to scout the fitness of the stepties, the pylons, the handropes. No flaw in the 'way would hinder Paell's journey home. This he could do.

Did his tightening of this rope and straightening of that steptie ease Lord Paell's last journey home? Neeli believed it did. That, when the long, weary procession reached the end of the bridgeways and trod the immovable dirt road that led into the shelters of Outer Camp, he had done well.

X • X • X

No one in Under or Over remembered who, in the far distant past, had built Outer Camp. Its shelters and corrals had been buttressed, repaired and expanded by both sides at various times since it lay precisely at the border. A place where traders pulled in wagons and safely slept between one long day's travel and the next. Where envoys and messengers could light fires against the cold. Where a road intersected that invisible line drawn to separate this from that, ours from theirs, known from unknown.

Once Golion acceded to Paell's request to be taken home, the healer had sent runners to Under, carrying the news their lord was found, was dying, was being brought back. It was, then, no surprise to see a contingent of Underions waiting for them at Outer Camp. To Golion's eyes, it mirrored the bringing of Arrant to this place not very long ago. Keen differences could easily be spotted. Pember and Zearia were not here to tear the heart from a grieving cousin. Where Kendle was now, no one knew, though he was certain he was not alone in caring.

Nor was Andeved present with his inevitable Oni. Paell had asked after the young man, but there was no knowledge of his whereabouts. Some odd shadow had crossed Lord Paell's face at that, a shadow that took long to pass over.

And this meeting offered the uprighted mind of one mortal man. That it might be tenderly employed for so short a time was as tragic as the foreshortened life of the impetuous almost-bride.

So Golion perceived the assembly that conjoined at Outer Camp and felt the sorrow and trepidation with which Chief Advisor Etcherelle, Under's menders and carriers received the litter for the rest of the journey home. He was grateful that no Underion even questioned Golion's need to continue with Paell, nor did they turn away Quist or Neeli. It was a mixed and nearly silent company that moved out of the halfway shelters onto the stony roadway. No one, Underion or Overite, was brave enough to mention that Lord Paell had slipped into unconsciousness.

X • X • X

The trail from the Second Chronicle House to the border was narrow and, in too many places, punctuated by boot-sucking mud holes. Two silent Oni, serious in their disdain for him, seemed to draw the wet, clinging fog with them. Andeved's rage gave him some inner warmth, but the flesh that held that rage was cold and tired. It was hard to maintain righteous anger when your nose ran and there were mud lumps and small, sharp stones in your boots.

When at last the gorse-spotted fen gave way to the tentative trees of the forest's edge, Andeved did not even glance back at the Oni. His back prickled with that being-watched sensation. They had simply stopped at a line only they could see and began to stand watch, making sure he kept going.

Still in view of the stony faced Oni, Andeved sat down on a fallen log and took off his boots. Grabbing a handful of broad leaves from a nearby banner bush, he wiped the mud and exasperating debris from the inside and outside of the boots. He made a big show of shaking the last bits of On from them before he put them on again.

Now Andeved turned to the deepening woods and, with a heavy sense of singularity, aimed his steps toward a more neutral gloom. Eventually his back stopped prickling and he knew he was out of sight of any Oni. But neither was he in view of any friend or a face he knew. For the space of many steps he felt his Underion-ness as he had not for a long while. The path beneath his feet was not stable stone. The trees moved in wind and made moveable breaches through which rain had begun to fall. He had a vision of Foodists bringing a feast to the tables: fragrant breads still warm from stone ovens, rich flavors of soups and roasts, cakes and fruits, cheese and cool drinks in misted cups.

Oh, it was not rain that wet his cheeks. It was the longing for what had been and would never be again. It was the loss of comforting trust. It was being a stranger no matter where he stood. That was what wet his cheeks as he walked alone.

How long he trudged in the rain he did not know. The sound of someone chopping wood got his attention. He knew the sound from Mote's provisioning of the tiny stove at the observation post. Could it be he had come far enough to be near the post? The flicker of hope was almost painful. Still he moved cautiously toward the sound, remembering so clearly being hunted when in company of Kendle and Mote. Carefully. Moving quietly. Peering through a wall of leaves and branches.

In a small clearing was a thin, wiry woman wielding a long-handled axe. Up she lifted it, then down with a smooth, swift motion. Bang-kettch. The length of wood cracked down the middle, the two pieces falling neatly to either side, joining an already generous pile of split firewood. The woman laid the axe aside and wiped her face with a kerchief she pulled from around her neck. Her cheeks were ruddy with effort and creased with a multitude of lines and furrows. A long braid fell down her back, though the braid was fuzzy with straggling hair loosed in the exertion.

"Are you going to stay in the bushes, or will you introduce yourself properly?" The lady looked directly at the patch of leaves and twigs behind which Andeved hid. Her voice, however, had a burr about it that softened the words so that, instead of being wary, he felt foolish to be crouching in a thicket spying on a chopper of firewood. And safe enough to come out into view.

"I heard you working." Andeved groped for an appropriate way to make a greeting without giving away too much. "I didn't know who...."

"Yes, well, you are not from here." She smiled. But Andeved had a tick of worry that she knew who he was. And not in a way that boded well.

"No one is from here but me. And my husband." She gestured vaguely behind her.

She did not seem to know he was from Under. She meant that she lived in a remote place. If that was true, it might be good. Perhaps in their isolation they had not heard about Kendle or the...troubles.

"At any rate," the woman continued, "you happened by at an opportune time. I may have been a little over zealous and split more wood than I can easily carry. Perhaps you might help me get it back to the house? I know for a fact that there is a lovely roast baking even now. Would that serve as wages for your help?" She tilted her head as if to suggest he was free to say yes or say no as it pleased him.

Nothing of his most recent life induced Andeved to trust easily, the prospect of betrayal was never far from him. Still, if he was observant, cautious, there might be something of help in this. And his mouth had convinced him to take the risk, for it began to water at the prospect of hot food from a warm fire.

For an answer, he picked up a few lengths of wood and let the woman pile more on his arms. She loaded herself with a bunch and headed down a small trail. Andeved followed.

Small bends in the path, first one way then the other. Rocks and roots tried to trip him. At first he worked to memorize the way he was being taken, but eventually realized the trail did not branch but ran uncrossed ahead of them. What did that mean? If it led toward the lady's home, where did it lead away to?

Very soon the path debouched into a clearing, in the center of which was a wooden house. It did not hang from a tree, nor did it rest on a stone foundation. There were stones involved, but they were stacked in a narrow column taller than the wall against which they rose. Pale smoke emptied upward and it was that which told Andeved its purpose. A chimney, a flue, like the oven vents of Under. Which explained the neatly arranged stock of wood to which he added his armload.

The lady brushed bark and bits of moss from her sleeves and then dipped a basin of water from a barrel at the corner of the house. When she had washed her hands and face, she folded her arms and looked at him. And waited. She seemed capable of waiting for a long time. Her scrutiny made Andeved uneasy, suspicious.

"Young man," she finally said, "I require some civilized behavior in my home. You might clean away the shards and grit of this work and your journey before supper."

"Yes, of course." Andeved's unease was compounded by embarrassment. She must think he had no manners at all. He quickly stamped his boots free of trail mud, dusted off his jacket as best he could and got a fresh basin full - though he brought the water to his face, not his face into the water. The better to keep an eye on things.

"There now." The lady beckoned him to follow her inside, through a door that was already ajar. She pushed it fully open, calling inside as she stepped through.

"Hammin. I have brought a lost traveler with me. And it is likely he has an empty stomach."

Andeved allowed his hostess to precede him by a few paces. With all the wood stacking and washing up done outside, surely anyone inside had been alerted to the presence of a stranger. If an ambush was planned, it might be now. Blinking quickly to adjust his sight to the darker interior, he cautiously went through the doorway.

Something huge rushed at him, grabbed his hand with such strength that Andeved gasped.

"Welcome, then, traveler. You are just in time to eat with us." The giant devolved into a large, smiling man with broad shoulders and black and white hair that stuck out in all directions like a wild bramble bush. He pulled Andeved toward a well set table. "Have a chair. Aimree, bring him a mug of cider. He looks dry as the last leaf to fall."

Aimree, for evidently that was the lady's name, did fetch a jug and brought it to the table along with a third plate, fork and mug.

"I think you startled the lad, Hammin. He doesn't appear familiar with hospitable mollucks like you." This brought a look of consternation to the man's face, which was quickly followed by a grin.

"My word, sweetling, you haven't called me that in such a long time. Am I blushing?"

Aimree snorted - rather indelicately Andeved thought as he sat down, though the mug of cider she poured looked redeeming. The frowzy-haired giant hefted a crackling roast from the fireplace to a huge platter on the table and commenced carving copious slabs of meat. And, oh, did it smell good - hot and savory with hints of herbs and the richness of long, slow cooking. The loaf of bread that Hammin laid on the table was still warm, releasing fragrant steam when Aimree cut it into huge slices. Though he had every intention of remaining vigilant, the meal before him was truly distracting. Concluding that vigilance functioned better on a full stomach, Andeved picked up his fork and put it to immediate use. Mercy was he hungry and truly, truly the food was surpassing good.

Andeved became aware that they were leaning back comfortably in their chairs watching him eat. Evidently Aimree and Hammin ate little, since they were finished already. More importantly, having eaten from the same platter, loaf and drunk from the same jug, they showed no ill effects. Perhaps he had stumbled on a reasonably safe refuge for a night after all.

"Hammin, I don't think we'll get a second meal from this. Do you?"

"Thinking not. Though there'll be most nothing to wash from his plate after. That's thoughtful of him."

As he was, at that moment, using the last bit of bread to sop the last drop of gravy, Andeved could not help but smile. "My apologies if I ate too much, but it was all so fine. I am quite full and quite grateful."

"Well, our son used to tuck into meals just like that when he was your age. Of course, he's all grown now and lives away to do his work." Aimree looked over at her husband in the way of mothers to fathers. Hammin gave a small sigh and ran his hands through the tangle of his hair.

"I had far less white in this mess then. What time does is not always kind."

But Andeved's breath caught in his chest. When Hammin had tugged through a section of frizzled hair, something was revealed. There, over one ear, a faint glow, a pair of folded wings. A flett.

X · X · X

If there were the smallest bit of dirt, the vaguest quasi-path, the most insolent squelching of mud they had not stumbled through, they did not know where it might be. In hours of light they walked and in hours of dark dreamt of walking. Always with the twitching between the shoulders so hideously familiar to prey.

When the sight, smell and feel of nearness to the observation post finally broke through the trudgery, Mote and Kendle found some small remnant of energy, just enough, to press on. Already the day had dimmed almost to dark, the hour when even shadows withdrew. The coming night had sent fog ahead of itself, gray and cold. But with the thought of a small, warm fire soon to be stoked, the furtive mist seemed to hide the travelers from any watchers, so that it felt more ally than foe.

There. The vine covered tree. Dark and quiet. At last. Mote took Kendle's hand from where it rested on his back and put it against the tree trunk. She knew immediately what it was. He could tell from the smile that briefly graced her weary face. He had brought them this far, to the place she wanted to be. He should climb up first, let her follow by touch, handhold by handhold, as he knew she could. But it took him a moment to find the strength for this last effort of the day. Then, fingers and toes found the notches and boles that took him up to the latch-less door. He swung it up and open and pulled himself through.

Kendle leaned against the tree, heedless of the rough bark, the twisting veins of cluster vines. She heard Mote push up the trapdoor, then heard rustling and bumping. He must be starting a fire. She could almost taste hot broth, feel warmth in her fingers at last. When some rest had been eked out, it would be good to tell him how much his help and companionship had come to mean. But there would be no warmth, no sleep until she made this last little bit of the journey, so she trailed her fingers across the treebark until the next notch presented itself. Hand over hand, foothold by foothold, Kendle pulled herself upward. Almost there.

A muffled sound. Was it a groan? Kendle froze. Hands gripped her arms hard, wrenching her upward. Voices, harsh, loud. Not Mote. Smells of others and the gabble of words she could not understand in tones she could not fail to understand. They were caught. Outliers caught in Over where they should not be, could not be.

Someone came very close to her, demanding something from her. She tried to answer, but knew it was in vain. With mounting anger in his voice, the unknown other grabbed her face, to make her acknowledge him. She heard her own scream before there was no more.

X · X · X

Four marchales, two lengths of rope and a single-minded adherence to orders. That is what had brought them to this miserable state. Mote found he could not even blame the marchales. He knew the captain, had gotten part of his training from her. Brekkan was respected by those she led, a principled woman. When the marchales had first been told that the observation post long ago held by Kendle's parents was where she might have fled, this quad was assigned to find it and find her. They had arrived just after he and the others had left for the ill-fated trip to On. But, in the absence of any orders to the contrary, the quad had taken up quiet residence, waiting patiently and, in the end, successfully.

In Mote's heart, there was only bitterness toward himself for stupidly leading Kendle into a trap. Toward the givers of orders that made enemies of friends. Toward the abomination someone had unleashed that took so much and gave such anguish. Most of the night of their capture Mote had spent trying to tend Kendle. The marchales had been shaken by the pain they unknowingly caused. The sight of a flett and Mote's angry explanation of the damage it had done was disturbing. So much so that Captain Brekkan fell into heavy brooding.

Still, when light came again, the captain found no other choice but to begin the trek back to Lodenbye. Kendle had revived to the extent that, though shaky and silent, she could walk for some distance, with help. Mote allowed no other to assist. He tried to bury the guilt of his failure deeply enough that Kendle would not sense it as she leaned against him for support. Once they reached passable bridgeways, he had to convince the marchales that Kendle could not manage their sway. That prompted much whispered consultation among the three guards and Brekkan. Eventually, but not happily, they all continued treading dirt.

So much time passed, walking slowly, resting often, silence broken only by calls to stop, to start, to eat or drink. Until after forever, but sooner than hoped, the leading edge of bridgeway stations and beginnings of hanging houses marked the return to Lodenbye. The captives had been brought to what had been home. Mote tightened his hold around Kendle's shoulders.

Because he had always managed on hope, Mote had never imagined a captives-brought-back homecoming. In the earlier days of his marchale duty he had helped bring wrongdoers here to be given justice, but this arrival was nothing like that. In point of fact, this was nothing ever before seen in Over.

Against a deep darkness that made mysteries of this and that, lanterns glittered and flared. Many lanterns, like captured stars, hung on pylons and stanchions. Throngs of folks paced the bridgeways, knotted in groups on platforms here and there, four to five deep outside the open doors of clan houses. Windows were wide open, light spilling past sills and shutters. Everywhere the sound of voices in debate, some forge hot, some bitter cold. Or swells of muttering, murmuring that broke against the louder forces like waves against rocks. Only one house did not show light, did not sway with unaccustomed company. It was shut down, but not invisible. A ring of lanterns and watchers surrounded the house of Pember and Zearia.

The constant movement, the unceasing noise, the forced light and ragged dark paralyzed the new arrived group. They could make no sense of the chaos. No orders given covered this.

"Captain Brekkan?" The voice came from behind and above them.

The captain turned around and looked up at the nearby bridgeway, blinking to clear the after-image of lantern light.

"Yes. I am, and in quad. You are…" Brekkan recognized the face, "you are Hilly, Golion's apprentice."

"Indeed. Just come back from the gesh camp. An injury, not terrible. And you have come from…?" Hilly stopped because she had just seen past the shoulders of the marchales. Saw a young woman turn toward her. Saw white-filmed eyes reflect back night. A momentary flutter of folded wings framing a face she knew.

"Kendle? Is that you? What happened?" The young healer climbed down the nearest stanchion steps and pushed past the guards to get a closer look. "No - there was one let loose before we--?" She took Kendle's hands in her. "I did not know we were too late to stop this. Oh, I am so sorry."

"She cannot understand you. The flett took her sight and speech, both the saying and the hearing of it." Mote pulled one of Kendle's hands from the healer's grip and brought it up to his mouth. "It is Hilly, Golion's apprentice."

Kendle pulled Mote's hand to her lips. Hilly startled to hear the gibberish that was spoken, but Mote nodded in comprehension.

"Kendle is confused by all the voices. Nothing is stranger than home made foreign, she says. But she asks if you might have been given healer's secrets that could help her."

"I...it is not that...there is much more to this than you have heard."

Brekkan laid a hand on Hilly's shoulder. "Do not hold back, healer. I have seen the pain this causes the lady. As a healer it is your duty to..."

"You misunderstand, captain. My heart cries out to help. But no secrets exist in Over to mend what ails Kendle. If there were, I would tell you anything, everything I have been told. It may well be," she pointed upward at the crowded, noisy bridgeways, "there will be no more secrets at all in Over when this night is done."

"What does that mean, healer - no secrets?" The captain's frown took shadows from the darkness. "I am bound by orders to bring Kendle to Over's Senior Secretholders, but no sign of life comes from their house and it seems to be guarded. Is that to keep folk out, or keep them in? "

Hilly pushed back a stray lock of hair, started to answer, then closed her mouth again. Again she tried to reply and this time managed a bit more of a response.

"While you were gone, Over became unbound, and we have become wild. Everyone who has tasted this new freedom has his own imagined system to impose. Some clan leaders, your own marchale chief among them, are...well, they are not to be found. Others stand with a loyal few against the chaos, though for what ultimate purpose remains unknown. Verbal assaults, bloody fights, threats, pleadings, tirades. There is true danger here."

From somewhere beyond the tenuous chain of lanterns came the sound of wood splintering, a door slamming, shouting. Hilly winced and then, with a sudden urgency, spoke again.

"You are tired. I am tired. And the explaining this needs will likely exhaust all of us even more. Best you come to my house and hear what has happened in more comfort and less chaos. Perspective is often better served with hot drinks."

The healer climbed back up to the 'way and waited as Brekkan decided that the suggestion was how to proceed, given night and disorder. Then waited as Kendle was carefully helped up and onto the 'way. Then was led, with as little bridge sway as possible, to the small, snug and, until now, quiet home at the edge of the town in the safety of the dark.

ⵣ • ⵣ • ⵣ

Hammin's frown of concern brought his chaotically haired eyebrows into a deep vee. "You are sure you are well? For a moment there I thought you were going to drop like a stone."

"No, I am fine. Truly. Must have eaten too fast. Or something like that." Andeved struggled to recover from the shock of seeing another person flett-ridden. Traditional wisdom said one flett in every third generation, never more, often less. He had seen three in one season. And unfledged ones, too, more than he could count. Once again the telling of time in the telling of tradition no longer held true, no longer strangled and trapped him. It was being stripped away, leaving him without a structure against which to lean. Or to rebel.

"Well, in answer to your question," Hammin handed him a soapy plate, "my flett came to me long, long ago. Before I met Aimree, when I was still a young man toiling as a 'wayworker as my father had been."

Andeved took the plate, dipped it in rinse water and set it on a wooden rack to dry. "So, you are an Overite, then."

"As you say. Then one day I was far out on a 'way that had been damaged by a fallen branch. It was after a tremendous wind storm that brought down old limbs and shallow-rooted trees. The forest was quiet again but for the sound of my own work. I clearly remember being deep into the rhythm of axe and the feel of muscles being used well. One huge branch that had barely weathered the storm felt the beat of my axe below and it was too much for it. Down it came."

Hammin's fingers, stubby and thick, held a dripping mug he did not seem to know was there, lost as he was in the living of a day long ago. Andeved gently pried the mug from the stilled hands. Just that small motion brought the present back to Hammin.

"Yes, so, as you might guess, it fell on me. Well, more precisely, as I tried to dive away from the worst of it, a broken limb stabbed right through me, like a splintered stake. The back of one leg began to feel warm. And wet."

"I hate that part." Aimree, sitting at a small desk across the room, shivered as she spoke. "Never like to hear it." She looked up from the book in which she had been writing. "To the better part of the story, husband, please."

Hammin's expression, which had shown remembered pain, softened. "Yes, to the better part." He stood up straight and finished washing the last of the dishes. Drying his hands on his shirt, which brought a sigh from Aimree, he motioned Andeved to a seat at the table. He lit candles against the darkening and, when both had scrinched around in their chairs until comfortable, took up the story once more.

"I was able to lever up the branch with my axe just enough to drag myself out from under. Sure enough, nothing broken, but something gashed enough that blood ran out like wine from a cracked barrel. It was not long before the world grayed and faded and I knew no more.

"I don't remember much about what came next, only that a long time later I awoke to discover I had been flett-blessed. The gash was almost completely mended and I was strong enough to stand, albeit still a bit shaky."

Aimree put down her pen and turned toward the two men. "See, there is a better part. And the best part is coming now."

Hammin grinned and motioned to his wife to take over the telling of the tale. So she did.

"The bridgeway Hammin was repairing was far up, almost to the border between Over and On. And so the First House of On was the closest for the getting of help. Imagine the sight - a blood covered, flett-glowing hulk of a man limping into the settlement in search of aid. It was memorable, to say the least. Certainly to me. I had just finished apprenticing as a tomeist and was on my way to the Chronicle House that morning to begin work. It is how we met, Hammin arriving with blood stains and a need to know and a much younger version of myself with ink stains and a need to capture what is known."

Aimree patted the books piled like towers on her desk. "Nothing more would have come from that meeting if it were not for the subject to which I had been assigned: the gathering and recording of any and all knowledge concerning fletts." She smiled over at her husband. "And there he was - field work on two legs."

"Now don't believe that it was all moonlight and sweet songs from then on." Hammin shook his head, looking quite like a mountain bear shaking off the long sleep. "The closer this good lady and I became, the less welcome I was. Even was told I was poisoning the purity of scholarship."

"To be certain," Aimree interrupted, "there was no poisoning the purity of anything, or anyone, going on. Just so you know, young man. Just to be clear."

Hammin sighed gustily. "True enough, though I had made some cunning plans to remedy that. Didn't amount to a twig's worth of firewood.

"Young folks are ridiculously transparent to their elders and every Oni past toddling could tell we would not be parted. But because Aimree's subject was of importance and she was a most excellent tomeist, we were allowed a special dispensation. We must remove ourselves from On so that we would not be a visually horrific example, but the study of fletts might still be continued in the field."

This time it was Aimree who sighed in the way of the contented. "Here we have lived, studied, loved, had a child who is now a man, who still makes joy leap up and dance in our hearts. Much has been difficult, separated from those who knew us from birth. There are days loud with the call of bloodlines, nights that shake with longing for what is missed."

Her voice trailed away. Andeved heard a great deal in the silence that carried a deeply wounding familiarity and a yearning for what was not yet his, nor might ever be.

Bang! The door slammed wide open.

"Son!" Two voices exclaimed as one. "No!" another yelled.

Against the darkness outside, his sweating face lit by the fires within, hard breathing like an air starved runner, stood a breathless Belwether.

Chapter Twelve

As she was still Chief Advisor, Etcherelle made the arrangement. It was she who directed the bed be brought into the Chamber of Ceremony and placed in the alcove next to the Water Clock. She saw to it that braziers had been lit and set on the cold stone in such numbers that soft warmth and muted light rose from their flickering coals. Once the menders had given her the truth of Lord Paell's state, she required them to keep away but for a brief assessment at the telling of each new hour. Only Golion had not objected to the constraint, and he a stranger.

The commands on her part were why she now sat close to the solitary bed in a borrowed chair. It was why she could take Paell's hand and, in softened tone, speak of matters she knew should have been broached long ago.

"Your parents loved you so well. How different it might have been had they lived. I served your father early on, so I knew him best. Dark did not belong to him. He turned an active mind to find what light there could be. It was an adventure just to talk with him."

Paell's slow, shallow breaths were a counterpoint to her voice.

"Your mother I knew less well, as she was made family later. But how your father loved her. And when you were added to the family, folk believed they beheld the perfect Lord and Lady and Heir. The hours were told faultlessly, rituals held precisely, masks of office bestowed with all ceremony. We expected we could buy providence with order."

Etcherelle marveled at the thinness of the lids that closed over Lord Paell's sight. It seemed she could almost make out the gold-brown of his eyes behind skin as taut as stretched silk. What had those eyes seen when masked by madness? She wanted to know what it had been like, yet was deeply fearful of ever learning.

"Ritual took your parents, you know. The accident occurred on a proscribed tour on which they dutifully departed and did not return. Was it this great grief that began the bending of your heart? I wonder at that by day, though at night the thoughts become formless, fearful dreams."

The Chief Advisor shook her head in dismay. "I want to think myself better than this. Better than to make your illness an excuse to list my worries."

"Do not worry." Etcherelle startled. He had spoken. And now his eyes opened, slowly and with some trembling.

"You were second mother to me, far-cousin. It was a disease took me, not a fault of your heart." Paell's whisper was so thin that Etcherelle leaned in so close to catch his words she could feel his breath on her cheek. "The flett, you must tell them, did its best to heal that disease. But it was itself taken by it. Tell Golion that, had it not been shaped by breeding to seek who they thought I was, we might have lived." Small tears, like distant stars, began to fall. Some from Paell. Some from Etcherelle.

"Conquer this, my Lord, my boy." The Advisor's breath caught in her throat. "We need you."

"I will be beyond pain very soon, second mother. You will grieve, and for that I am sorry. But take a second fosterling in my place. The ridiculous boy who loves so mightily. He will, we must hope, be better than I."

"No, stay. Please." But Etcherelle knew that all the breath had been used. Words would never come again from Paell, late the Lord of Over.

Then she wept. In this too brief a privacy she mourned the boy she had lost, the lord she had served. Too soon came the ceremonialist to tell the hour. Then the menders to confirm the end of pain for he who had been their charge. Then the full-masked, long robed caretakers that managed the terrible mundanities required when one who had lived was no more. They took away the shell that no longer held Lord Paell. And sent one of their guild to the edge of the Chamber of Ceremony to ring the change.

The great, bronze bell hung high in the vaulted ceiling. Until an hour such as this, the bell was draped in cloth so dark it was almost impossible to see. The eye could not hold the shape. Now, undraped, tolling began. Slow, deep and disturbing peals. So that all of Under knew it was bereft of its lord. Echoes, receding into the stone itself, whispered the name of the lady recently welcomed and more recently fallen. 'Paell' spoke the toll. 'Arrant' it echoed. Until the sounds became sighs and then ceased so that even the corridors themselves knew nothing but loss.

X • X • X

Nothing but endless trudging, Kendle thought, as she wearily put one foot in front of the other again and again and again. No gold light playing through green leaves to brighten a tired heart. Not even the dimness of dusk or restful dark of sleep for her now. But for the grief, guilt and fury of that first run into the deeper forest and a too short sanctuary in the old observation post, her life had become a white-blind march from places she could not see to things she could not comprehend. Step. Step. Step.

How many paces from her walk into the hewn-rock Chamber of Ceremony in Under? Then she had carried a box with what she had been told was a tender bride gift. How many steps from the terrible night that had taken her cousin? Then she had plied the forbidden-to-her healer's skill when it was needed most. And how far from the arrival of the little hunter sent by her uncle and aunt? Now she carried a flett bent to terrible purposes made for her alone. What a fool she must have seemed, to be so dutiful and so trusting.

Her hand was gently taken and brought to lips she now knew by touch and by the magnificent gift of comprehension they gave her. Mote framed words.

"They have gotten a molluck and cart, Kendle. You will be able to ride the rest of the way."

Kendle suddenly felt embarrassed by her plunge into despair. She should have known Mote would offer just the right gesture at precisely the right moment. He had earned her trust over and over again. And marched just as long in exile as she. If this journey had taken much, it had given a great deal as well. Mote was one of the treasures that never would have been found but for adversity.

Kendle brought his hand to her lips.

"I have not told you nearly often enough how grateful I am to have you with me," she breathed into his palm. He said nothing in return, but helped her locate the cart's edge and climb onto the seat-bench. She could feel the tipping of the small cart as he clambered up after her and clicked at the molluck to walk on. It seemed a prudent idea to link her arm through Mote's. For stability in the lurching ride onward. Interestingly, she could feel the tides of his blood bashing against his ribs.

X • X • X

Belwether blocked the doorway or Andeved surely would have fled. The boy's loathing flayed his heart. The parents, clearly aghast at the instantaneous reaction of both Andeved and their son, were speechless. Despair burned in his throat. There was no time to reconcile all of this, for the Hunters had certainly found his trail by now. With a lurch, Belwether shut the door behind him and, still blocking the way out, lowered a too heavy pack to the floor with a thud.

"Let me past, let me out you..." Andeved groped for a name to call his former shadow. The boy took a step toward the door, raising his fisted hands in a show of menace.

"Now wait a time." Hammin stepped between his son and his guest. "There cannot be good reasons for such hard greetings."

"No?" Andeved ignored Hammin's restraining touch. "Ask your good son for his good reasons. Ask him why he bound and gagged me like a vile wrongdoer when all I had done was accept his offer of help. Plead with him to tell you why he cruelly abandoned friends in dire need. He is a cold betrayer, a deceitful heart, who falsely gained our trust." Andeved's voice cracked with emotion, "My trust." He broke off, too overcome to speak, turned abruptly toward the wall where his travel pack leaned. With shaking hands, he tried to tie up what few things he could take on the trail.

Belwether could barely breathe. For once his skill at pithy, pointed wordings failed him. Squatting down, there in the doorway, he undid the thick straps that bound his pack. Carefully he lifted out a large leather-bound tome and laid it gently on the floor. It took all the strength he had left to manage the restraint that the huge book deserved. Then he retrieved another volume. And a third, then a fourth. By now his mother had moved toward the growing pile, gasping as she did.

"Those are mine," Aimree finally managed to say. "All four of them I did. With that one," she motioned vaguely toward her desk, "they are the whole of what is written on my field of study." Kneeling, Belwether's mother touched the spines of each tome, the long and wide ribbon of titling and murmured their names: *Fletts: Origins. Fletts: Patterns of Birth and Death. Fletts: Physical Characteristics. Fletts: Feeding Habits.*

"How did you get these, Bel? Not even I could remove them from the Chronicle House once they are placed there." Her tone had hardened into sharp concern and she asked her question looking squarely into her son's eyes.

Belwether flinched. "I stole them out."

Aimree took in a rasp of breath. Andeved raised his head and his fingers paused in their work of departure. Hammin took an involuntary step back.

"It was the only way. You know the penalty for this theft and I beg you to forgive me for bringing them here. I fear my disappearance has already been discovered. If they see the books are missing, too, then it is death for certain."

Aimree's hands raised to cover her chest in the way that mothers do when a child is in pain. "Why, Bel? Why take this terrible risk? It cannot end well, son."

"The fletts, mother. There was one given to Lord Paell as a gift from the bride to be. It was carried to Under in a box. Once the box was opened, the flett overflew a huge cavern full of grossfolk. But it chose Paell just as the gift givers intended."

"That is too much for chance. It does not happen that way." Aimree began to rock back and forth on her heels.

"This I knew as well, from listening to you when I was still a boy at home. The flett bond was a shock because it was clear the Overites knew the creature would choose Paell. But that was but the first unnatural bond."

"The next bond was even more perfidious and I was there, too, to see it happen. The girl, Kendle, niece and foster daughter to Pember and Zearia of Over, had also been made outcast. She and her allies, of which I am one--"

"Was. Was." Murmured Andeved in bitterness, his face still turned away.

Belwether stumbled a moment hearing the terrible accusation one word could make, "--we had taken sanctuary in her parent's old flett observation post."

Aimree stopped pacing. "I know of their work. It was good study they did. Much of what they recorded I have used in my collections. What a terrible loss when they went with the fever. And you say Kendle is their daughter?"

"Aye, and a strong one she. Perhaps it was that strength threatened Over's highest, I do not know. But I do know they sent a hunting flett bred to track just the one person, track and then ensure she would never be a threat thereafter. When the flett bonded, it also turned Kendle white-blind and unable to speak or hear anything but babble."

Andeved, his face still turned away from Belwether, began to shake his head from side to side, to shake away pain.

Squaring his shoulders, Belwether strained to put what words were needed together. His seldom taxed throat ached with the effort.

"The flett that attached to Paell took on the illness of his mind. But in doing so, the flett itself went mad and began to die, in hideous ways, while still bonded. It was to find a way to remove the unnatural flett and heal the physical harm it had done that Andeved brought his companions to On, to the First House."

Aimree sighed. "Not well received I warrant. They are not... open."

"No, not open. Closed to them and the aid they sought. Open to accusations of heresy and treason to me. They required a reading of the Reticulum."

Hammin startled. "You must have known, son, a reading of the destiny web was surely possible. How could you subject your companions to that terrible danger?"

"My Attached," Belwether addressed his parents, but could see that the boy had turned toward him, listening, "had been forced to leave Under. But he made good work of a cruel dismissal by seeking out others who also held, however flawed, a passion for living the truth plainly and ardently. When those others were also cast out, he did not hesitate, but followed as a friend and ally into exile. I was

duty bound to follow the boy. And so I did, though I would have
gone with him even had I not been constrained to do so."

Some brush of noise rattled outside. Belwether continued,
speaking even faster than before. "Yes, he is young and pushed-
pulled by the heated thoughts of his age. But he endured an
upbringing by weak and harsh parents, cared as he could for his
lord cousin who descended into madness as he watched. I began to
understand why years ago the Reticulum had seen him as a Pivotal
Piece. He was strong enough that, if I pushed him away cruelly
enough, he would survive the questioning because he would speak
the truth as it had come to him, like a blow of an axe. He had to
truly despise me, hate the coldness of On so he would be allowed
to live. And so I would survive to be taken to the Third Chronicle
House where I found most of the flett volumes are stored."

In the light of the lamps and the glimmer of the hearth fire,
beads of sweat shone on Belwether's face and, more strangely
and rarely, tears gleamed in his eyes. "Kendle must not be left to
endure this kind of living horror. Nor should Lord Paell rot with
his decaying flett. Mother, please, you must have knowledge to
aid. Hurry to answer, I beg you, for I would not have you pay the
price for my acts. If you find blame for what I have done, know that
already I have lost my work, my home and all those who once called
me friend. Let this be full payment. It is all I have."

Even as Aimree caught her breath to answer, Hammin moved.
He strode across the room and took down two packs from pegs on
the wall. As he made toward the books piled in front of the doorway,
he rumbled out directions.

"I can carry three of the volumes. Bel, you take the fourth and
the one your mother is working on over there." He waved toward
the desk. "Aimree, there will need to be supplies for the long and
swift walk."

Then the huge bear that was Belwether's father stopped and
turned to Andeved who still crouched over his own pack.

"Whatever darkness you have endured on your journey to this point, young man, put it away for now. None of us will live should the Hunters of On find us. Nor will Over shelter us as we come with damning knowledge. To bring aid to your friend and family, we must survive. To survive we must run. And we can only run to Under."

The room, the whole of each life held in that room, hung suspended. Andeved stood up. He tried to look up but could not raise his eyes to meet the waiting gazes of the others. There was a sound in the trees, in the fireplace a log cracked and sparked, but the loudest noise - the one that was not air or fire - was the silent movement of the boy's head as he made his answer.

CHAPTER THIRTEEN

Prickles ran up Mote's spine. He'd fully expected the huge doors of Under to be shut tight, the way he had first encountered them. But when the molluck-drawn cart crested the hill and began the downsloping way to the gates, they were met with a gaping entrance, wide open, unguarded. In truth, the doors hung a bit askew, as if impossible winds had slammed them open.

Though Brekkan and her marchales had looked carefully all along the way, there had been no sign anyone had exited Under and come up the road they used. No one coming out? Anyone able to enter? It made Mote apprehensive. Still, it would be helpful for Kendle to be able to ride the cart past the doors all the way into the great entry hall. With caution and some hesitancy of which Kendle, judging by the tension of her hand as it tightened on his arm, had become aware, he clicked the molluck forward, down into the dark, cavernous hall.

No lights were burning, no sentries present to direct the cart toward an empty stall. While Hilly kept a watchful eye on Kendle, Mote commandeered a pen for the weary molluck. He had to pull feed and water from the scant supplies brought with them as there was no grain or fresh water to be seen. After some discussion, that echoed oddly in the deserted entry hall, it was agreed that bringing a quad of marchales in uninvited might ignite suspicion among the sheltered Underions. Brekkan ordered the other three marchales to stay on watch by the great doors of Under and then she and the others turned toward the interior hallway and walked into the empty silence.

Hilly slipped into a position next to Mote and Kendle. She looked more confident than Mote felt, no doubt in part because she'd never been to Under before. He could tell she was keen to meet up with Golion and piece together what they knew about removing fletts. Perhaps the senior healer had brought the ailing Lord Paell through the worst after all and Kendle would benefit from that. And, though Hilly had not spoken it aloud, Mote knew she hid a healer's urgency. The more time passed, the less likely a good outcome.

There was noise ahead of them. Distant sounds incomprehensible by virtue of rebounding too often against stone walls. But it was enough to make Mote feel somewhat more hopeful. It could be one of Under's many ceremonies, perhaps a gathering in celebration of Lord Paell's recovery. It could be a vigil to hope for recovery, if the healer's touch had not yet fully worked. It surely meant that Under had not been stripped of its folk in some terrible way. That possibility had briefly shivered through his mind.

"I hear voices." Kendle had pulled Mote's hand up to her mouth. "Can you understand what they are saying?" But since he had no good answer yet, he just shook his head and kept walking. Better that than try to create an answer from what was not yet known.

Now some lights glinted in the ascending corridor. From down a branching hallway came an Underion, practically flying past them with all the signs of urgency. The masked person barely gave them a glance before she disappeared down a subsidiary corridor. Not even time to hail the runner.

Forward once more, taking a winding stairway slowly for Kendle's sake, until they could hear the sounds more clearly, could even glimpse ahead of them the doors, again wide open, to the Chamber of Ceremony. For a moment the interior of the great hall swam and squirmed in Mote's eyes, and the sound from it was like many trees crashing in a high wind. It took an effort to decipher the reality: the massive cavern and all its balconies swarmed with what looked to be every Underion. A tide of talking rose and fell from the many-headed crowd.

Over the top of the multitude, Mote could barely make out who and what was on the dais at the far end of the cavern. He recognized Under's Chief Advisor who was, with great animation, speaking to the crowd and gesturing toward the man and woman who stood next to her. The noise of the crowd was so great that Mote could not make out what Etcherelle was saying. But he could see the final occupant of the distant dais. On a catafalque draped with white cloths lay a body. Mote's heart sank. Next to him, Hilly groaned in disappointment. Kendle, who could not see the evidence of failed healing, grasped Mote's hand to implore him to describe the scene.

But before any explanations could be made, they were hailed by someone behind them. Turning around, it was with great relief they recognized Senior Healer Golion, who looked as surprised to see them as they were to be found by him.

"What are you doing here?" The man was disheveled and beads of sweat ran down his face. "It's all of a jumble here. We – "

The crowd in the Hall gave a great shout, though some shouted 'yes' and some 'no'.

Golion pulled Hilly along with him, directions to the marchale captain flung over his shoulder. "The mender's chamber, down a level. Much quieter." He ducked his head just a bit. "Maybe safer. Come on."

With no other plan in the face of such unexpected turns, Mote guided Kendle and Brekkan followed. Not knowing, but hoping.

The Mender's Chamber was cold, lit with lamps that burned starkly white. It had its own distinct smell - like frosted herbs and beneficent acid. That odor, of attempted cures and attempts to wipe away evidence of failures, was what made Kendle grip Mote's arm with painful anxiety. He realized she must know they were entering the very place where her cousin had died not so long ago. Perhaps she even thought they had come here to... Mote found his mind would not put words or pictures to what must be done to save Kendle from the hateful winged worm. It was a relief when Golion began to speak. This, at least, he could translate for Kendle. He brought her hand to his mouth.

"We all believed Paell would not awaken from the deepness into which he had fallen on the journey here. He was laid by the Water Clock for the final watching. But he did wake, and briefly spoke with his Chief Advisor. Then, just as the Hour of Lessons was called, he truly left for all time." The healer shook his head wearily and muttered to himself: "Not in Under but a sliver of hours and already I speak in measures of time."

Golion took in a breath and straightened his shoulders. "There has been no opportunity, or even any desire, to tell of Over's part in the bending of fletts. As it is, Underions blame us for simply bringing the creature in the first place. It has soured hearts and accusations of mortal carelessness have been made. Chief Advisor Etcherelle, blessedly, has tried to pacify the hottest of the accusers. But should the truth be made known...." The healer glanced over his shoulder at the chamber's shut door. "When I came across you outside the Chamber of Ceremony, I had just been finding those who came with me to gather in the great entry hall. Telling them we must be prepared to leave. Soon."

The tense and whispered echo of the healer's news, Mote's translation on Kendle's palm, trailed behind but eventually came to a stop. Neither Golion nor Hilly could manage to look directly at Kendle, though they knew all too well she could not see them. Could not see the remorse that twisted and tore across each face. If they could not stay, could not use this exceedingly well appointed chamber, could not have what benefit might be had from the knowledge each fervently hoped Andeved might still bring, then the only eventuality was a hideous, agonizing and much too long end-journey for their companion. Already Kendle showed signs of mounting distress. Yet even now she kept her head raised and her hands steady as she brought Mote's hand to her lips and spoke into his palm.

"It is hard to explain how little I desire to walk another step, to be pulled from place to place, endlessly hunting help, chasing failed purposes." Speaking aloud to others what Kendle could say to him alone, broke Mote's heart. His voice faltered even as she continued. "But it is so clear that each of us from Over is in great peril if we stay here. We cannot have that. The only possible choice is to go out. Again. Though, if Over itself is not safe for us and On will not have us, where will we go?" and here her voice also shattered. Her mouth closed into a tight line and she drew Mote's palm away from her face. She did not let go of his hand, but held on to it with both of hers.

The merciless silence that came then lasted but a moment before it was broken. By noise in the hallway just outside the door. Scuffling, murmured words. Tugging at the latch. Too quickly for evasion, the door flew open. From the dimness of the outer hallway, shadows struggled to shove their way in.

Andeved threw himself into the room. Then came a bulk of a man with a huge pack slung on his broad shoulders, followed closely by a determined looking woman of age panting raggedly but supported by a grim-faced Belwether.

Shock.

Mote hurriedly named the arrivals for Kendle. Their first impulse was to embrace Andeved with elation. So they did, with Golion and Hilly looking on in relief and anticipation. Then the recognition that he had come in company of the traitor Belwether chased much of the joy from their greeting. Especially when seeing the tautness of pain and fear pulling at Andeved's face.

Several folk tried to talk at once, but it was Andeved's voice overrode all the others.

"We've got it. We've got what information there is of fletts the knowledge hoarders of On have tried to hide away. Anything that might help Kendle is in these books - and Aimree." He gestured toward the woman who was already pulling volumes from packs and placing them on a table. "It was only a hope that Kendle might be on her way until we entered Under, found the marchales and they told us it was true." A swift smile, a momentary lessening of tension, passed across Andeved's face. Just as quickly, it left.

Golion stepped toward Andeved with an expression of concern and began to speak, but the young man silenced him with a gesture.

"There were others in the hallways as we entered who told us they have been directed by you to gather in the great entry hall and make ready for what might well be an escape. Because," and here Andeved lost for a bloodbeat the steadiness that had held him, "because my cousin, the Lord Paell, will never again say the hours. He's gone. Dead." The last word fell from him with all the terrible amazement that the young, who have not had such loss before, so keenly feel. Part the unexpected blows of grief, part the first terrible intimation of personal mortality.

This time Golion would not be stilled. He moved next to Andeved and, putting a healer's hand on the boy's shoulder, spoke gently. "You need to know that, at the end, Paell became himself, became the cousin you knew of younger years. Though the flett that had been made for him destroyed itself and Paell's body, yet the lord's mind cleared, his eyes saw truly, his mouth spoke of good and in calmness of spirit."

Andeved raised his head, searched the healer's face and words and found a measure of comfort. Kendle, who heard what had been spoken from Mote's whispers, began to quietly weep. It could only mean her own death, this telling of Paell's end. That she might find quietness of heart in the midst of her body's pain was of small comfort. Beside her, Mote gathered tears in his palm, some hers, some his.

Aimree, who with Hammin's help had now laid out all her volumes, broke into the too heavy moment. "Please, please if we are to do our best for Kendle, then we must start immediately. Time is a mortal enemy in this."

Golion shifted his focus to the table of books. "I have now some limited experience of removing a flett," he began cautiously, "but if we are to be of true help to Kendle we need more than third-hand knowledge from an unknown archivist."

"These are not cold pages limned by an indifferent scholar," Hammin burst out, his face taking on anger-ruddiness. "My wife IS the tomeist. She wrote every word with hard wrought wisdom. Much of it firsthand." He reached up and drew back one side of his wild mane to reveal the flett that had residence there. "This knowledge has been bought at great cost. Our son risked his life and lost his life's work to bring it out of On. My wife and I, on his word alone and for the sake of strangers, have committed knowledge treason, the penalty for which is death. These are no idle scratchings that caused us to be hunted to the very doors of Under."

Belwether, who again had moved without notice to Hammin's side, laid a hand on his father's arm and spoke in his quiet rumble. "He didn't know, father. Now he does. Let him do the work at which he is so skilled. It is Kendle who must be served in this."

Hilly moved to Golion's side and tugged at his tunic. "Time is the only enemy in this chamber, Healer. I will lay out the instruments and potions. Will you prepare Kendle?"

Mote, who had struggled to translate all of this for Kendle, left out the reference to instruments and potions. Still, she gasped when she realized Belwether must have known all along who and what must be brought out of On - and at what price. Yet again she gasped when she understood that the time was now, even as a chastened and tightly focused Golion gently helped her climb onto the stone slab that was to be his workplace and her fate.

"I will stand by my wife," Hammin planted himself between the door and the healing table, "should any who mean harm try to enter." He looked to be immoveable.

"Aye, sir." Andeved moved his travel pack against the far wall. "And we will stay guard in the outer hallway." He glanced at Captain Brekkan, who moved toward the door in agreement, then at Mote. But Mote shook his head, still holding Kendle's hand in his. Andeved gave only a slight nod. He turned toward Belwether. But the Fool-no-longer was no longer there.

X · X · X

From his vantage point in the shadowed corner of the highest balcony, Belwether could still easily hear the Chief Advisor beseeching the populace of Under. He could still clearly see Sere filled with wrath and the fear that fired it, Glitter hopelessly adrift in the currents of calamity. And could too clearly understand the galvanizing finality of the white-draped bier.

Etcherelle moved toward where the emptiness that now was Lord Paell lay. "He was," she paused, hoping the uneasy murmurings of the crowd would cease, "he was, in his last moments, free from the terrible influences of an unwholesome flett," the name of the creature stirred mutterings, but the Chief Advisor rode over them. "and from the troubled mind against which he had long fought. Our Lord, our Paell, he came at the very last to such sharpened clarity that it cut my heart to hear him speak." The mutters fell away. "He spoke of his youth, the loss of his parents, our care of him after. He spoke, with such tenderness, of you. Of the Under that once serenely told the hours, held ceremonies in respect, whose folk put hands to worthy work, carving out of stone seemly lives."

Sere began to pace restlessly, distracting attention from Etcherelle's declamations. This disrespectfulness of movement made Belwether catch his breath, though he mocked himself for being surprised at Andeved's father. How many years had he watched Sere berate, belittle, scoff, rage? What had troubled Paell always seemed a gentle illness when placed next to Sere's black humors. As if to stress the comparison even more, Sere stopped his pacing in front of the catafalque and trampled over Etcherelle's voice with his own.

"How nice Paell was so fond of the Under he ruined, so loving in his feebleness. But the naming of the exile Andeved as heir is surely proof that his insanity had no cure."

Belwether groaned. There was the confirmation of his dread. The boy turned so recently a young man would be abused, flayed, dismissed, cruelly rent in this war of words, this struggle for succession.

"My lady wife coos after this absent son - it is a mother's flaw to prattle on about children. We can forgive her that. But we cannot allow such nonsense to poison the judgment we must make. Glitter is the nearest blood kin to Paell's line and, though she is my spouse, I will be honest with you - that line is spent. Done. Bred out. Let the guild leaders meet and decide who next will lead us."

"Aye," came shouts from the crowd.

"No," erupted from others.

Mirror bells sounded beneath the shouting. The light in the Chamber of Ceremony became brighter as the hour of turning had arrived. Then the distant, deep bell began its toll. No matter the press of events, now was the time decreed for a final journey. All must be put aside as the funerary procession took the former Lord of Under to the distant, deep, cool, dry tombs cut into the side of the Cavern of the Timeless.

Ⴟ • Ⴟ • Ⴟ

Captain Brekkan closed the door to the healing chamber behind Andeved. Silence. Standing in the hallway. Awkwardness.

"I mean no offence, Andeved," Brekkan finally began, "but exactly how are we to protect those inside? If Oni Hunters come this far in, we have no deterrents at hand. No weapons, if it should come to that."

Andeved shook his head, color rising into his cheeks. "I thought you would be equipped with...something. You are a marchale after all. I just thought...."

"Marchales carry truncheons when ordered to do so. And those orders are an extreme rarity. We have some skill in physically applied restraints, but you must have noticed, surely, we are armed only with derived authority. Yes?"

"Yes. Yes, it is just that--" Andeved glanced over his shoulder at the closed door, "--if there is a need to..."

Brekkan broke in confidently. "From what I know, the folk of Under incline to rigidity and arguments in trouble. My own people of Over fall back into chaos and revelations. Neither attack with other than words, though words can maim, even kill. Still, no weapons against flesh hold a place in our histories, nor do I believe will any be wielded even now."

"No weapons against flesh?" Andeved exploded. "Then what was it killed Under's Lord? What would you call the flett destroying one of your own people? Kendle would call it a weapon against flesh. If the rest of Under comes to know that it was Over twisted the fletts into arrows of death, will *histories* keep us from retribution against flesh?" He ended breathless, hardly managing the terrible anger that washed over him.

Brekkan took a step back. "No, no, young lord. I did not mean to look away from the abominations bred by the darkest of Over. But our folk hate what was done as mightily as yours will when they learn of it." The marchale narrowed her eyes, pinning Andeved with her intensity. "And if we listen through anger and truly hear the fear that feeds it, we will know – all of us – we are complicit, each of us witless accomplices in what crimes have been wrought. We would not see them, looked away, blinded by a surfeit of self-pleasing shrugged off the knowing that would have required a doing."

A stunned pause. Andeved's mouth worked soundlessly. He began to rock back and forth where he stood. The marchale reached out to lay a hand on the boy's shoulder. He jerked away.

"You think I have not already blamed myself for what I did not do?" Andeved's voice was raspy and tight. "I knew my cousin was sick in his mind. And, though he was both family and friend, I did nothing. Said nothing. Never let on to Over that Paell was not well enough to wed. Even when Bittercalls bent the stone with their wailing."

"You were a boy then." Belwether rumbled, appearing at Andeved's side. "You are not one now. Do not let the good young man you have become despise the disregarded boy that you were."

"How can you say that? I betrayed you when you never did me. You tried with me from the day you arrived, but I...I—"

Belwether stepped in front of his once assigned. "Enough. Stop up what threatens to overwhelm. Confessions will not stay Hunters. And they, make no mistake, are sent to find and kill their prey. Kill us."

Tonn, tonn, tonn. Through the corridors came the tolling of the funerary bell, deep as grief, calling the living to walk away with their dead. The sound hit Andeved like a blow.

"That is the signal to gather for the funeral procession," Andeved's hands opened and closed into fists, though he did not seem to notice. "All of Under will walk the dead...my cousin...to the outer burial caves. No one of Under is likely to come by here during that time."

Belwether took the marchale by the arm and turned her toward the way out. "In the Great Entry Hall there are axes, prods and other things that might serve as weapons. Arm your quad and intercept the Hunters."

"If it should come to that." There was the hope of avoidance in Brekkan's voice. But the eyes of the Oni who held her arm disallowed such a hope. So she pulled from his grasp, gave a terse nod and swiftly walked away outward.

From within the healing chamber came a high, terrible cry. Andeved reached for the door, but Belwether moved to block the entrance.

"All that can be done," the Oni murmured, "is being done."

Andeved could not, for a long moment, take his hand from the door. Then he nodded, slowly. "I know. But a side of me wants so fiercely to do something. Something brave, a deed that really and truly matters. The other side of me knows how stupid that is, like a child playing at being grown, pretending to be good as if that made one so."

Belwether took Andeved's shoulders in his firm grip. "Listen carefully, lordling, for this must, by circumstance, be brief. Would you task a child with the saving of a people? With understanding the many ways grossfolk delude themselves and ruin others? Would you? No. Not ever. Then why do you assign those heavy burdens to the child you were?

"When I first came to Under, newly assigned, I found a boy who had been left to raise himself. One parent so unfocused as to be dangerous; the other a prisoner of dark and cruel humors. No child should have to be so alone in the midst of so many. But you found ways to thrive. It surprises me still to see the strength you somehow found and made of such good use."

The Oni drew a deep breath, removed his hands from Andeved's shoulders. As if that had opened a gate, tears began to run their course down the young man's face. He swiped at them roughly, willing them to cease and yet yearning to hear more of the words that had loosed them.

"If there should come a day empty of peril, Andeved, I would tell you of all I have not done, of the evil of Oni knowledge hoarders, those who play at weaving fate. We would shed our guilt, come to peace with our own destinies. Though it is far from fair and puts time out of joint, today is not such a day. This is the day you learn Lord Paell, in his dying breath, named you heir. Your mother deems it a task too worrisome for her boy. Your father brands Paell's bloodline unfit and demands Under choose a new one." More gently, the Oni finished the telling. "For all their faults, Oni do often see the timepoints upon which history turns - and those who stand, alone in their fate, on those points. You are such a one, Andeved. I am so sorry."

A noise of scuffling, swift and disturbing, careened around the corner of the hallway leading up-inward. Then quiet, then the wush-wush of something being dragged. Andeved turned toward the direction of the sound, listening intently. Belwether reached into a tunic pocket and drew out a wickedly curved knife. From the corner of his eye, Andeved saw the movement, saw the harvesting knife glint in the muted gold of mirrored midday light.

"I would beg the Maker for time to talk of this," the Oni whispered, "but I think it will not be ours. Let me be the one to wield this, if it comes to that. You should not yet have to decide such a thing."

At the end of the corridor, three figures appeared: two wrapped in black and one, tied and silenced, dragged between the Hunters. From the captive, a mask of messenger hung askew to show eyes wild with fear. The Hunters gave no evidence of being surprised to see who stood before the chamber door, but continued moving toward them until they stood not a dozen paces away. They stopped, and with casual brutality, dropped their captured messenger at the edge of the hallway.

Andeved's indrawn breath rasped against his tension. "If you have come to take the books, then you will have to wait." He thought he sounded steady, but the tides of his blood broke so hard it seemed his whole body shook. "The knowledge is being used to heal. We cannot allow you to take what is required to save that life."

Both of the Hunters focused on Belwether. Neither seemed to have heard Andeved nor even recognized his presence.

"You, Oni. We are come for the knowledge and for you." One of the Hunters took a single pace forward, but it was enough to cause Belwether to step out with the harvesting knife held at his side.

The Hunter shrugged. "Those who are not of this treason are not our concern." He gestured at the bound messenger tossed aside, still alive but shaking in panic. "This one directed us to where you were. Not needed now and let to live. We are, as you must know, weapons of On, but we are sharply aimed. You the thief, the stolen knowledge - these are the targets. The rest are nothing. Less than nothing to us."

"So you say," Belwether held the blade, and himself, steady, "and yet what defines target to you. The healers who even now use the treatments - are they now considered containers of 'stolen knowledge'? Or Kendle, the one healed? Or perhaps my mother who archives the secrets, or my father who loves her, loves me? They are not nothing to you. I am not the only target of you weapons-that-walk."

Both of the Hunters reached behind a small swirl of cloak and brought out, each, terrible, long handled, double-bladed axes.

"Truly you are a fool, Belwether, to make this harder than it should be." The Hunters moved apart and carefully, inexorably came nearer. "Get that nothing boy out of the way. He is not our concern."

"Nothing boy?" Andeved's hands clenched into fists. "Did your masters not tell you that I am named Under's lord? Or did those bloated spiders consult their destiny web to find only what they wanted to believe."

"It does not change what must be done." The Hunter nearest Andeved suddenly leaped forward and swung his weapon, the sound of the axe rushing through air like the hiss of a snake. The edge ripped across the boy, slicing through cloth and into flesh. Andeved dropped to the floor, clutching at his chest. Faster than thought, the other Hunter made for Belwether, bringing his weapon up to cut away the hand that held the harvesting blade. But the Fool, in his way, was not where he had been. He was where a Hunter's side was open to the curved knife, a side that was opened by that curved knife. The enemy fell with a gasp of surprise and sudden, unstoppable spouts of blood.

Belwether turned to take on the remaining foe, but that Hunter was already raising his axe for a final blow. Time slowed so that it was hideously clear every possible movement to save Andeved would be far too late to interdict inevitable death.

Blurred motion of the boy's arm. Upward. A grunt, hesitation in the downward stroke. The Hunter began to topple, like an ancient tree, his hands spread wide, the weapon loosed to clatter on the hard stone. It was not until he lay, blank face upward, that Belwether could see the long, thin healer's tool planted flag-like where the tides of blood had once beat.

A hot, metallic smell rose from the spreading pools of black-red. Odd and awkward extrusions, slashes of bone white lay in terrible view. Two dead and two living, all four bodies wearing stains of flesh and of blood. So swift a moment to produce such horrors.

Groaning, Andeved struggled to his feet, pressing one hand to the long cut across his chest. With the other hand he cleared blood from his eyes. But then he could see what lay in front of him. The evidence of a kill. Kills. He staggered back against the wall and retched. Hard. And again.

It was a passing of time, a not-silent pause, before Belwether realized he still held the harvest knife. With a wrenching shudder, he threw it down. In a paroxysm of haste, he tore off his ruined cloak and flung it over the body of the Hunter he had....

No. Looking away. Seeing the blooded lord-to-be sick, cut, needing a healer. He could help with that.

He made himself move to the boy's side, took him by the arm and turned him toward the healing chamber door. "Come away. We should see to your wound."

Andeved straightened up and wiped his mouth with the sleeve of his shirt.

"No."

"But you've been cut. You need a healer."

"No. They can't be finished in there with...with Kendle. No one interrupts that, not them," he did not look at the fallen Hunters, "and not us." He looked up at the Oni still standing. "Or what was this for?"

Movement and a moan. The messenger, still bound and gagged, struggled to free herself. With sudden urgency that tasted of relief, Andeved went to her and bent to untie the strips of rag that silenced and restrained her, then helped her to stand. Her legs were shaking, but then, so were his.

"They came in where the collapse made the opening." The messenger's voice was breathy with the remains of fear. "I shouldn't have led them down-outward. I knew it was the direction you had gone, but they..." She tried to glance at the fallen Hunters but could not.

Andeved kept hold of her arm, as much to steady himself as her. He reached out and carefully pulled the mask of office away from her face. "I know you. You are Leesil, Wellan's daughter. We had the same tutor for ceremonies class two seasons ago."

Leesil nodded. "I am. We did." She straightened up and carefully pulled her arm from his hold. "I am so very sorry. I didn't mean to... they had weapons of the flesh." She shivered. "Truly. I thought I would be dead. You saved my life."

"You are safe now. That is what matters." He found words and a direction had somehow risen for his use. "But we need your help, if you believe you can manage it."

Leesil nodded, her lips pressed in a grim line.

Andeved turned back toward the Oni. "There is no more reason for Brekkan and the quad to guard the entry hall. But they might bring a cart and straw to," a catch in his throat, "to remove the fallen. Yes?"

"Yes. Yes. But at least wrap your wound." Belwether tried to move farther into the hallway, but slipped on the bloody floor and had to grab at the wall to stay upright. "Though you must hurry. The funeral procession will start soon."

"Yes. And I must be there. For my cousin-friend, and to win the safety of us all."

Belwether stopped moving altogether and fixed his gaze on Andeved. An expression that mixed calculation and conclusion flowed over the Oni's face, leaving a deep knowing in his eyes.

It was in that moment Andeved knew that nothing was, for him, ever to be the same. Already distance built itself around him, the distance of the leader, the solitude of the one. It pierced his heart, but it steadied his legs.

X · X · X

"Here. Here." Aimree jabbed at a page. "Clearly, a flett will succumb to the same deep sleep as its host. And that means," she began to read aloud, "no movement or action other than those normally occurring during sleep can be brought by the creature in that state."

Golion, hunched over the opened volumes shoulder to shoulder with the tomeist, nodded in agreement. "This is what a healer hates to hear, but needs to know." He straightened up, stretching to loosen the knots in his back and moved to the raised table on which a quiet, determined Kendle lay, Mote and Hilly close by.

"Here is what we know and what we propose," Golion spoke slowly so that Mote could relay his words to Kendle. "Knowledge we now possess - great thanks to Belwether and his parents - informs us that, by constricting the feeding tubes... No, don't call them that." The marchale paused, fingers still against lips.

"Say, instead - by constricting the connection points it is highly likely the creature will instinctively release its complex bindings to the host. Just the precise amount of pressure at the proper point, applied long enough to distress the creature without injuring it, is required. Once loose, it will attempt to reconnect in a different and, to it, better place on the host. We will prevent the flett from that attempt and so it will, in essence, remove itself. This should avoid the damage force would cause."

Kendle brightened at that, unable to see the healer's grim expression as he continued.

"What the books also affirm, however, is that the creature will not struggle to release itself if it is under the influence of deep sleep. Because fletts...draw...from the host, it means the host cannot..."

Mote stumbled to silence, unable to go on. But Kendle, understanding too quickly, lost all brightness. Using the young marchale's shaking hand to cover her eyes, she took in ragged breaths.

Hilly, who stood by with a cloth soaked in sleeping potion, looked down at what she held, now worse than useless.

Hammin, standing guard beside the door, shook his head slowly side to side, like a great pained beast. Aimree turned away from the word-heavy pages, a deep frown creasing its way between her eyes. Only Golion presented a composed expression – until Kendle abruptly brought Mote's hand to her mouth and spoke. Clipped, urgent sounds.

"Do this now. Quickly. Before I lose the will to it." The stunned marchale blurted out his translation of the words, a mirror to Kendle's courage.

Golion moved closer to her, sharpening his attention to a deep focus. "Hilly, keep the prepared cloth at hand. Once the flett releases, Kendle may be put into sleep. Aimree, stay close to snatch the creature once it is freed. You will know how to handle it then, I trust. And Mote, keep hold of Kendle. It will be painful, but she must remain still enough for us to manage the doing of this."

No answers, only action. Mote caught hold of Kendle's arms, though whether his grip of her was tighter than hers of him was not apparent. Aimree shut all books but one. That one she kept open to a page with a drawing, bringing it over to where Golion could easily see it. Hilly took up a tray of needles, gut and salves, and laid down the soaked cloth for later.

Carefully, the healer set his fingers to probe where creature and host met. Avoid the flett's body – that would cause pain. Find instead the hollow horns that burrowed into flesh. Follow them down as far as touch could go. There. Now lean in against the tubes, harder until they give, flatten. Now hold just that way. And wait. Wait.

Kendle began to pull away from the pressure, moaning. Mote and Golion both kept hold. No movement from the flett.

Pushing down. Kendle's entire body went rigid. Pressing. Blood seeped from Kendle's eyes. She screamed. Unmoving flett. Unmoving flett.

Terrible bubbling sounds in Kendle's throat. From Mote a gasping sob. Silent, unmoving flett.

Beneath his finger, Golion felt the beginning of a tremor. A hideous wriggling. As if a rope were being snaked just under Kendle's skin. So slowly. Bringing up blood from the two holes, But, yes. Upward, outward.

"It comes. Be ready." The healer nearly shouted, though he did not lessen the pressure of his now blood-slicked fingers. Aimree tossed away the unneeded book. Took up a lidded, metal box.

Sound like corks pulled from jugs. Flicker of wings trying for flight. Banging of an iron lid being closed hard. Groan of Kendle sliding into unconsciousness. Tip, tip of a needle stitching up holes in flesh.

When, at last, what could be done had been done, there was a stillness in the chamber, a tentative quiet in which breath was caught, eyes were shut for a moment against the too bright images of blood and necessity that had burned them.

Mote carefully unwound himself from Kendle's arms. He discovered that his legs were ready to give out, as if he had run too far too fast. But there was one thing he had to do before he could rest. Shakily, he took a fresh cloth from Hilly's tray. Blotting away the drying blood from Kendle's eyes. Tenderly cleaning around two patched holes behind her ear, below the curve of her skull, where lately a creature had been. With the touch of light in a dark place, he smoothed back her hair. She never stirred as he did these things, though he thought, perhaps, her face lost some of the lines pain had drawn.

Wearily, the healers, the scholar and the defender set about to put the chamber to rights again. The box that held the unnatural killer was tied shut with strong knots and bitterness. Books were put away in packs. Muffled sounds of talking and moving outside the doors made for worry. For all that, the only choice now was to wait. Believing the best. Denying the darker fears that gibbered within. The seeming endless wait when action is done and only hope remains.

CHAPTER FOURTEEN

Seven grossfolk looked down at the straw they were spreading in the hallway, watching it sop up what remained after death had come and gone.

Brekkan and the other three marchales, profoundly sobered by the evidence of what they might have had to do, moved the bodies of the Hunters into the cart.

Belwether worked silently, knowing that the dark red beginning to stain the honey-colored straw was, in part, his doing. All the reasons why it had been necessary, inevitable and justified tumbled around in his head like boulders in a flood.

The messenger found she was becoming more and more angry, raging against On for sending killers, against the Hunters for invading her home and her own sense of self. Leesil threw down her fistfuls of straw with the fury that masks fear. The belief of her youth, that she was invulnerable, that she could always defend herself without betraying others, was gone.

Surety of stone. The words mocked Andeved while he watched the brittle straw soften as it drew blood into itself. Everything he had known, his understanding of where he stood in his world, had slipped sideways and it was proving exceedingly difficult to grab onto anything that felt solid, true, right. Yet, even in that uncertainty, a part of Andeved trembled with anticipation. Though much had been lost, much was now possible and he dared to believe he could be that Pivotal Piece the Oni seers once named him. Because he had also discovered how very dear the places and, even more, the folk of his life were to him.

With the cart now emptied of straw, Belwether dusted off his hands and looked over at Andeved, caught his eye, nodded once and turned away without a word. Back to the entry hall, to prepare the bodies of the Hunters for return to On. And to clean from his clothes and himself the stains of mortality.

"This duty done, we stand ready for the next, Lord Andeved." Brekkan, too, brushed off her hands, taking longer than the dust required. "Is there a possibility that other Hunters were sent, or that others will follow?" She heard both apprehension and resolve in her voice and wondered at the odd pairing.

"No, there should be no more Hunters for now, though once this is known, surely then more will be sent. I asked that of Aimree, and Belwether, even as we fled from their home to mine. To here." The words seemed to catch in Andeved's throat. But he drew in a breath and continued. "Even so, it would be of great value to us all if you would take over guarding the mender's chamber. Keeping those working within safe, whether from Oni or Underion threats, remains a serious task."

"Done." Brekkan motioned her quad members to positions at each end of the hallway. "And you will be here to intercede with your people? I believe they will not take kindly to strangers blocking the way to their own healing chamber."

Andeved shook his head. "No, but I will ask our messenger to stay with you. She knows what has happened and why the healers need to remain undisturbed." He turned to Leesil. "No better hands than yours for this."

"You are not staying here?" Leesil twisted her thoroughly bedraggled mask of office in her fingers. "You could explain better than any..."

"I need to join the funeral procession. That would clearly be the duty of," he paused to find a word, "a new-named Lord." That last was said with a sad hesitation.

"But there is a faction, led by your own father, that fiercely refuses Paell's naming." Color rose to Leesil's cheeks. "You are called exile. And worse. Stay here and your defense will look brave. Go toward them and you look brazen, arrogant."

Andeved shrugged, a bit of the boy showing through the man. "I think you may prove uncomfortably correct. Nevertheless, it is the best thing I can think to do. So..." He turned toward the up-inward direction of the corridor. "So..." His voice trailed away even as he squared his shoulders and started toward the uncertain illumination of the hallway's turning.

Bronzed with light mirrored in from the fading outer day, the stairways and halls were both familiar and strange. Andeved knew his way, by memory and by sight, and yet sight betrayed memory. Corridors that had once seemed endless, wide and high-vaulted now looked bounded, lowering. Once unfailingly constant, now only cut stone. The sense of loss that had, of late, been his unasked-for companion pulled down at him until he felt he would topple into deeps of dark. He reached the place to which his need to become clean had brought him.

The door was slightly ajar. He paused with his hand on the latch, feeling very much the intruder but wishing fiercely for the peculiar comforts of home. Stepped inside. Turning right, down the short hall, to his room. Ducking past the curtained entry. Startled to see that nothing had been changed. The books left untidy on the small desk were still stacked askew. Cover linens rumpled, bed unmade. A sock hung, limply alone, over the edge of an open drawer. What he wanted to believe was that his mother left all as it was awaiting her son's return. Likely she had just neglected the room, endlessly distracted by the oddments of her fecklessness.

Nonetheless, clean garments and an encounter with soap and water was the goal. It could be achieved. Andeved rummaged for items less wrinkled, taking them to the washroom. He stripped off his ruined clothes, scrubbed the stains from his skin. Scrubbed hard even after the water in the basin held all the red.

When at last he had wrapped his wound, was dressed in fresh clothes, mismatched socks and dry boots, he poured the last basin of wash water down the privy. And threw the blood-fouled clothing down after it. Let the gesh make of it what they would.

There was one more thing he needed and, for it, he went to the storage room that held those things not good enough or too good to be used day to day. In one of the trunks he found what he sought. Made from the shearings of younger goats, the vest was a soft pleasure to touch and a warm comfort to wear. It had been given to him not so very long ago by his cousin. Paell, late the lord of Under. Andeved ran his fingers over the deep-green dyed wool, tilted the polished shell buttons to catch the light. Wearing this now would be his visible respect, even if only he knew it to be that.

Worried that one and all would already have started walking the dead, Andeved hurriedly did up the last of the vest buttons and turned to leave, catching his boot on a pallet jammed against one of the walls. A narrow, hard but neatly made bed. The dim, cramped space that had reluctantly been made for Belwether, there among the dress clothes, dried fruit, unwanted gifts and dusty jugs of some past season's wine.

Andeved shifted uneasily, ashamed that it was only now he was truly aware of even the smallest part of what his Observer endured. Alone among the many. Deliberately relegated to small spaces designed to encourage invisibility. Unable to decide for himself how to spend a single hour. No other course but to walk behind another's destiny. All the same constraints against which Andeved raged in his own life.

It was so very clear at that moment. Obvious that the discomfiture he felt with Belwether was not only because of Andeved's rage at the necessary betrayals at the Chronicle Houses. No, it was the sharp contrast between what he and the Oni had made of the same obligations. From imposed attachment, Belwether had drawn loyalty; from forced observation, wisdom; from proscribed duty, strength of action; from restriction, boundaryless affection.

Had he done as well? Andeved thought not. He saw the boy he had been as reactive, given to fits of anger, irresolute. He yearned to lay those attributes at the feet of childhood and leave them there forever. A more encouraging accounting could be made of the young man he had been trying to become of late. Some actions of merit here and there, the great and recent goodness of friendships, moments of clarity before action, and somehow earning a word of admiration from Belwether.

A chiming of bells and a dimming light caught Andeved's regard. The Hour of the Last Turning. Time to light lamps, the work of the day done, the prospect of rest to come. In this case, a rest that would last forever.

Because the ceremony was bred into his bones, though the Ceremonialist recited in a distant room, he could hear the litany.

> "In the Hour of the Last Turning,
> The Lord of the Under reflects and remembers
> That beneath the above
> And over the below,
> The lives of the people turn
> With the tide and the light.
> Turned, turning.
> Hour of the Last Turning."

He voiced the reply aloud:

> "The lives of the people.
> Turning. Turning."

And then walked out of his childhood home toward the Chamber of Ceremony. To reveal his return, claim his naming, mourn his cousin.

X · X · X

Andeved had been forced to take a place near the head of the procession and it did not sit easily with him. The Chief Advisor stood on one side of him, silent and sad; his dithering mother on the other, babbling on and on about nothing of substance. He'd already shut out the often disrespectful mundanities she spouted in a whisper loud enough to be heard by most everyone near them. He felt well and truly alone in spite of being surrounded. And the warmth of the vest over his dress tunic was making him sweat. Which made his wound burn from the salty sweat trickling into the bandage.

The Ceremonialist was trying, in vain, to manage the crowd and the ritual. Though she wore the full mask of her office, it did not give her the power that all could hear from Sere. His voice cut through the milling folk, sending this one here and that one over there. Andeved winced as his father grabbed on to Paell's wrapped body, shouting at a clan leader tardy to the scene.

When the jostling was done, the people quieted, it began: The walking of the dead. His cousin's body, swaddled in bolts of gauze, rested on the shoulders of the clan leaders. The Ceremonialist found her voice and, though it was more tentative, less confident than the crowd expected, called out the words:

"Who is it we carry? Who shall we mourn?

Who was this Lord but one of our own.

Who, being born, is now being borne?

Who will be ever safe in the surety of stone?"

Into the silence came the response from all the people of Under crowded into the entryway of the long tunnel to the tombs:

"We know it is he. We knew long before.

Lord Paell as he once was, now is no more.

The lives of the people, turning, turning.

The lives of the people, turning, turning."

Andeved wanted to shout: Liars, stupid liars. You should have seen he was broken. Broken. But the agony in his heart made words impossible. It was just too late for his cousin-friend, for those of Under who marched in lockstep to the telling of the hours.

"Let the lanterns be lit, for we must travel where there is dark," the Ceremonialist called out over the heads of the crowd and glimmers of light blossomed like small flowers along the whole length of the procession. A drumbeat began. Measured. Steady. Slowly, the procession began, every swaying step in time to the beat. The only sounds were the thumps of the drum and the rustle of the walking.

Andeved kept his eyes fixed on the Ceremonialist's back and tried to forget who and what followed him. But he had determined to be the stubborn rebel even now. For he trudged toward the Cavern of Timelessness with a naked face, no mask to say what he was. Nothing to hide behind. And stepped in counterpoint to the crowd, his syncopated footsteps echoing strangely loud between drumbeats.

The tunnel to the tombs was long and cold and dark. Long before they arrived at the cavern's entrance, Andeved felt the haunting. Not the shiver of spirits or the ghosts of the dead. He did not believe such things existed. But behind him, the endless line of mourners had become almost a living thing, a darkly crimson snake. With needle sharp fangs, venom carried in hidden places, more and more strongly considering a strike. He shivered so violently, that he lost the rhythm of his step, nearly stumbled but for the hand that steadied him. Belwether was there of a sudden, then gone in the next moment, once again unseen in the shadows that flickered on the tunnel walls.

The quality of the sound and the silence changed from contained to uncontained, from tunnel to cavern, from the living to the dead. They had finally entered the Cavern of Timelessness, the distant, deep, cool and dry immensity that held the fallen of Under. Sere snapped at the other clan leaders, getting them to stop near the back of the cave, shouldering the other bearers until they took the positions he deemed correct. The immense procession reformed itself, with all orderliness, into a single line, somberly filing past the carried corpse, each Underion reaching up to just once, just briefly, touch that portion of gauze that covered Paell's head. Touch after touch after touch, until the wrapping became grimy. It took the better part of an hour and the entirety of Andeved's endurance before all had paid their respects.

The last time Andeved had been in this cavern, he had just lost his aunt and uncle, Paell's parents. Both at one time. He was so young then, so distraught, he might be forgiven for not remembering where they had been placed. And yet he could. There, head-high in the center of the cavern, the section of wall that would be seen first upon entering. The wall that looked so much like a honeycomb made by bees with no interest in sharp angles. Hundreds and hundreds of cylinders carved with gesh bile straight back into the rock, as long as a person was tall, each stopped up with a memorial stone plug - a hideously mundane name for such a thing - etched with names, family connections, the bright day of birth, the dark day of death. Except the one newest circle. Full of emptiness now, waiting to provide a last rest. Andeved shivered.

The Ceremonialist, wearing the deep gray robe and full mask of office, stepped up on the plinth in the center of the cavern. She held her hands, palms up, in front of her. The crowd, which had been jostling to find the best views, turned, every one, toward her and fell silent. She raised one hand and then let it softly fall on the other, back of the hand to palm. And again, and again until she held a steady rhythm like that of the water clock. Tap tap tap, tap. It was taken up by everyone else except those who bore the body, and Andeved who bore his own grief.

Over the collective tapping of time, the Ceremonialist began the antiphony of history:

"Beyond impassable mountains

Once was a grace-filled land of
Rivers, trees, fields and towns,
Our home as it had been.
Ash, poison, rage and death
Was what it had become.
Those of power fought for more,
Uncaring of those with none.
Dread and devastation were the
Spoils of their warfare.
Lands burned, seas boiled.
Women, men, children, all
Reduced to deadly dust
By the tyranny of mages."

And the tapping crowd responded:

"The lives of the people, turning, turning.
The lives of the people, turning, turning."

The Ceremonialist continued:

"In the dimness just before the dawn,
A meager few, a hoping few, fled.
Picked and bled a way across
The unforgiving mountain.
Through the smallest, cruelest, only pass,
They climbed and crawled their way.
The few of the few who made it through
Put the powder of destruction
Into the powdery snow,
Lit the very world on fire

And closed the only door."

And the tapping crowd responded:

"The lives of the people, turning, turning.
The lives of the people, turning, turning."

"We have learned the lessons of disaster.
 Learned them well:
Never forsake the surety of stone."

tap, tap "Never forsake."

"Never descend into formless chaos."

tap, tap "Never descend."

"Never submit to the tyranny of mages.

tap, tap "Never submit."

"Never yield to the power that tempts."

tap, tap "Never yield."

"Order, stability, safety and calm.
These are the virtues of Under
From the first to the last."

tap, tap, tap "From first to last
That we might last."

The Ceremonialist continued to lead the crowd in the tap of time while the guild leaders, who bore what had been Lord Paell, made their way toward the new-carved hole. With such care as they could take, the bearers pushed the wrapped body into the cylinder feet first. Pushed until only the slight grimy gauze that marked the many farewells could be seen. Then two wallworkers brought the memorial plug and hoisted it into place, tapping it tightly in with muffled hammers, pounding softly in time to the marking of time. When the wallworkers stepped back, their macabre mission completed, the Ceremonialist spoke the final words of the committing:

> "We, who have loved and lived
>
> Beside our Lord Paell,
>
> Commit him, who now needs no more surety,
>
> To the great unshaped and unending
>
> Void of timelessness."

A soughing, an almost contented sigh breathed through the crowd of mourners, as if it were a single, satiated beast. What was appropriate to be said, had been said. It had been orderly. That made them safe. But Andeved did not feel comforted or secure. The Ceremonialist was looking straight at him, motioning him to come forward. His stomach took a bad twist, his knees locked into place. He could not, would not, move. He knew what was coming next and wanted no part of it.

Someone gently took Andeved's arm. It was Chief Advisor Etcherelle, wearing her full-faced, blank-featured mask of office. A lantern lifted nearby and glinted off a shining tear that dropped from behind the edge of her mask. He knew that her sadness was for the person Paell. But he also knew that the tug she gave his arm was apologetically determined. Her whisper found him: "We are here for you, Andeved. We always have been, always will be." The words unlocked his legs and, with support from the Chief Advisor, he managed to walk to the central plinth and step up. Immediately, he felt the crowd's regard hard upon him with a relentless hunger for order, for safety and calm at all costs. The virtues of Under to which they aspired and from which they built their own prison.

The Ceremonialist spoke another ritual:

"Though we have committed a Lord of Under

To the void, Under will not feel that void,

for Paell was but the latest in an unending line.

As his predecessors before him,

He named an heir, the next to wear

The Mask of Office."

She held up the half-face mask of the Lord of Under. The pleybird feathers broken in the tragedy of Paell's final days, had been replaced. In the same order, at the same angle, of the same color. Andeved couldn't take his eyes away from it, remembering too well how Paell's trembling made the feather-ends tremble. No one else had noticed. Except the Fool.

"The Chief Advisor," Etcherelle began, "stands witness to the naming of the heir. As our much loved Paell lay dying, his mind at last clear of taint, knowing full well the burden it would be for the next in the unbroken order of Lords, he named Andeved, his cousin, his friend." Etcherelle had to pause and clear her throat. "This is that same Andeved, come to ensure that the people do not walk away Lordless from this place. See the office as it passes."

At that, the Ceremonialist placed the mask on Andeved, tying it securely at the back of his head, catching hair, painfully, in the knot. For a moment, Andeved was grateful for the mask, grateful that Under could not see his wince, his pooling eyes. Oh, mercy, there would be one who saw. But instead of battering him further, the thought gave him some strength. Strength enough to lift the mask and pull it away, along with some of his hair. He held it in front of him, trying not to find particular faces in the crowd that might keep him from what he had practiced in his mind to say in this moment.

"As ritual requires," Andeved was shocked at how weak his voice was, "this one takes the office as is required." He took in a deep breath for the next part. "But I will not wear the mask of office." Uneasiness rose from the people. "Paell, my cousin and my friend, wore it and it covered his illness and terrible decline. Because most did not want to see the person that struggled behind the mask. Most wanted a surety in this stone that did not depend on a mortal, fragile being. So the help that Paell needed could not get past the impassible mask. I am very young to be named, I know that. I did not want this office, you should know that. But since it is declared mine, I declare I will do this duty with a naked face. So we will truly see one another, and can truly help one another. That will be a deeper order than ordered hours, a stronger surety than any stone." He came to the end of his words, nearly breathless from the strain of speaking this rebelliousness, to find that the Chief Advisor and the Ceremonialist had each taken him by a hand. They lifted their hands, held them out before them like offerings and said, in unison, "There is a Lord of Under. This is the Lord of Under."

There was not a person, young or old, who did not know that those words ended the ritual of the passing. Yet it was a long time before anyone moved, before anyone turned to the homeward tunnel, but almost immediately, mutters and groans, questions and the staccato shuffling of incipient disorder echoed in the immense cavern.

X • X • X

By design the mender's chamber was kept brightly lit and dry. It did not depend on the turning mirrors that illuminated the rest of Under by day, nor were the cold and damp of season or night allowed to intrude. Lamps that glowed white had been lavished throughout the room, tended into evershining by apprentices who, by this duty, took their first lessons in perpetual readiness.

Enough warmth to drive away the dank was most welcome, but Hilly found a certain mercilessness to the glare. She could see all too clearly the gray paleness of Kendle's face, the two spots of darkness seeped into formerly colorless bandages, the eyelashes stuck shut by the remnants of pain. Ruthlessly dispassionate, the brightness refused to hide the deep concern on Golion's usually impassive face, or the coiled tension in Hammin's pacing and the tapping of Aimree's ink-stained fingers.

Only Mote had found a form of surcease. After he had cleansed what he could from Kendle's face and neck, he had climbed up on the table next to hers and, in a descent almost as abrupt as hers, fell into sleep. Hilly understood the marchale's exhaustion derived not just from physical duress, though that had been prodigious, but from an intensity of caring. How she hoped that both Kendle and Mote were healing in the depths of their slumber.

Of a sudden, Hammin stopped pacing. "I truly, truly hate - *hate* - not knowing. Can we at least crack open the door and see what is going on?"

"Possess yourself with patience, my dear," Aimree spoke over the drumming of her fingers. "And perhaps speak a bit softer so as not to wake those who rest."

Click. Rattle. Click-click. As if it knew what was wanted, the door creaked open. Just a bit. A hand, then wrist, then arm appeared. Hammin grabbed the arm and jerked the rest of the person into the room, ramming shut the door and leaning against it with his bulk.

"Hold. I only bring news. I swear." It was Brekkan. To the immense relief of everyone. Though the quad leader kept her hands open and raised until she saw recognition from each of those in the room who did not sleep.

"Apologies for the rough welcome," Golion began, "but I am sure you understand our caution."

"Of course. Most especially after seeing the end of an Oni hunting."

Across the room Aimree gasped. "The end. What does that mean? My son...?"

"Your son lives, as does Andeved. It is the Hunters who do not." A shadow passed over Brekkan's face.

Aimree rose from her seat at the book-strewn table, coming to where Brekkan stood, grasping her hands. "Then we owe you a great debt for what you have done for us."

"Not I. Nor my marchales." The quad captain paused, hesitant to impart the next of the news. "It was Belwether and young Andeved managed the doing of it. Though I would have spared them that deed had I been able."

Hammin shook his head in dread wonder. "How can this be? Hunters are honed to their duties, even to killing if it comes to it. My son knows nothing of that - and Andeved is but a boy."

"Yet it was done. And that measure of safety was won." Brekkan gestured in the direction of the hallway. "Now others come to enter this room. The menders of Under are returned from taking Lord Paell to his last rest. They come carrying a child taken ill, needing the tools and measures their healing chamber offers."

Golion and Hilly glanced at each other, an instant assessment of what was needed. And instant agreement.

"Of course the menders must enter." Golion spoke with his deserved authority. "We will assist if we can. It is only right."

Brekkan nodded, then added the last of her news.

"The menders know of Kendle's condition. It caused some consternation, Under having just walked their lord to his grave. The lord done down by a diseased flett. A gift of Over. As we are of Over."

The captain's words fell like stones into the room. She turned and pulled the door open wide.

In rushed a man holding a small boy in his arms, a woman at their side. Close behind came two of Over's menders who, with a minimum of words but a clear display of competent concern, indicated a table upon which the father laid his son.

From the far side of the chamber, Golion watched as the menders assessed the child, noting as they did the boy's flaming cheeks, wide dark-rimmed eyes and shallow breaths. High fever. Too common in the little ones, swift to strike and frightening in effect. Mortally dangerous if the cause could not be found and addressed.

But the child was in good care, for Golion had immediately recognized Head Mender Dawley as one of those attending. They had worked together to ease Paell's going and found mutual regard in the sad endeavor.

Addressing the illness is precisely what the Underions did. Cool cloths were brought and applied where the blood tides surged closest to the skin. Dawley peered into eyes, ears, throat, focused and thorough. The boy's parents, standing just out of the way with arms around each other, winced each time Dawley touched their son's arm, leg, or tipped the boy over to tap his back. It was all they could do to allow the examination, though they knew it was for the best. The fever-glazed child, not knowing the need, struggled feebly against the intrusion.

Then, in a quickness of confidence, Dawley pointed to several small angry-red spots just below the boy's knee. "This looks like a reaction to shreemoss sap. Has your son been near a moss hag?"

The mother knew immediately. "Yes, yes. The way we walk the dead had to be cleared in places for so many to go. Several sections showed new cuts in old growths. Ceeley could have brushed against shreemoss as we walked. But many folk could have done. No others were brought down with fever. Are you sure?" Father and mother alike bore the signs of that terrible complexity of anticipation and the deep call of blood to blood children make to parents.

Dawley gestured at his aide to fetch items from a dispensary. "A very few of us take badly to the sap. The lesions on Ceeley's leg and his high fever look very like this reaction. We'll know more as we treat for it." And with that the Head Mender applied an ointment to the inflammation. The aide had also brought a mug with water into which Dawley sprinkled a compound. He held the mug out to the parents.

"He needs to drink this, all of it, and I think he will take it better from one of you. It is not too much, and the taste is not unpleasant."

There was a small pause in which courage was gathered to do what yesterday had been mundane and unremarkable.

"Of course." The mother took the mug while the father held his son in his arms, bringing him upright so that the boy could drink. And the deed was managed, with words of comfort and encouragement uttered by parents to soothe both child and self.

"Excellent, very good. You did well." The Head Mender nodded in approval. "Now here is what we do next. We will bring stools for you to rest on while we watch Ceeley." He gestured again at the aide who bustled off to fetch the seating. "Look for his breathing to deepen, his skin to feel cooler. Keeping him calmly resting will help his body use its own strengths."

Though neither parent took their eyes off their child, they must have, in some deeper sense, understood Dawley's intent. Each took in a breath, worked to loosen the tension of their shoulders, and settled onto the procured stools. Golion smiled to himself at the Head Mender's compassionate cunning. No others know the child better than the parents - and no others so sorely need a task to blunt the edge of panic from the inevitable waiting.

Then Dawley walked over to the far ledge to wash his hands. And just like that, Golion became aware of what a physically comic figure the mender cut. Bandy legs supporting a paunch-heavy body with narrow shoulders topped off by a line-creased face and a bulbous nose. How had he not noticed this before? It would take some effort not to betray a reaction - especially now that the Underion was approaching the tables where Kendle and Mote lay.

But no drollery was possible, not even remotely, when Golion saw the Head Mender's grim expression. Behind him, Hammin stirred, taking a pace forward. Hilly moved closer to Kendle. In the three breaths it took for Dawley to reach him, Golion had gone from cautious calm to foreboding.

"How dare you allow...this--" Dawley hissed, gesturing toward the company attending Kendle.

"This?" Golion startled at the vehemence of the Head Mender's tone. "What is this but bringing someone ill to a place of healing? Just as you brought the boy. It is what you and I do, Head Mender. What the heart and the mind of a healer compels."

"No, it is vastly and terribly different. Murder entered Under when you, an outsider, allowed these fugitives and thieves entry. Our young messenger tries to say the act is defensible. But nothing warrants weapons against flesh. There is taint among us now that never was here before. On you is all the guilt. You and the dark hearts of Over." Dawley clenched and unclenched his fists, struggling to stay articulate in the grip of his rage. But he could only spit out the last words. "Get out. All of you. Take those stolen archives with you. They can only draw more death."

Mote stirred, roused by the shouting. "What is happening? Kendle? Is she...?" He sat up, remainders of fatigue slurring his speech.

"She still sleeps," Hilly spoke with a quiet urgency that made Mote's eyes widen. "But much has happened and we are being told we must leave. All of us. Now."

"But why?" The young marchale rubbed his eyes. "Kendle cannot be moved. She is deeply wounded. Do the healers know we are being told to leave?"

"It is the Head Mender demanding it, Mote." Golion's voice held a sharp edge of accusation. "Turning away the sick, refusing the curative knowledge we have brought. I cannot fathom it."

Dawley bristled at his peer's words. "Refusing knowledge? Not so. Only refusing stolen volumes of flett lore. Which is knowledge none of Under would ever have needed if Over had not brought a blighted creature to infect our Lord Paell." The mender bit down on his words. "The late Lord of Under. Driven to madness and death by Over's gift."

"Water." A cracked voice feebly interrupted. "Please, water."

Comprehension of what the raspy request meant came quickly to Hilly, Golion, Aimree and Hammin. But especially to Mote, who jumped off the table where he had slept and took back his position at Kendle's side, his eyes now wide open.

"I can understand you again. Can you understand me? Please say you can."

Though Kendle's eyes remained shut, a small, and to Mote incredibly lovely, smile alighted on her lips.

"Yes. Oh, yes." She breathed out the words most desired. Around her, the companions of her trials sighed with relief. Hammin was brought to tears which he brusquely wiped at with his sleeves. Hilly brought a mug of water and, helping Kendle hold her head upright, gave her the drink so clearly requested. Then she produced a damp cloth and began gently to clean the sticky residue of milky tocsin from Kendle's eyes.

Head Mender Dawley, who had barely restrained himself while the others clustered around Kendle, waited no longer. "She is awake. There is no need to be in this place any longer. Leave. The surety of stone is not yours now or ever."

Hefting her pack onto her shoulders, Aimree strode toward the obdurate mender, shaking her finger at him the whole while. "You, sirrah, have authority over this healing chamber and the care of your own patients, but you cannot speak for the whole of Under. Unless Under's new named lord decrees it, we will not be made to flee. Not while our own patient is still in a state too fragile for it. I will gladly take the offending books away, but Kendle stays."

"Wait." Kendle fought to get off the table and stand upright. Her battle went badly and she began to fall, dizzy with still perilous wounds. Mote caught her, bending to support her almost entirely.

Kendle blinked. "Look. I can open my eyes. I think, with some help...if it is best...I could travel."

"Don't be foolish," Mote blurted out his distress. "You are not well enough."

"Listen to your marchale," Hilly stepped between Golion and Dawley, but addressed Kendle. "You should not take the road yet. Nonetheless, there is good reason for the rest of us to leave." She glanced at the importunate mender. "Those few, very few 'dark hearts' you accuse from this distance have only now been revealed. The discovery of their corruptions has thrown the *good* folk of Over into disarray in much the same way Under strives to acknowledge your late Lord's madness. You wish us gone so that you might protect the lives here in your charge. So be it. But Kendle stays. She is as much in your care as any other here who seeks your healing."

Hilly's pronouncement stunned Golion as well as the Head Mender. But it was Golion who recovered first and, his jaw set in a stubborn line, grabbed his travel pack and slung it over his shoulders.

"Indeed, we will need Brekkan and her marchales with us. But Kendle and her companions are under Lord Andeved's protection and will stay."

Before Dawley could protest, Golion and Hilly made for the door, collecting Brekkan and her quad on their way out.

A mountain moved in the room. Hammin, his face a study of pure determination, swept Kendle up in his arms. "Make a path for us, Mote," the big man rumbled. "Find us a chamber that does not contain such a molluck-headed coward."

Kendle turned into Hammin's chest, allowing him to carry her out the door, into the hallway, startling the still present messenger. Hammin followed Mote into the up-inward hallway, but they began to hesitate at each intersecting corridor. Quickly enough Mote felt the need to get a better sense of direction. Though he was reluctant to press her, he knew Kendle had been up and down, inward and outward along the labyrinthine passages of Under when in the Lady Arrant's party. Or in Andeved's company.

"Kendle?" Mote touched her shoulder, trying to be gentle but needing to connect. "Do you recognize where we are?" No response. "Are we headed in the right direction?" Kendle stirred, but kept her head tucked into Hammin's chest. "Is there a place we can safely wait for Andeved?"

Kendle's mouth opened. Closed. Opened to say, "I don't know. I can't tell."

"Does anything look familiar?"

"I don't know, Mote." Tears began to fall from Kendle's wide-opened eyes. "Though the world is no longer gray-white, it has become dark. I am still blind."

From behind them a voice came, hesitant. "I know a place that might serve."

CHAPTER FIFTEEN

The rebelliousness of his earlier years had, at least, provided Andeved some useful skills. He was employing one at that moment: Hiding in the shadows, an art he had studied to improve by observing Belwether's perfection of it. Looking down a lesser used hallway and through an open door, he could see arrayed before him the most of Under's folk. Evening lamps made the huge refectory glow golden, their light catching the hominess and, even among the many, intimacy of sharing the memorial meal. Foodists brought platters laden with still sizzling roasts, bowls heaped with cool, crisp fruits, boards warm with yet uncut loaves of bread whose yeasty redolence nearly brought Andeved to his knees with memories of the past and the hunger of the now.

At spots along the trestle tables families clustered, oldest and youngest in no ordained order save that of companionability or care. Some benches held guild members having animated trade-talk between mouthfuls. At this dinner, since it followed the walking of the dead, small silences, like the scudding shadows of passing lanterns, moved from place to place as an honor to the departed. Here and there, solemn toasts were made, stories were told of the man and the leader now gone from their midst, while others could not bring themselves to words and let quiet speak for them. This night, however, there was also a bitter taste of tension in the meal.

There, in a far corner, Andeved saw those he both dreaded and desired to find. Their heads together, turned away from the rest of the room, were the leaders of the guilds. One among them Sere, Head Terracetender, his father. Even from this distance, the glowering presence that had pervaded his childhood was too easily recognizable. As usual, Sere leaned back from the knot of his peers, arms crossed, mouth turned down, eyes half shut. It made the heat rise to Andeved's face just to see the way his father managed to exude rage without using any words.

But there, in the shadows, motionless and unnoticed, the breath was shocked out of Andeved. For with a terrible and instantaneous clarity, he saw himself outside the Chronicle House, posed in the same way, wordlessly raging. Like father, oh, mercy, like son. So it came to him with a rush: as he had been, so was Sere. Beneath the fierce anger lay fear. His father was now, and had been for a very long time, afraid.

"This reunion will likely take a grievous toll." Belwether's rumble startled him more than ever before. "But best it is witnessed."

"What are you doing here?" Andeved shook his head. "I thought we agreed it would be safer for you to be elsewhere. No Oni will be welcome now. May even be," he struggled for the words, "may even be actively unwelcomed."

Belwether looked away, as if there were something too bright to behold. When he looked up again, compassion had softened his expression and there was a touch of sadness in his eyes.

"Understanding just makes it so much harder, does it not? To acknowledge the needs masquerading as whims, the dread festering beneath anger, shallow sentiment instead of deeper and riskier emotions shakes us profoundly. How much easier it would be to purely despise, to never doubt the righteousness of our own calculations and wield good, as we see it, like a club."

Andeved sighed deeply. "I want to storm the walls, denounce the breach, collect vindications like treasure. Because there is wrongdoing, there is good to be gained, evils to be redressed."

"Yes. Yes, and you will work toward those aims, my Lord." Belwether hazarded a smile. "And you will come much closer to that which is worthy if you never cease to assess how you translate good into the deeds of each day." He shook his head. "Which advice I wage a daily battle to follow myself."

That made Andeved smile, too. But it was wiped away by the sight of someone at one of the nearest tables pointing straight at him. Then others glanced his way, whispering to those nearby. Whispers that spread through the refectory in waves. Shadows failed him and he was left exposed to the merciless gaze of the public eye.

In the center of his heart came a strange peacefulness, a welcome quiet. He did feel his heart race, his palms sweat, his chest labor to take in breaths. But he could view those things from a place of calm observation. Time slowed, then sped, then stopped, then began again as Andeved directed himself forward. He watched himself walk between the long rows of tables, acknowledging those who greeted him, noting the scowls of those who did not.

He saw Etcherelle rise from a far corner, beginning to make her way toward him. The part of him which found time malleable gave thoughtful assessment as to whether it would be politic to have the Chief Advisor near him in this. He relayed his decision against that by a slight motion of his hand. Her eyes widened, then she stopped where she was and watched him with unwavering focus.

The guild leaders, long practitioners of crowd reading, heard the change in the collective dynamic. They ceased talking amongst themselves and turned to discover what was happening. Andeved, seeing them begin to stand, readying themselves for words, knew the moment must become his now or it never would. With an almost painful clarity, he found a brighter casting of light, laid a steady hand on the shoulder of a woman nearby to ask if space might be cleared on the tabletop, enough that he could climb up on it and be seen and heard by the whole of room.

Without hesitation she nodded and then directed her near-seated family to push aside the mugs, dishes, platters and bowls. She, herself, rose from her seat on the bench and indicated he might use the space as a step up. Throughout the brief moments of arrangement, Andeved read the language of her motions, her words, her eyes - and found that, beneath the sense of community that prompted accommodation, lay a suspension of opinion, a hope for and fear of what was to come that balanced the scales of thought into uneasy neutrality.

Years of pleading a case to authority for the turns of his youth, cajoling and humoring those who might give him what he needed, stoically taking deserved and undeserved punishments, learning to read the moods of his mother and father, all this flooded Andeved and informed him. With no outward sign that he did so, he found the brighter light of a large lamp overhead, calculated the range of the tabletop, noted that his father was stalking toward him, saw that Belwether remained at the far doorway, heard murmurs rise and then fall.

Now.

"Thank you for the honors undertaken today in remembrance of Lord Paell. I loved Paell. He was family to me and, in younger years, close companion in the way of a much admired older brother. But my cousin fell under an illness. A disease of the mind. I could not bring myself to speak aloud of his peculiar behaviors. By looking away I told myself I shielded him. In truth, there was just not enough bravery in my boy's heart."

Andeved paused, turned toward another side of the refectory. The side where, along the far wall, the guild leaders stood.

"None of us had enough bravery. So that this seeming kindness brought us, by twisted and unacknowledged paths, to bring our world down upon itself. We overbred the gesh in a desperate hope that the rich soil their bile and our stone combined to create could nourish crops enough to feed us all. When that faltered, instead of naming and solving the crisis, we simply did more of what had been a failing: carved out stone for soil until the stone itself could stand no more. Look only to the rubble of the upper level to find evidence of the deaths our stubbornness brought us."

Through the room, uneasiness stirred. Folks shifted on their benches, frowned, looked away from those seated near them. Andeved's father stopped short as if he had been had struck by a blow.

"Likewise, when Under made an alliance of betrothal with Over, Paell's madness was deliberately hidden so that the negotiated access to seeds, timber and the meat and labor of mollucks might not be upset. Did this kindness serve us well? Those we might have asked were done to death in the dealing. The Lady Arrant, our Lord Paell, the crushed wallworkers."

The hearts of the people balanced on a blade's edge.

"You know me well. I have cadged second servings from every Foodist, talked past Terracetenders to find daylight and ripe sweetrounds, heard the same lectures as every child of Under does in the wake of a prank gone public, haunted the dusty stacks of Under's archives, at an early age became an Attached. You and I passed in the corridors, ate at the same table, said together the turning of the hours."

Rueful nods. A few fond chuckles.

"Until the day my cousin bid me go to Over on his behalf. To spy out the secrets others kept. He feared for us and for that which, in his clouded mind, he believed was now his: the whole of Under, *and the entirety of Over.*"

Murmurs swept across the room. Here and there were heard louder exclamations of dismay, surprise, denial, rebuke. "He lies." "The boy is mad." "Let him speak." "What does this mean?" "Take him down." Andeved gathered it all and made from the conflicting tangles a sense of the whole, with an awareness of those outliers whose reactions defied reason: blank stoniness, hands curling into fists, shouts that battered against him.

"It was madness that took Paell from the duty of a Lord to the imperiousness of a king."

Several of the guild heads, including Andeved's father, once again started pushing toward him. Though they had to shove their way through the agitated crowd, their progress toward him seemed inexorable and malignant. With the urgency born of imminent brutality, Andeved took in a deep breath and, raising his voice to carry even to the walls, spoke into the storm.

"But you and I are not mad. We would not plot to take another's home, deceive those who have what we covet, or violate the telling of other's hours."

Those who were forcing their way toward Andeved renewed their efforts, more violently than before as there were now those who tried to block them, those who called out for calm, for order. Now the progression was marked by the shattering of plates, the screech of benches shoved along the stone floor, cries of unexpected pain.

"The secretholders of Over fashioned a flett intentioned to make our lord malleable in benefit of their own needs. Yet the creature served us well. It tried, desperately, to heal Paell. It could not save the flesh, but when it was removed it took with it the dark disorder of Paell's mind. At the end, the remnants of reason, the tattered banner of a noble lord, again rose to the light. He could love us again as once he did. Could see the truer, higher--"

The table Andeved stood on was shoved. He waved his arms in a struggle to keep his balance. Somewhere in the mass, a child laughed at the ungainliness. And that single sound, which in a different hour might have been a balm, broke the restraint of community. Shouts turned incoherent. Andeved's father reached him and grabbed his leg. A mug, then a bowl were thrown. The mug hit his shoulder. The bowl missed but struck the woman who had made him a place. Blood began to flow from her head.

A carving knife flashed through the golden lamp light, turning over and over in its seeming languid flight. End over end. Bits of meat, like small predictions, dropping away as it soared. Finding Andeved at the same moment his father pulled his leg out from under him.

It was a surprise to be falling. Unexpected to look down at a blade buried in his flesh. Only when his head met the stone of the floor was he dazzled by pain. And that was but for a brief and terrible moment for, swifter than the taking of breath, darkness found Andeved and he knew no more.

X·X·X

Mote had begun to hate the unyielding stone of Under. It did not sway in counterpoint to his footfall as bridgeways did. The corridors smelled of damp and dust so that he longed for a deep breath of breeze-tossed, loam-scented air. The only green to be found in these endless halls was the feeble luminescence of jinncar moss that, to him, shone like the color of unripe apples--the kind that made you sick.

And still they moved deeper into the darker halls. It was noticeably colder this far back, cold enough his breath misted. Even held tight against Hammin's chest, Kendle had begun to shiver uncontrollably. His concern, never dormant in this unyielding place, rose even higher. Had he been wrong to trust the messenger? Where was the girl leading them?

"Here. In here." Leesil ran ahead and began to push on high, wide metal doors that looked too massive to be moveable. Yet they swung inward with only the slightest touch. Through the opening came a soft exhalation of warmth. Yellow-orange light flickered cheerfully in a large pot-bellied stove just past the doorway, though it cast only a limited circle of illumination beyond which was featureless dark.

Still, any reservations Mote had melted in the prospect of putting Kendle in front of a well-stoked fire.

Hammin and Aimree must have felt the same way, for they followed Leesil without a moment's hesitation. Aimree spotted padded benches and cushioned chairs that she quickly arranged into a soft, warm bed upon which Hammin gently settled Kendle. Mote laid his cloak over her, gratified to see she had already stopped shivering.

"Bonn. Bonn," came the toll. Leesil had taken up a metal bar and hit a large hollow cylinder. The sound drifted back, disappearing into darkness. It took a while for echoes to commence, a sure sign the place was immense.

Mote ran over to the messenger and grabbed the bar from her hand. "What have you done? Raised an alarm?" In his anxiety, he had raised the rod. Leesil shrank from him.

"No, no. That calls the archivist to us. This is Under's archives. It's the safest, most--" she struggled to find the right word, "--the most overlooked place in all of Under."

From the shadows beyond the firelight came a voice. "Indeed, that is true. Quite sad, really, but quite correct." The old archivist emerged into the light, his long robe swirling up dust as he walked.

"Ah, Bertrynd," the messenger shivered in relief. "Who knew we would see each other again so soon?"

"Though I think you do not bring a message," the archivist eyed the four strangers, "strictly speaking at any rate."

Aimree could not contain herself. "Archivist? Under has archives?"

Bertrynd tilted his head, looking very much like a tall, curious bird. "Yes, of course." He waved his hands vaguely about. "A modest collection of books, scrolls, exhibits, documented experiments, artifacts. Not that many folk find their way down-inward to see them."

"We had no idea Under had such a thing." Aimree's eyes were brighter than the firelight. "I am a tomeist, myself. Do you think... would you...well, might you show me the archives?"

"A tomeist? How unexpected. And how entirely pleasant." The archivist clapped his bony hands together in elation. "Allow me to bring up the lamps so that...."

"Wait, wait." Mote interrupted before Bertrynd and Aimree were completely lost in their scholar's rapture. "First measures first. You must know how matters stand if you are to grant us sanctuary."

"How matters stand? Let me see," the archivist folded his arms across his chest. "Lord Paell has passed, naming Andeved as heir. Under is divided into opposing factions that, now the funeral obligations are done, may well become, shall we say, heated." He shook his head ruefully. "You all, saving our good messenger here, have been a company. Companions to an Underion and that choice has brought you, outsiders all, here under what must be dire circumstances. The Underion is Andeved, unless I miss my guess." He paused for a moment to gauge the reactions of the group that stood before him. "Am I close to the mark?"

Leesil was the first to recover speech. "How could you know all that? Messengers only brought news of Lord Paell's death. Nothing more. No one comes here. You don't leave. How...?"

"I have my ways, child." Bertrynd smiled, and the smile showed some pride along with the reassurance it was primarily intended to convey.

Leesil looked down at the mask she clutched in her hand. It was beyond bedraggled after the rough handling she had recently received. With a shrug and a sigh she threw it away into a dark corner, of which there were many in the fire lit foyer. "Pointless face covering. It seems we messengers were sent on fool's errands when we came here."

"No, not a fool you. Each message brought me value with it. You did not tell me news as much as the weight and import of that news. For that service, I was and am grateful."

Mote, even more fretful than before, interrupted the archivist. "Yes, yes. But there is more. Belwether breached the knowledge stores of On and took volumes of flett lore from the great Chronicle Houses. He did it to save Paell and to--" Mote's voice broke as he gestured toward the sleeping Kendle, "--to save this lady of Over from a flett made to hunt and kill her." He took in a breath. "Though it was too late for the healing of Paell, the knowledge brought in the volumes and in the person of Belwether's mother," he swept a hand toward Aimree, "did keep Kendle from death."

Bertrynd had gone pale with Mote's recitation. Now he brightened. "Then the knowledge came in time to be of good help, yes? It is the reason, truly, information is gathered at all."

"Perhaps that once was true." Hammin's rumble reverberated in the antechamber. "But now it is kept for other reasons: dominance, control, the insidious pursuit of power. The Houses of On are most deadly determined to reserve their knowledge. They sent Hunters to ensure it could not be shared. Even to the murder of those whose need for it was greatest."

Bertrynd blanched. "Oni Hunters? Following Andeved here? We must take steps, make a plan..."

"Too late," Mote's tone was grim, his eyes dark with what they had seen. "Hunters came for us. Found us at the healing chamber." He glanced but barely at Leesil, who flinched at the reproach. "The lordling and his Oni protected us. At the cost of their own blooding."

"Andeved has murdered?" Bertrynd hissed the question.

"No." Mote nearly shouted. "Not murdered. Killed those who sought to murder, so that we would live. These books, these archives - they are not idle collections of careless thought. They codify what can be, and what can be made to serve. Who, and what, they serve..."

A thinly stretched whisper slipped into the dim light. "Where are we?" Kendle, awakening, asked. "Is it safe here?"

Mote looked hard to the master of the archives.

"That is the question of the moment. Is it safe here?"

The chamber entire held its breath for the response.

CHAPTER SIXTEEN

There was no thought in what Belwether did. His body took over, pushing him through fists, knees, elbows, feet: an aimed determination parting the milling chaos. He rammed past a woman who was using a platter as a shield, gentled by a father carrying a child to safety. The closer he came to where Andeved had fallen, the more densely pressed the crowd.

"Aside! Aside!" But words did nothing. His head down, he put his shoulders into it, made himself a rock hurled against living walls. Until at last he broke through and saw what took his breath from him without a blow being struck: Andeved, motionless, held in his father's arms. Some nearest them cried out: "The heir has been killed." "Find a mender." Others shook their fists, shouting, "Murderer." "Usurper."

Struggling with the weight of his son, Sere heaved himself to his feet and lurched forward only to be blocked by those who would protect and those who would condemn. "Help me. My son--" Here, somehow, the Oni and the father saw one another. His eyes wild with pleading, Sere cried out through the terrible madness of the crowd to Belwether alone. "He still breathes."

Belwether needed no more. He motioned Sere to follow and turned again to ram, shove, push and plough a way through the feckless throng. The battle to gain the doorway had its costs, but the Oni did not stop to count them. Light shifted, he stumbled forward, caught himself. A corridor stretched before him. They had achieved the hallway. He turned around, desperate to know if Andeved had been carried through. Yes. There, in the grip of the sweating, gasping Head Terracetender was the boy. Knife still protruding, blood oozing over his father's arm to drip onto the cold stone floor.

Belwether caught in a rasp of breath and tried, with the frenzy of haste, to take Andeved from the tiring father. But Sere roared defiance and, though his legs trembled with effort, lunged forward. Now a few people who had managed to fight through the doorway made a vanguard, urging the laden father toward the not too distant Council Chamber. Someone he did not recognize grabbed Belwether's arm, wrenching him forward as well. "Do not trust him," the unknown man hissed into the Oni's ear. "Stay with them." And he roughly shoved Belwether down the hallway, then turned back to close the door to the refectory and, with several others, lean hard against it, buying time.

Confusion layered itself on top of Belwether's already roiling dread. *Distrust whom? Sere? Andeved? Someone else yet to come? Who was so brave or so foolish to believe they knew him, knew his heart enough, to direct him so?* But no questions of the mind stopped the Oni's feet from propelling him to the Council Chamber. He just managed to get into the room before the door was slammed shut behind him and a heavy bench was pushed in front of it, blocking any further entrances. At least for a time.

Sere had staggered to the immense council table, but could not make his arms unlock. Several of the dozen folk who had herded, guarded him this far took over. One appeared to be a mender, for she issued commands with that kind of authority. "Bring cloaks, vests, anything that can pillow the boy and cover him for warmth. Tauven, go down to the Mender's Chambers and get me a wound kit. And bring back others to assist. Light that lamp - I need to see.

Get Sere to sit down over there. Keep him clear." And then: "The boy still breathes. Give me room to work."

Belwether knew he should be relieved, hopeful - and he was. Andeved was getting care. Perhaps in time. Everything he could do he had done. But still his hands trembled with helplessness. There was nothing for him now but to wait for whatever would be. Every lesson he had learned in becoming a disinterested observer fell away. When the mender felt around the place where the knife had entered Andeved, pain cut through his own chest. As the mender grasped the knife, tugged once, again, and then pulled the offending blade out, he groaned for the pale, motionless boy.

"Ah, that is better than I thought," the mender muttered. Then she turned to grab the arm of a man who stood nearby. "Here," she ordered, "use this cloth to hold the bleeding." She cut away Andeved's shirt, which brought a concerned "Oh" and a quick moment of assessment when the slash across his chest was exposed. Nonetheless, she brought the man's hand toward the knife wound. "No. Here. And do not push down too hard. The knife stuck in the bone that runs across the upper chest. Too much pressure and the bone may break."

The mender stepped back and, shoving aside any in her way, went around to the other side of the table. She cautiously approached to view the place on Andeved's head oozing a wide, dark ribbon of blood. "Hmmm," she murmured in the tone menders have that strikes dread in those who hear it.

With fingers trained to explore the worst of circumstances, the mender touched the edges of Andeved's head wound. Her focus was intense, her mouth a thin, grim line. Belwether could not breathe. Time ceased. Light dimmed, blurred. He ached to hear the mender speak, and despaired of hearing the words.

Sere leaped up from the seat imposed on him by the mender's orders. "Speak! Speak!" His agitation burst out in demands. "Will he live? Will he wake? Tell me. Now. Speak!"

"Hold." The man nearest Sere grabbed him. "Let the mender do her work."

But Andeved's father would have none of it. "It is not your son, Duggins, lies between light and dark. It is *mine*. *My* son."

Flushing with anger, Duggins yanked Sere farther away from the sadly burdened chamber table. "The same son you vomited into the outerness like a sickness? *That* son, terracetender?"

Sere recoiled, his face losing all shade but a paleness so abject as to look almost green in the high-lit brightness.

"Ignorant wall-worker, *apprentice* Duggins." Sere's fury made him almost breathless. "Judging me by the platitudes you hold as truth? You know nothing, nothing. I send my son where I will, why I will." He leaned in so close to Duggins' face that the wallworker stepped back in alarm. "You are as demented as Paell was, small man, for the people have taken on the madness of their leader. All but I. I alone require the guild leaders - idiots - to fulfill their duties. It is I keep the populace fed, the hours told, the tomorrows possible."

Across the chamber a man, so like an older Duggins that he could only be a brother, shouted: "That is your madness, old man."

Sere spun toward the cry, pulled short by the wallworker's vise grip on his arm.

Belwether startled at the violence of the action and the accusations. Nothing seen or heard during his years in Under presaged this ripping away of public masks, or that such passion lay so close beneath the placid structure of everyday.

"I am mad, Chasen?" Sere spit the words toward Duggins' brother.

"Aye, old man. Mad to take the lordship for yourself. It is power you want, Head 'Tender. The abuse of which I daily suffer working in your visq-fowl coops."

"You *suffer*," Sere drew out the word in a sneer of derision, "because your incompetence deserves it. How else are the gormless brought to a state of use? So intoxicated with your own self you are unable to grasp the workings of the world. The late Lord could not, he was mad. My wife, presumably next to be heir, is a...a pleasant moron. And our son, who lies on this table: irresponsible, immature, incapable of leading anyone anywhere. Truly, hen-keeper, who of the bloodline - Paell, Glitter, Andeved - would best serve you?"

The mender straightened up from her station at Andeved's head, and that action brought all attention to her. "May I remind you that there is a cruelly wounded boy here who may, or may not, wake and live. We can only wait for what will be. But be warned, your shouting is no curative. Take your battle elsewhere while those of us who care to heal work on."

Belwether forced himself to fade back, desperate to be overlooked in the mandated exodus. He flattened himself against the wall as Chasen pulled the bench away from the doorway and then went to help his brother drag a flailing, protesting Sere past and out the door. He sought shadow as Tauven returned with the demanded wound kit and two others, one of whom was Head Mender Dawley. Hardly dared to breathe, so great was his need to stay. Should Andeved...nay, *when* Andeved woke, he would be near. This he owed the young man. This and more.

X • X • X

Hammin had always thought himself immune to what he, in childhood, called 'the squirms'. He could look on things foul or disgusting, the creeping or the crawling, the fetid or merely hugely distasteful with equanimity. Not so for this. While they were only desiccated flesh and bones pinned to a board, something about the dissected fletts was thoroughly unsettling. It would not do for the others to realize how undone the displays made him, so he loudly declared his intention to stand guard. Somewhere else.

Not that Aimree and Bertrynd actually noticed his discomfort. Or remembered that, tucked above his ear, he had a live version of those flayed carcasses. The two scholars huddled over a wide study table far back in the depths of the immense archives, completely absorbed in the books, scrolls, stone tablets, jars, boxes and artifacts. When the rest of their company learned that Kendle was still blind, albeit in a softer darkness, the archivist admitted to some stored lore. Aimree had hefted the volumes they had brought. And, swift as turning a page, the two of them had disappeared down rows and aisles lit where they went by hanging globes.

Hammin sighed. It was inevitable that, once permission had been given to shelter here, his wife would not be able to resist seeking out what she did not know. As long as he had been with her, the pull of that desire was as strong as her need to give that knowledge back in useful form. Perhaps in a form that would restore Kendle's sight.

At least it would be easy to find his way back to the warm stove. He just had to follow the track of illumination back to the entrance hall. It reminded him, in an odd way, of following a blazed trail. Except that the only trees here had been shredded and pressed into paper long ago.

When he turned the last row-end and came again to the warmth of the stove, Leesil nodded at him but continued to address Mote and Kendle.

"He's a season younger than I so we were seldom together in classes or such. But Andeved always looked to have...how to say this...a very strong sense of self. At least that is how it seemed to me."

Kendle smiled. "Aye, it seemed that way to us as well." Then her smile turned into a more somber expression. "Though he has been sorely tested of late. Of that there is no doubt."

Mote shivered, in spite of the stove's radiating heat. "When what you know in your blood and bones to be real, to be the certain way of things, changes..."

The young messenger covered her face, her hands rubbing hard. "It burns, like gesh bile on rock. And I hated seeing it. Seeing myself betray you. I never thought... I dreamt myself strong, but when the moment came, I acted the coward. And seeing the killings, the too much blood and the emptying eyes of the dying."

Hammin felt his heart breaking for the young woman so recently met. And for Kendle and Mote. For the lordling, and his own much loved son. This is how wisdom starts, he thought, with the discovery of how much it costs to take that perilous road. He moved to where Leesil sat hunched over in her desolation and put his hand gently on her head.

"The folk I love the best, admire the most, are their own most severe judges. It is why I trust them with my own heart."

Leesil looked up, her face fresh streaked with tears. Hammin kept his hand softly where it was.

"You did all that you knew to do," the big man willed his deep voice to be an audible comfort. "Now you know more, though the knowing of it was thrust violently on you. There is a journey of worth before you. Do not let the darkness take that away."

"Darkness," Kendle sighed, "I know some of that. It means I will not see your face, Leesil. Nor the great trees of Over, the melded greens and blues of sky and grass reflected in a pool." Now her voice trembled. "I will no longer see those who are dearest to me." She lifted her hand. Mote touched it.

"For this, I hate the darkness." Kendle's voice strengthened. "Despise what it seeks to do. But just because I cannot see what I most love does not mean it is gone." Pounding on the archive doors. Hammin hands turned into fists. He frantically searched for anything that might protect them. The long metal bar used to ring the entry bell was the only thing he saw. He grabbed it, hefted it once to test its weight, and moved toward the doors.

"No, no." Leesil rushed past Hammin and placed herself in his way. "Let me see who this is. I am of Under and will not draw unwanted notice."

Hammin's eyes must have betrayed his doubt, for the messenger gestured toward the side of one of the huge doors.

"I'll only open it the smallest bit." Her tension, and her earnestness, displayed themselves openly. "And you can stay hidden and be ready. In case."

Behind him Hammin heard movement. He turned to see Mote and Kendle slip into the shadows. Silently, he nodded and planted himself, like a living doorstop, two paces in front of the entry.

Leesil undid the bar and cracked open the door, peering out into the hallway.

"Oh, it's you."

The sound of a voice, indistinct. A man's - young man perhaps from the timbre of it. Hammin could only clearly hear Leesil's side of the conversation.

"Yes, I came to bear words to the Archivist but have yet to find him in these endless shelves. And you?" Her tone carried the grievance of the young and impatient.

Words rose and fell on the other side of the metal door. Then Leesil almost disappeared through the opening, but as quickly pulled back in. Hefting a large basket she swung to the floor.

"Really? When did that happen?"

More words, rising in pitch, increasing in swiftness.

"Yes, yes. You are most likely right. I will stay and keep the Archivist here, too. I am sure Betrynd will appreciate what you have done, Rully. Thank you."

Leesil closed the huge door and slid the bolt into the lock once again. She pounded twice on the metal door, which rang with the effort. From the other side came an answering two knocks. With a sigh that held something of relief, the girl moved to pick up the unwieldy basket. But Hammin's cautiousness drove him to get to it first. He carefully flicked up the latch and lifted up the lid. His face took on an odd expression.

"It's food." Leesil offered. "One of the Foodists brings the Archivist his daily meals."

"Just making sure," grumbled Hammin. He looked defiant about his caution - and pleased by the appearance of edibles.

Mote reappeared at the edge of the yellow-orange circle of stovelight. "Is it safe to come back out?"

In unison, Hammin and Leesil said "Yes." But Leesil continued after that. "But it is not safe to go back out. At least that's what Rully says."

The messenger glanced at the edge of the shadows where she had thrown her bedraggled mask of office. But the darkness did not yield up that former covering. Her news must be told with a naked face.

"He also says that there was a terrible and violent conflict during Paell's memorial dinner. He says he barely escaped unharmed with the Archivist's delivery and now he's warning everyone he sees to stay hidden and safe."

She paused. How hard it was to have to speak this message to these three. From some part of her, only now awakened, strength came and with it compassionate tears. She drew breath.

"And he says that, in the fighting, a knife was thrown. He was told that Andeved...that he is...is dead."

CHAPTER SEVENTEEN

Deep dimness. Blunted voices from a distance. A faded, uneasy sleeping without sleep. No time, no heat, no cold. Someone moaned. Ragged rifts of unbearable brightness slit the gritty gray. No body, only eyes. Which, not knowing until that moment were so slightly open, he closed against the brutality of light and sound.

The pain of the embrace brought him back up. He heard his mother wail. "Oh, my boy - my sweet, baby boy." It cut through him like a knife. Knife. There was one coming at him. In him. Agony blossomed in the shoulder upon which his mother pressed, and in his head, beyond enduring and then, as suddenly, lessening. The weight of the maternal lifted. Another voice pounded in his ears.

"That is your son's wounded side, lady. Be careful, please." Head Mender Dawley must have pulled his mother away, which relieved Andeved. Though not enough to open his eyes and return to the terrible business of clarity.

"You aren't doing anything," Glitter's complaint echoed off the stone walls of the room. "You should be saving this child. He didn't know what he was doing. Everyone needs to understand he is just a boy. Why are you letting him die?" Upward rose his mother's voice, in tone and in volume. Even behind closed eyes, Andeved could see her waving her arms in frenetic punctuation.

"We have done all that can be done, lady," Dawley offered, keeping most of the irritation out of his voice. "He cannot be moved. We can only wait and watch."

"That isn't good enough," Glitter began.

"You know him best." Belwether. His rumble did not jar loose more pain. It soothed. "Only the lordling's mother would know what would aid him to recover. Yes?"

"Ye-e-s." The response tasted of dubiousness and distraction.

"Some favored childhood item, a bit of clothing from a happier time? You would know what might help - might bring him comfort."

Even in his fugue, Andeved recognized Belwether's strategy and knew his mother would not.

"There is that shirt I made him. The collar is sort of crooked, but he loved that about it. Except he wasn't fond of the color, he said. A lively shade I thought it." Her voice began to recede. "Now where did he put it? That boy never could..." And in just that way, the lady Glitter was gone. Though he still could not bring himself to open his eyes, Andeved could not resist the smallest of sighs. He should not have done it. Someone would notice he was awake and make him emerge from the relative safety of unconsciousness.

A hand on his arm. A small, signal squeeze. Then Belwether's rumble.

"She meant no harm, Head Mender. But it does seem best to keep the quiet for your patient."

"Quite correct." Dawley sounded almost as relieved as Andeved felt. "In fact, let us dim the lamps and let the boy rest until he awakens of his own accord. And pray he does so."

"Let me stand watch with him, Head Mender. There must be others who were hurt in that...during what happened. You will be needed, I doubt not."

For a moment, all Andeved could hear was the loud sound of his own breathing. A rasping that made his head hurt. More.

"Agreed." Items clinked as they were picked up. A case snapped shut. "If Andeved wakens, get word to me. It may be a long wait."

The mender paused. "It is my hope...." But he said no more. His boots clicked on the stone floor and other footsteps followed until the door banged shut on the echoes of them all.

Andeved sank into the restored peacefulness. For a most welcomed time, neither he nor anyone else required anything of him. Only the pain that surged with each blood tide demanded attention. And it was best addressed as a sole focus. Before he once again embraced the deep dimness, he heard Belwether say softly, "Take your time to awake. Too much has raveled. Be well first. Take your time."

Andeved slept.

X • X • X

Now they sat far back in the maze of shelves and cases, far from the warmth of the big-bellied stove. The heat and light so recently of comfort now seemed dangerous, obvious, vulnerable. Even in this almost-forgotten place.

They had fallen into silence because talking had resolved nothing. Too much was unknown, especially now with the likelihood their only ally in all of this was dying, or dead. Ally. The word had been used instead of friend, instead of his name. Ally was twice removed from the intimacy of grief, from the immediacy of loss and the unthinkable probability of a similar end.

It was a mother's voice broke the impasse.

"I still think the archives are the safest place for the time being. Under ignores it. Over and On don't even know it exists. There is no sanctuary in Over. It is in chaos. And even though one of us is...gone...when On discovers my son, my husband and I are still alive and in possession of tomes of the known, they will send more Hunters." Aimree's hands twisted and untwisted. "I have to find Belwether. My son is an Observer whose Attached is no more. This is loss in itself. But what he did will cost him his life as well if I cannot find him."

"*I* will find him, mother." The expression on Hammin's face was as hard as the stone that enclosed them. "It is mid-of-night now, which gives me the best chance of moving through Under unseen." He looked at his wife. "The fewer who go, the less likely detection. The more likely I will find Belwether and bring him here without harm."

Aimree opened her mouth to protest, then closed it abruptly, glaring at Hammin. He was right. He was best suited for this particular task. It was maddening.

"You will take too long, be too often seen, if you have no guide." Leesil stood up, straight-backed and determined. "Messengers know all the ways and, as well, I would not be remarked." Her lips pressed into a thin line, brooking no debate. It made Hammin unbend enough to nod his agreement.

But hearing the kind bravery of one so recently met caused tears to once again slide from Kendle's unseeing eyes. For so long, through so much, she had not found safety enough to have what her parents had called a healing weep. Now it seemed she could not stop it. That lack of control shamed her, but the tears were softening the places that had become hard. The cold air that chilled her wet cheeks told her she was far from heat and, she hoped, light. Just to make sure, she pulled up the blanket that had been draped around her and fashioned a deep hood. Seeing and being seen. Such different things.

Seated or pacing, Mote could not contain his restlessness. Huge cavern, this archive. And yet it closed down on him, more by the hour. Harder and harder to breathe or stay still. Nor could he stand to hear Kendle's crying. He had done so much to make their disasters bearable and now what he had thought fixed was unraveling into a sodden mess. The junior marchale he had been, never imagined the kind of grueling work required by adventure. Fairly thankless it was too, and seemingly endless. Unless ended by a knife's point.

From a well-worn chair deep in the shadows the Archivist watched his guests. Only vaguely. For Bertrynd's heart was cruelly broken. That boy who brought an inquisitive mind and quick smile - Andeved - would come no more. He had nursed the hope that the boy might turn his fierce curiosity into a life's work. Be the archivist Bertrynd could only aspire to be. Bring the folk of Under here to learn. Take knowledge up and out. At this thought, the old man let out a breath he did not realize he had been holding. Liberating a very few tomes on a single subject had brought swift death and the threat of more. No dream he held dear remained. He felt the cold through his robes and his body ached with it.

X · X · X

For the first time in memory, Under's refectory was disarrayed. Mid-Dark and no cadre of Foodists had cleared what remained in the aftermath of Paell's memorial meal. The silence was unprecedented, bereft of the slap-slap of washbrush on tabletop. What had spilled from mugs had begun to dry. Fat from the roasts congealed on platters grown cold in neglect. And in several places there were dark drops. On one table, a splash of blood and a trail of it leading away. Horribly easy to follow.

Through the tunnels of light mirrors, an icy, cold draft blustered its way into Under. In the refectory, the very air shivered. A spoon and a knife blew loose and clattered loudly to the floor. The echo took long to die.

X · X · X

Beneath the branch and leaf canopies of Over, torches flared into trails of acrid, oily smoke. Even at mid-of-the-night the bridgeways were congested with crowds shouting, arguing, fighting. Mocking and jeering, though it could not be said with any certainty at whom or by whom. The house of Pember and Zearia remained quiet and dark, lit on the outside only by a ring of lanterns.

From some other place, a wind began to agitate the canopy of trees. A wind that set the very air to shivering. The darkened house began to sway. The motion took long to die.

X · X · X

Behind the high, heavy draperies, the Reticulum hung still and immense. Wooden beads, varicolored to denote a person or place or time, clotted at intersections of the destiny web. There was, as always, a Chronicle House guard stationed on the outside of the rafter-high curtains. Useless against the wind that came, brutal, focused, so strong as to be full of intent. Its howling seemed full of warning.

The huge curtains fell, undulating. Onto the guard, the mass and weight of them driving any further breath from him. But that was not what stunned the soon roused scholars when they ran in to see what had happened. No, what paralyzed them was the sight of dangling cords, snapped strands, scattered beads. The destiny web was broken. Fore-knowledge took a very short time to die.

ACKNOWLEDGEMENTS

I can't even imagine how many books I have read over the course of my life. But I want to thank each and every author of each and every book for the gifts they have given. My father, in that earnest and academic way he had, introduced me, in very early days, to Shakespeare and Lord of the Rings. Talk about gifts – especially because they were presented as possibilities (i.e. "You might like this. Let me know what you think."). It made it even easier to love the new worlds, new words. Miss you, Dad.

Speaking of heart, mine sends out bountiful thanks to the Pendragons. These fellow authors have stuck with one another for years now, giving support, compassionate but honest critique, advice, consolation, sanctuary and unreserved friendship. Kay, CJ, Lisa, Jim and Chandler (in order of appearance) are The Best.

But this book would never have made its public appearance without the publisher and book designer: the bearded and talented Alex MacLeod. Did I mention that my kids, and their kids, are creative, informed and almost always snarky? Consider it mentioned. Kudos also to Roslyn McFarland, of Far Lands Publishing. She delivers cover art that rocks (in this case literally) and has the patience of a saint.

Are there others to acknowledge? No doubt. But you know who you are and how much you mean to me. Besides, I have two more volumes in this trilogy in which to add names to the honor roll. Hold Fast.

ABOUT THE AUTHOR

K.E. MacLeod is a Pacific Northwest novelist who writes fantasy and imaginative fiction. Somewhere in her sordid past she's taught English, speech and acting. She also lays claim to having performed in and directed plays ranging from Shakespeare to modern drama, produced and provided on-air talent for educational television and radio, and narrated a symphony production of Peter and the Wolf. Then there were the years working as an administrator in a community mental health organization. Result so far: accumulation of words, written and spoken; drama in real life and on stage; deep respect for those who walk a hard path. All of which resolves itself into a sense of humor - which is the single most potent survival tool.

PREVIEW:
THE WAYS OF OVER

UNDEROVERON BOOK TWO

CHAPTER ONE

It wasn't as if he had never written before: reminders to himself, a list of ingredients for an elixir, bits and pieces of life that needed noting. But not like this. His fingers ached and there was a sharp pain between his shoulders. No doubt the act of treason this sort of writing was, that it could lead to exile or worse, made him feel so apprehensive. The unrelenting tension of the target.

Golion put down the pen and tried to massage the stiffness from his hands. But when he looked down, he saw he'd only managed to rub the ink stains deeper into his skin. As was his custom when catching himself on the brink of a mortal error, he gave himself an internal scold.

For a senior healer you can be a consummate fool. Hide the pages. Use aether spirits to remove the ink from your fingers. Old enough to have some wisdom by now, yes? Is that not what you seek to capture? Remember what is at stake.

He unfolded himself from the desk chair, gathered the pages and stuffed them into a leather pouch that was already straining at the seams. Having fastened it with strapping, he carried it down the length of the central meeting and work room and into the bedroom at the back of the hall that was his, by right as senior healer. The Healer's Clan House barely swayed with Golion's pacing. Which was somewhat disappointing. His stay in Under, with its unrelentingly hard stone passages, had given him a new appreciation of Over's hanging dwellings and bridgeways.

When he had, long ago now, moved into the clan house, the one piece of furnishing upon which he insisted was his bed. He was too old and grumpy to put up with anything less than a comfortable night's sleep. And, of course, there was the other feature he needed. Tracing the carved wood of the headboard, his fingers sought and found the hidden latch. Unseen hinges made no noise as the tall, wide door that looked to be a panel of the bedstead opened. Golion crammed the pouch between others like it, so many now that they threatened to spill out every time the compartment opened. But they did not. He could still close the door that held his healer's secrets within. Knowledge that, if all went well, would soon be the property of all.

A sigh. A straightening of the back, flexing of tired fingers. Golion went back to the central workroom and finished putting his desk and ink stains to rights. But the smell of the aether spirits made him a bit dizzy. Though it was night's darkness that waited outside, the healer prescribed himself draughts of fresh air. He turned down the lamps and stepped out onto the decking outside the hall's front door. Took in a deep breath.

"Up late, healer. Eh?"

Golion startled so badly he nearly lost his balance. As it was, his blood tides pounded hard. He squinted into the darkness, struggling to adjust his vision to the dimness.

"You surprised me, uh…"

A woman stepped out of the deeper shadows, close enough to be recognized.

"…uh, Quess, isn't it?"

"Aye," the woman's voice was just a little too loud for the quiet of the night. "Marchale Quess it is. Making my rounds. Saw the lamps lit in the clan house. Quite late." She paused, as if to wait for some explanation. He made none. She waited a mite longer, long enough that Golion began to feel apprehensive. Tiny beads of sweat started a journey down his spine.

Quess sniffed. Sniffed again.

"Healer's work is never done," Golion almost blurted it out. Then took hold of his anxiety and continued in a calmer voice. "What with the recent – uneasiness – there have been a multitude of injuries. Restocking potions, salves, bandages, whatnots – well, it takes time. And late night lamplight, I'm afraid."

The marchale narrowed her eyes and looked him up and down in such an insolent way that Golion bristled with irritation. Then fear. The aether spirits.

"Mmm. I suppose those potions and whatnots take all sorts of ingredients. My mother used to make a tonic from helios 'shrooms. Smelled like sick up. She said it was good for me. You think she was right?"

Golion attempted a smile. "I make it a rule never to argue with a mother's good intentions. And a broth cooked down from helios meshroons is certainly nutritious – despite the odor."

Quess waited a beat too long to smile back. She straightened up, putting her hand on the butt of a truncheon tucked into her belt.

"Good even, then. Back to my rounds. We want to keep those injuries and – uneasiness – down to a pinch." The marchale walked slowly over the bridgeway leading from the clan house. Watching her leave, setting the 'way to swaying with her stride, the healer's confusion blossomed. Had he been that close to discovery? Or was the marchale purposefully turning a blind eye – or in this case, an undiscerning nose – to what she surmised was being done? It was less than one moon's cycle since he had returned from the bloody chaos of Under. A double handful of days back in Over and he still could get no good sense of the sway.

He realized he had been staring in the direction of the house that belonged to Pember and Zearia. Where were Over's senior secretholders now that one of their most wicked secrets had been revealed? It was a question everyone wanted answered, but no one spoke aloud.

What was that? Golion peered through the darkness, relying on the lanterns hung here and there on bridgeway posts. *There. Yes?* The prime secretholder's dark and shuttered house hung, as was their right, from the most advantageous limb on the city's central tree. It had moved. Just the tiniest bit of sway.

The senior healer leaned heavily against the doorpost. Now what?

■ · ■ · ■

Brekkan could only move her thoughts. The rest of her was motionless in the stance of a marchale on report. Though she was not, in actual fact, on report. Only summoned into the presence of the head marchale, Clan Leader Shawen. That was all. *All?* If Captain Brekkan had been in a position to roll her eyes, she would have done so. But the slight rocking of the field office announced the arrival of the clan leader. Through the opened door came sounds of barked orders, stamping feet, the thwack of wooden truncheons hitting straw-stuffed targets.

Head Marchale Shawen closed the door behind her. Closed it carefully, deliberately. She rounded the map table and stood facing her captain, not yet having said a word. The silence, and the unblinking scrutiny that was contained in it, continued a disquietingly long time. Though Brekkan kept her eyes dutifully focused on a spot just past the leader's head, edge-vision gave a chance to scrutinize in return. Thin, sinewy build, narrow face, sharp features, bursts of gray, wiry hair. All as it had always been. Except not. Something was changed. Around the eyes? The mouth? Had Brekkan been less disciplined, this would have been the perfect opportunity to squirm.

"Let us not put protocol between us, Captain." Shawen motioned to a camp chair. "Do sit and let us talk." A pleasantry uttered in the head marchale's thin, cracked voice did not feel very pleasant. Nevertheless, Brekken sat down and managed a nod of thanks.

"You are in the way of having a wider perspective of our situation," Shawen made a vague inclusive gesture toward the window behind her.

"Situation, clan leader? Meaning the increased activities of our training camp?

"Training camp?" The marchale leaned across the table. "Do not be disingenuous with me, captain. I have neither time nor patience for games with words. By 'situation' you know I mean the chaos that threatens Over. And by 'wider perspective' I mean your observations gathered in Under." Shawen stood upright again, crossing her arms.

"Of course, head marchale." Brekkan shifted in the hard chair. "I have made a report of the conditions my quad experienced while in Under. Including our failure to return the declared fugitive."

"Not one fugitive, captain. Two. Kendle and the young deserter, Mote."

The pause that followed this delineation was sharp and accusatory. Shawen kept her mouth in a thin, grim line, nor would she speak further. Accusation and silence was a technique that Brekkan had seen used before, though never with this icy skill. It was then she recognized what had changed in the clan leader. Beneath the outward sameness was a sort of shrewdness, a deeper calculation that had not been manifested before. That it was in response to the events of late there could be no doubt. Was it being wielded to the benefit of Over?

"I take responsibility for the actions of my quad. Leaving the debilitated girl to the menders of Under was my decision. And to be clear, we did not know Mote was declared a deserter or that we were ordered to bring him with us." Brekkan did her own inner calculation and elected to play the accusation and silence game herself to feel out Shawen's motives. "The revelation of Pember and

Zearia's flett breeding, the unnatural twisting of innocent creatures into weapons of the flesh, was too powerful to let past decisions remain unexamined. Our training places reason above violence always. It was my hope our actions honored that training."

Then Brekkan leaned just so slightly forward, a questioning but respectful expression firmly set on her face. And waited. Because the first to break this silence would lose. That was how this game was played.

Waiting. Neither turned eyes away, made even the tiniest gesture. Waited for the other to speak and, thus, reveal. Capitulate.

Shawen's eyes narrowed. Her mouth curved into the beginnings of a smile. Then the door of the field office slammed open and, in unthinking response, the head marchale glanced away and barked out her irritation at the junior marchale who had stumbled in.

"What is it? You were told…" She stopped, realization that she had been the one to reveal, to lose, written in subtle but unmistakable signs across her face. But the junior marchale, panting and trembling with his errand, could not contain his message.

"Word comes from Ressa. The Ressans have closed the roads. Against us, their own. They say they will not send…supplies. They say Over is divided until order is restored."

Brekkan read the face of her superior as the news was spoken. And discovered what was boldly written across it: now that Pember and Zearia were brought down by their own misdeeds, Shawen fiercely desired to climb up and over their failed leadership, to become more than a clan leader. Ambition had tightened the flesh of her face and it did not bode well.

■ • ■ • ■

It was just that kind of rain. Great splats of it, in gouts that fell straight down. Cold. Relentless. Mote rather enjoyed it. The usual dripping, hardly-more-than-mist rain of Over made the green slickery and lush, the dirt rich with dark color and a deep loamy smell. But a hard rain washed everything new. Of course, standing directly in it wasn't entirely pleasant, as the multitude of icy drips that found their devious way down his neck conclusively proved.

What was unique about this particular downpour was that it was falling into Under. Down it came through the huge, ragged gap made by the collapse, bringing soil and brush and debris cascading from the edges like a circle of dirty waterfalls, creating muddy rivers that oozed, meandered and, now that it had been raining for over three days, flowed down the stone corridors and stairways into the many caverns that constituted Under. Since no one in Under was experienced with what they called *upper-outer elements*, Andeved had turned to Mote for help.

"I have no training in roof building," Mote explained for the third time in as many breaths.

Andeved tried to shrug, but winced instead. His shoulder, still bandaged from the knife wound, had not healed enough to allow for such a gesture.

"So you say," Andeved tugged his hood further forward against the pelting rain. "But Under has no roofs, at least none not carved from stone. Over does. And you live with rain and rivers." He turned to his friend. Lowered his voice. "They are watching me in this. Too much depends on it. A test of the 'boy lord.'" Andeved snapped off the title with full bitterness.

Mote shifted uneasily, the pressure to aid his companion bearing down; alongside the knowledge that his and Kendle's continuing sanctuary in Under might be weighed against their usefulness. He squinted thoughtfully up at the immense gap above. But he got no ideas, he only got wetter.

"Well," he finally managed, "marchales use tents for our camps. Perhaps some sort of tented roof-like…" he struggled to name this constructed construction of his, "…sort of shelter thing might be stretched across…" But he stopped, his mind racing ahead of the concept to see the flaws in it.

Andeved glanced around at the many mud splattered workers attempting to deal with the situation. And shook his head.

"Yes. I mean, no. We have nothing that would stretch that far – or materials to construct tent poles long enough to support what would otherwise sag and break with more rain." He gave a thin smile to Mote. "But it was a good start." He gestured vaguely upward.

"A message for you, Lord Andeved."

They turned to find Leesil. The young messenger wore no mask of office but such a very serious mien. Serious enough that Andeved knew, though Leesil was delivering it with a naked face, the tidings were going to be official and difficult.

"A citizen of Under sends word he has proposals to deal with the flooding." Leesil did not speak in the louder, measured tones of a messenger. That she pitched her words low and directed them only at the two in front of her was not a good sign.

"Such offers should be welcomed. Shouldn't they?" Andeved tried to maintain the composure expected in a leader.

"Aye, lord. When Chief Advisor Etcherelle heard the proposals, she concluded they should be welcomed."

Andeved nodded. "But the proposer would not be?"

"It is most especially difficult to dispassionately evaluate ideas coming from a source not prized for…" she paused to carefully choose her words, "…well-tempered opinions or consistently constructive advice."

Mote threw up his hands in surprise and dismay. "No. Truly? He has the arrogance?"

"So," Andeved's voice was strained with a painful need to understand what must surely be both a useful and a terrible machination. "So, my father wishes to help?"

Leesil nodded, wordless in the acknowledgement of Andeved's dilemma.

"Well," Mote sputtered, knowing what the man had done, "just go back and tell him to-"

"Tell him I will come speak with him." The firmness of the Andeved's voice made Mote rock back on his heels.

"You cannot even be considering this. Can you?" Mote realized he had gotten louder in his distress. Some of the workers had turned to the sound and that was not going to be helpful. He lowered his voice, though managing volume did not negate intensity. "I mean to say, your father is head terracetender and all, but—"

"But this is not about what Sere," Andeved's choice to use his father's name was telling, "has or has not done to me. Any ways to salvage our home must be considered." He looked to Leesil. "I assume Chief Advisor Etcherelle is awaiting me in the company of the Head 'Tender?"

Leesil nodded. Her eyes stayed fixed on Andeved with an expression Mote could not read.

Well, then," the young lord squared his shoulders, "I will join Etcherelle for the…discussion."

Mote moved to accompany his friend, but Andeved laid a hand on his arm.

"No, Mote. This is mine to do."

The marchale tried to protest but Andeved rode over what words he might have said.

"And yours to do is this: Go back to the Archives. Ask the others to search the records again for anything that might be of assistance. Perhaps Kendle remembers some solution, or Bertrynd could conjure up a lost bit of knowledge that will do."

The request – no, it was a thinly veiled demand – hung in the air. It was the flush of coloring on Andeved's cheeks that decided Mote.

"Of course. I'll go now."

And the marchale turned toward the down-inward stairway, slogging through the worsening mudflow, deeply apprehensive about what pain this *discussion* would create. But also understanding that Andeved was not yet ready to let others, even close companions, witness it.

■•■•■

"I see you do not wear a mask of office, Leesil." Knowing who and what awaited him, Andeved was struggling to get hard-beating blood tides under control, desperately hoping a distracting conversation would help.

The messenger gave him a sideways glance. "My old one was rather shredded, if you recall. And it did not seem as though a mask was appropriate anymore." She frowned. "Unless it suits you, my lord, to reaffirm such a practice." Her tone slipped, for the moment, into the cadences of official messengering.

"No, no. Far from it. Hiding behind regalia is a terrible idea." Andeved stopped talking, keenly aware that he was on the brink of a nervous ramble. Also aware that he had come close to insulting Leesil's decision which, if truth be told, had been given his own outspoken permission. He attempted to paste an expression of support and strength on his face. Though what that looked like he had no concept. Nor wished for a mirror to see the result, this being difficult enough.

"Good, then." Leesil continued leading him toward what he dreaded. "Besides, I am not the only one to forego masking. You'll see." She gave him an encouraging smile, for which he was very grateful.

Except that the messenger had now stopped in front of a doorway, gesturing to him that this was where his advisor waited. Potentially two advisors. How he hated the war between the duty to enter and the need to flee.

"Thank you for your message and your company to this..." Andeved could find no word to describe what might be inside. Then he felt the lightest of touches and turned to see Leesil had placed her hand on his arm. She spoke no words, but there shone enough encouragement in her eyes that he could borrow some bravery from it. Enough to push open the door and enter.

His father sat at the far end of the meeting table, half in shadow, arms crossed in front of him, no look of warmth on his face. Only a one-sided smile that, Andeved knew from long experience, held absolutely no humor.

Etcherelle rose from her chair, a gesture of respect toward the young lord that Sere did not make. Neither wore the mask of office, not the Head Terracetender's green and brown leaf trimmed half-mask nor the Chief Advisor's full-face unembellished ivory mask. Both were here in capacity of their position, yet they prepared to counsel with naked faces. It was unprecedented, welcomed and unnerving.

"Please sit, Chief Advisor." Already beads of sweat had started to roll down Andeved's back. "I understand the Head Terracetender proposes methods to restrain the flood." He looked only at Etcherelle, but felt the scorn of his father's wordless disregard.

"Indeed, the Head 'Tender has told me that he does have a proposition that may help."

"Will help." Sere's voice came sharply from the shadows. "Will fix, even make good use of, the mud and rain." He leaned in toward the light. "I assume that you failed to find solutions yourself, or you would not be here. Talking with me."

As much as it galled him to admit it, his father was right. He had not thought of a way to do more than slow the onslaught of muck that was filling the upper corridors.

"No one has yet devised an answer. And not having heard your idea, I cannot say if it is of value either." Andeved felt shame rise up to heat his neck. He tried harder to resist the mortally aimed darts of his father's opinion.

"Of course," Etcherelle put her calm tones between the two men. "So, it is time to hear what Sere proposes. Yes? For the rain continues and the influx worsens."

Neither Andeved nor Sere spoke for a very long time, each weighing their blood bond with the other in the way of fathers and sons. It was the older man made the first movement, drawing a parchment from his tunic and spreading it on the table in front of him. And then waited, increasingly impatient, for the other two to come close enough to view the plans. Which Etcherelle did first, and Andeved, deeply reluctant but impelled by duty, followed.

Pointing here and then there at his drawings, Sere made his explanation. Use stone set on stone to ring the outer-upper edge of the hole and stop the inpouring of mud. On the floor of the space below the gap, mortar a stone wall to hold the soil already in the deconstructed room. From the rim of that mortared wall, bring a spillway that would take the excess water through to the terraces. There it could be used to nourish the crops with the rest allowed to plummet to the sea below.

"But what of the pit of mud held in the upper chamber?" Chief Advisor Etcherelle had leaned over the parchment, keenly engaged in understanding what was laid out there.

Sere sat back in his chair, the one-sided smile again installed on his visage. "It will serve to grow food, of course. Fresh soil, rainwater, light shining down. Meshroons at the edges, and light-seekers in the middle. It solves more than just the effects of this rare storm. It gives Under space to grow more and – with the fresh soil and any volunteer seeds and shoots that came with it – more robust crops. It turns the tragedy," he gave the word a bitter emphasis, "into usefulness. Now tell me I am not the one to solve this. Tell me what I propose has no value."

It was what Andeved had dreaded: His father had, indeed, solved this problem. And in such a manner that there was no possibility of argument. No way to dismiss or disparage the plan without causing greater harm to those of Under depending on them for guidance and protection. He would have to set aside every slight, rant, meanness, cruelty and coldness with which Sere had plagued him for the whole of his life. Set it all aside, swallow his pride, restrain his barely discovered sense of self and accept, gratefully accept, his father's solution.

Andeved looked up, steeling himself to catch his father's eye. No longer one-sided, the Head 'Tender's smile had stretched into a thin-lipped smirk of triumph. It was an expression to which the son had been subjected many times. This time was one too many and it severed the vein that had, through childhood's darker hours, fed shame and loathing to a boy's heart. Untethered from the ever-present force of denigration, Andeved felt, for a giddy moment, as if he were light enough to float away. Something of that new freedom of soul must have shown, for the triumph on his father's flickered, faltered.

"This is an excellent plan, head 'tender." Though the strain to do it cost a great deal, the young lordling pitched his voice low in a pleasant cadence. "Let us bring direction to the workers best suited for accomplishing each task. Most, I assume, will be 'tenders under your authority. To construct mortared walls like those that buttress the terraces, claim the soil, redirect excess water."

Andeved turned to his Chief Advisor. "Etcherelle, perhaps you could see Sere is credited with developing and implementing this fine idea. The people should know to whom they owe thanks."

"Y-yes. Of course." Etcherelle stammered in confusion, momentarily looking more the youth than Under's heir.

"Of course," Andeved sat down now, finding his legs had begun to shake, "we shall have to consider how to manage the questions that most certainly will arise at the announcement of Sere's solution."

"Questions?" A grimace of distaste crossed the head 'tender's face. "Such as which laze-abouts will have to shovel mud? Or how many shielding hats will be needed for the cowards who fear falling up into the air?" He shook his head in derision.

"Oh, yes. I suppose there will be questions of that sort." Andeved made sure his hands were beneath the edge of the table so that his whitened knuckles did not show. "Though what I meant was how to address those who ask why, if you knew what to do, you did not act immediately and stop the destruction. Or those who wonder whether the head terracetender knew Under's crops and herds were weakening for a long time but said, or did, nothing. You understand, those kinds of questions."

Sere rose, furious, spitting out a barrage of words.

"Knew? Of course I knew. Oh, I tried to convince the guild heads – morons, all of them. They wouldn't listen. Or if they did believe disaster was approaching, they just scurried around grubbing for guild glory. Did anyone else see that it was the whole of Under in peril? Certainly not Paell, so weak, so self-involved. Nor you, Chief Advisor," Sere pronounced Etcherelle's title with malevolent sarcasm, "you did nothing but coddle Under's lord and call it counsel."

"Enough, father." The force of Andeved's words tore at his throat.

"Not enough, boy. No, not nearly. Because it was I only began the plan to save us. Pressured the geshherders to extract more bile. Forced the wallworkers to paint more stone with it so that, from the space it carved out, came more fertile soil for the failing terraces. Not my fault they could not gauge what stone would hold and what would not." He looked away in disgust. "And yes, it was I who put my mush-hearted wife up to insinuating into Paell's vacuous head a duty of marriage with Arrant of Over. Whose bride gifts would be fresh seeds, stronger breeders for the herds - a stronger breeder for the failing house of Under."

Etcherelle gasped, shock taking the air from her as if she had been hit. But Andeved schooled himself to the appearance of calm, tried to put on an Observer's face, one worthy of Belwether on his best days. He could not, of course, see the expression of his efforts. And his father was too far gone into rage to notice. Old ways for fresh disasters.

"The foundation of what you say regarding our crops and flocks is very true. You have every right to be concerned. Your deep knowledge and long experience served you well in seeing through to a perfect way to harness the unprecedented influx of rain and debris."

Sere balled up his fists and frowned so deeply his face was slashed with darkness. But as was his way, he now waited for those he despised to speak their weakness and then beg for help.

"Truly our guild heads have not looked beyond their own interests. And our former lord, now gone, came too late to clarity." Andeved carefully took in a breath, wrestling to shut out the terrible pounding in his chest. "Where you have failed, father, is in thinking yourself the only means of salvation. Of turning your moral conclusions into tyrannical imperatives. So that even the most desperate would forego your assistance just to avoid your arrogance."

But here the lordling's voice began to break under his pain. "Why, father, do you hate all others, even your own wife, your own son? Why scheme to save Under when there is no one in it you do not scorn?" The young man caught the edge of the table, for all the world as if he were spinning into a fall. "It is why the guild leaders and the people risk a boy lord rather than a solver of problems. Because they have come to despise you as fully as you despise them."

"Then, so be it." Sere rasped out his response, "They will die of their choice. More the fools they."

It seemed to Andeved that there was no more air in the room. Breathing was too hard. So he rose from his chair, turned his back in dismissal and left. Left the room. Left the red-raged man that would always be his father in the custody of a pale, aggrieved Chief Advisor. The hot release of tears, the pounding of his fists against stone, did not start until he had somehow found his way to his room and pulled the heavy draperies across the doorway.

Made in the USA
Middletown, DE
13 September 2022

10388044R00170